Dear Reade

They say t   same all over.
Whether it's a small village on the sea, a mining
town nestled in the mountains, or a whistle-stop
along the Western plains, we all share the same
hopes and dreams. We work, we play, we laugh,
we cry—and, of course, we fall in love . . .

It is this universal experience that we at Jove
Books have tried to capture in a heartwarming
series of novels. We've asked our most gifted au-
thors to write their own story of American romance, set in a town as distinct and vivid as the
people who live there. Each writer chose a special time and place close to their hearts. They
filled the towns with charming, unforgettable
characters—then added that spark of romance.
We think you'll find the combination absolutely
delightful.

You might even recognize *your* town. Because
true love lives in *every* town . . .

Welcome to *Our Town*.

Sincerely,

Leslie Gelb

Leslie Gelbman
Editor-in-Chief

❖ ❖ ❖

OUR·TOWN

HARBOR LIGHTS

LINDA KREISEL

JOVE BOOKS, NEW YORK

HARBOR LIGHTS

A Jove Book / published by arrangement with
the author

PRINTING HISTORY
Jove edition / July 1996

The Putnam Berkley World Wide Web site address is
http://www.berkley.com

ISBN: 0-515-11899-0

A JOVE BOOK®
Jove Books are published by The Berkley Publishing Group,
200 Madison Avenue, New York, New York 10016.
JOVE and the "J" design are trademarks
belonging to Jove Publications, Inc.

PRINTED IN THE UNITED STATES OF AMERICA

10 9 8 7 6 5 4 3 2 1

HARBOR LIGHTS

❖ 1 ❖

Silchester Island,
Chesapeake Bay
1885

"DEAD FISH!"

"I love the smell," Eleanor Folsom told her sister.

"Yick!" Alice sniffed again and screwed her rounded face into a horrible grimace.

Eleanor drew in a deep breath and savored the odors of saltwater, creosote, seaweed, and dead fish.

"That's what freedom smells like," she murmured.

Spending the months of July and August at her family's summer cottage had always brought relief from the sweltering heat of Baltimore and the strictures of society. But she felt she only truly comprehended the meaning of the word *freedom* now, when she was finally out of the clutches of Bradley Butler Randolph.

Even as she felt her tense body relax, she could feel the slight shudder through the brass handrail as the yacht jostled against the pilings at its berth at the Folsom Yachting Club. She gripped the handrail more tightly to keep her balance, and hoped this wasn't an evil omen. The well-maintained steam engine purred to a stop.

As her family had traveled across the Chesapeake Bay, Eleanor had enjoyed the sounds of the rhythmic slapping of the green waves against the dark wood and the raucous cries of the seabirds flying overhead. Now the shouts between the club attendants and her father's own crew as they tossed lines back and forth to each other drowned out the gentle sounds.

She stood to the side and waited with her sister for their formidable father to pass by. Winston Stanford Folsom III offered his elbow to his wife, then descended the gangplank with the stride of true royalty. Why shouldn't he? Hadn't his money funded the building of the Folsom Yachting Club? Hadn't his presence on this tiny island turned it into a fashionable—and exclusive—summer retreat for Baltimore's wealthy?

Eleanor grimaced. There were times when her father fumed with anger and frustration that the inhabitants had stubbornly and inexplicably, to his way of thinking, refused to sell him the entire island outright.

Eleanor and Alice followed more humbly in his wake. Then they were left standing alone on the pier while their father proceeded to tend to one or another of the many pressing matters involved in coming ashore, and their mother badgered the household staff as they unloaded enough baggage to see them through the next two months.

"I don't see the carriage," Alice complained, looking up and down the white gravel drive bordered with bright potted flowers.

"Reed'll come," Eleanor assured her, although she didn't think that would really bother Alice. "He's very dependable. And besides, he wouldn't dare not."

"I don't even see a wagon for the baggage."

"Just be patient," Eleanor told Alice.

She might as well be talking to one of the seagulls, she decided. Thirteen-year-olds so rarely listened to their big sisters.

"You know everything always goes exactly as Father plans."

Alice nodded, her long dark braids swinging in the sunlight and salty air. "Usually."

"*Always*," Eleanor corrected. She hoped her father's plans always worked. If it weren't for her father's influence with powerful friends, she didn't know how she would have managed to keep Bradley Randolph at bay and keep the gossip from the society column in all the newspapers.

Alice, hands on hips, observed their surroundings with little nods of approval. "It's not bad around here."

"Yes, it's very pretty," Eleanor answered quickly, eager to move her mind onto any subject that didn't involve Bradley.

Everything was a splash of color. Clear blue sky overhead and tall green sea grass growing at the edge of the land. Neatly raked white gravel drives and paths, red geraniums in terra cotta pots standing out against the taller blue and purple irises, yellow and orange marigolds boldly poking their heads over the borders of white-painted rocks, and multicolored pennants flapping in the breeze.

She was glad for the wide-brimmed straw hat that shaded her eyes from the bright sunlight. She couldn't wait until they arrived at the summer cottage, and she could enjoy the cool breezes across the water as she sat in the shade of the wide veranda.

"I guess I can stand it here for two months. After all, *our* side of the island is the prettiest," Alice proudly declared.

Eleanor looked at the pristine whiteness of the Folsom Clubhouse. Yes, it was beautiful. In the distance she could see another building—wood once painted white but now grayed by the weather and black with coal dust, with rusted chains hanging from grimy cables. Several of the wooden roof shingles were missing.

Definitely not as beautiful as their side of the island. This was the side of the island the people lived on year-round.

How could they tolerate such ugliness in their drab lives?

"*Our* side of the island doesn't smell like dead fish."

"You're an insufferable little snob." Eleanor tweaked one of her sister's braids.

"I am not!" Alice protested. "You don't think these people really enjoy the smell of dead fish, do you?"

"Of course not. But it *has* to smell like that here. That's how these fishermen make their living."

"Excuse me, miss," the masculine voice cut into their conversation. "We're not fishermen."

Eleanor turned quickly. In all the hustle and bustle involved whenever her father's yacht arrived anywhere, she never really singled out any of the men on the docks. Why should she? But now, as she watched him standing behind her, she wondered how she ever could have missed this man.

He was rolling up a rope, looping it over his palm and under his elbow. Each twist moved the fabric of his shirt across the distinct muscles of his arms and chest. He wasn't even watching what he was doing. It was very plain to Eleanor that the man was watching her very closely.

How long had he been eavesdropping? What had prompted him to interrupt her and her sister?

She wasn't used to being approached by strange men—especially workmen toting ropes. Mother had taught them early and well how to keep unwanted men away. And it usually worked.

She lifted her chin proudly and stared him coldly in the eye. "I beg your pardon. Are you speaking to us?"

"I don't mean to be rude and contradict you or your . . . um, sister, I guess, miss."

"She's my sister," Eleanor told him with a slight nod.

"But, you see, we're not fishermen," he repeated.

"Then what are you?" Alice demanded impudently.

"Hush, Alice."

Eleanor glanced around, trying to hide her nervousness. She didn't spot either parent, but that still didn't mean they could stand here chatting to just anyone—especially a workman.

Alice knew as well as she did they shouldn't be talking to this man. But if they were caught, Eleanor knew she, as the elder sister, was sure to catch all the blame. And Alice—curse the little rascal—knew it, too.

"We really should be going," Eleanor urged her sister.

"Going where?" Alice demanded. "Right now we don't have anywhere to go, or anything to go in."

Eleanor could feel her cheeks beginning to warm with embarrassment. Confound Alice, exposing her for a bare-faced liar!

"I want to know," Alice insisted. "If you're not fishermen, mister, what are you?"

"We're watermen," he answered.

He seemed so proud of the statement, Eleanor thought. What was so special about a waterman?

He grinned at Alice, then turned that same grin on Eleanor. His even white teeth against his tanned skin shone like pearls that might have come from some of the Bay's own oysters. His eyes were the same pale blue-green as the water beneath them, and twinkled like the sunlight bouncing off the lapping ripples.

Eleanor noticed her sister giving him a quick, scathing glance up and down. Alice *was* a little snob—and much too young to appreciate what was before her!

She, herself, would have taken her time, studying the broad thighs beneath the trousers, and the expanse of muscular chest straining against the plain, blue cotton of his damp shirt. He was taller than her father, even taller than Bradley.

Whatever these watermen were, they must work very hard at it. Either that, or Mother Nature had simply endowed this man with more than his fair share of all that was right and good with the masculine physique.

She didn't know what he was or who he was, and yet she found herself wanting to know more when she really shouldn't care at all.

She felt guilty having such an interest in this stranger. She'd had very little interest in Bradley—and even less as time wore on. None of the other young men of her acquaintance had caused such feelings in her. She wasn't prepared to acknowledge those feelings right now, so soon after her escape from Bradley. She certainly wasn't about to admit—even to herself—that she could have those kinds of feelings about a mere workman.

She just knew she needed to get away from this man.

She grabbed Alice's elbow and gave a little tug. "We really should be going. Mother and Father will—"

"What's a waterman?" Alice, undaunted, demanded of the stranger. "If I stuck you with a pin, would you spring a leak like an old bucket, and water would squirt out until there was nothing left inside?"

The man laughed—a deep, rumbling chuckle. He reached up and raked his browned fingers through the waves of his sun-bleached hair. Like the mane of a tawny lion on the beach of some wild, desert island, Eleanor speculated, purring like a kitten when stroked, and yet always there was the underlying danger that he would spring. . . .

"Well, miss, you sure aren't imaginative none. . . ."

Still grinning, he turned to Eleanor. Her heart skipped a beat. If only he knew what she was thinking of him, he'd quickly amend his opinion. Her imagination, surely, was a match for Alice's any day.

He nodded his head in her sister's direction. "Is she always like this?"

"Oh, oh, no. Alice can be quite nice when she wants to," Eleanor managed to mumble. She wasn't about to reveal the family's tribulation to a total stranger.

"Liar," Alice accused. "You should hear what she calls me when other people aren't around."

"Oh, Alice, hush!" Eleanor scolded. She could feel the flush on her cheeks warming even more.

"Somehow I get the feeling your sister deserves it," the man told Eleanor.

She managed to smile up at him. She never imagined she'd be so bold with a complete stranger—and a mere fisherman at that. Or waterman. Whatever.

She turned quickly to her sister. "We really should be getting back to Mother and—"

"But I still haven't found out what a waterman is," Alice insisted. She planted her feet firmly on the pier and placed both fists on her hips.

"A fisherman just makes his living fishing," he told her.

Alice looked disappointed. "I think I could have figured *that* out on my own."

Gradually his gaze returned to Eleanor, and he completed his explanation.

"*Waterman* is an old, old English word for someone who makes his entire life from the whole Bay."

Then his blue eyes took on a mischievous sparkle.

"In the summer we go out in our bugeyes—"

"In what?" Alice demanded.

"And we catch rock, shads, and blues."

Alice frowned and her eyes were glazed with puzzlement.

"Why do you catch rocks?"

"We catch sooks and jimmies, too, and a few spongers—but we throw them back," the man continued without answering Alice's question. "After all, nobody wants spongers, do they?"

Hesitantly Alice replied, "Um . . . um, oh, no."

"And it's better for the next harvest."

"Of course." Alice had to agree.

"We hunt canvasbacks and geese in the fall, and in the winter we harvest mobjacks and manninoses. Do you see the difference?"

He grinned at her, awaiting her reply.

"Of course. I'm not stupid," Alice told him with a haughty lift of her pale eyebrows.

But Eleanor could notice the hint of uncertainty in her sister's voice. She couldn't blame her. Sooks, jimmies, manninoses, spongers—she'd bet none of those words were in her Webster's dictionary. The man left them with more questions now than they'd had at the start. None of it made any difference—or much sense—to Eleanor as she watched him grinning playfully at Alice's consternation.

"If you'd like," he continued, looking at Eleanor, "I could take you out on my bugeye and show you some sookies and jimmies."

"I don't get in any bug's eyes! What do you do in the spring?" Alice asked.

If Eleanor knew her sister as well as she thought she did, Alice was definitely eager to leave a subject that puzzled her. It was just as well. There was no way she was going to allow her sister to go off with a strange man to look for strangely named creatures that most probably didn't even exist. Worse, if Alice *had* taken it into her head to go, there was no way she could stop her.

"We fish for sturgeon and we plant our own kitchen gardens—watermelons, tomatoes, cucumbers. You know, my mom used to put up the best watermelon and cucumber pickles—"

"That's it?" Alice exclaimed, slapping her hands at her side.

"Isn't that enough? I know it keeps most of us pretty busy year round."

"Watermen work on the water. Big deal."

"Alice!" Eleanor exclaimed.

"I mean, I thought being a waterman was going to have something to do with mermaids or pirates. Not bugs' eyes!"

"Father says Alice reads too much," Eleanor tried to explain.

"Oh, if you want a tale of a tub, you'll have to go see Unk Moore," the man told her.

"Who?"

"He's a really old man who usually hangs out at Moore's General Store."

"Don't you *dare* think of going into town," Eleanor warned her sister. She was half tempted to grab her braids, just to keep her from running off wild. "If you want stories, there are lots of books in the library that haven't been read in almost a year."

"On theories of industry and economics?" Alice exclaimed.

"Now, we really should be going."

She turned to the man and more calmly said, "I thank you for kindly explaining—sort of—to my ungrateful little sister about watermen and what they do. Good-bye, Mr.—"

"Eleanor! Alice!" Mrs. Folsom called across the gravel drive. Her voice was pleasantly musical, but Eleanor could hear the underlying threat, a skill their mother had developed from many years of practice.

"We've got to go," Eleanor said, trying to hide the frantic desire for flight she was experiencing.

"Oh, poop," Alice grumbled.

"Don't use such language!" Eleanor scolded. "At least not in public."

"But Mother's spotted us—and it's all your fault."

"*My* fault? Little liar!"

Alice turn to the waterman. "See?"

Eleanor's anger and embarrassment were growing by the minute. Her anxiety was growing in direct proportion to her mother's approach.

"*You* were the one who insisted on stopping and asking rude questions," Eleanor accused.

"Yeah, and now we'll have to spend the first day of our summer explaining why we were breaking Rule Number One."

"What's Rule Number One?" the man asked.

"What do you mean *we*?" Eleanor demanded in an angry whisper. "This was your idea. *I* wouldn't have done such a thing."

She hoped very hard that, in the face of their sisterly argument, the man would forget his question and just quietly go away.

"Oh, poop. You never do anything anyway," Alice complained.

"What's Rule Number One?" the man asked again.

Alice said nothing. Eleanor wished she'd never said a thing a lot earlier. As usual, her sister started the trouble, then left Eleanor to explain their way out of it.

"I . . . I don't think you'd understand," Eleanor mumbled. Why did he have to ask? How was she going to explain this to him?

"If your sister can understand that watermen don't spring leaks, I think I can understand these rules of yours."

Why did this man have to be as stubborn as Alice? She'd already tried tactfully to leave him alone. Now there was nothing else to do. This one wasn't going to be easy.

"Well, they're not exactly *my* rules."

"But you abide by them."

"I . . . we have to."

"Yes. Rules are rules. So what is it?" He crossed his arms over his chest and frowned at her—with a twinkle in his eye. "And I warn you, I'm as persistent as the young lady here when I want an answer.''

''I'd already figured that.'' With a sigh of resignation Eleanor conceded, ''Oh, very well. But just remember, you asked for this.''

He eyed her, waiting.

''Rule Number One is . . .'' Unable to meet his unsuspecting gaze, she stared at the weathered wooden planks beneath her. She drew in a deep breath before continuing. ''Don't associate with the islanders.''

He continued to watch her, but his fine lips drew into a tight line. The sparkle vanished from his eyes. He nodded.

''Yes,'' he replied very quietly as he picked up another rope and began coiling it over his hand. This time he was paying a great deal of attention to what he was doing. ''I do understand. I think I've actually known this for a long, long time, but thank you for explaining it to me so clearly anyway. Sorry to have bothered you, miss.''

He turned his back to her, intent on his work.

''Oh, please, no.'' Eleanor raised her hand and almost placed it on his broad shoulder, hoping he'd turn around, hoping he'd give her one more chance to apologize. It was so tempting to touch him—and she *had* to make him understand. ''You really don't understand. Please—''

''Eleanor! Alice! Ah, there you are, my dears.''

Eleanor drew her hand back quickly.

Mrs. Folsom interposed her wide body between her daughters and the stranger. For such a large woman, she was actually rather nimble when it came to coming between her daughters and any man who didn't meet her strict specifications, a skill that also came from many years of practice.

Her back, her ruffled parasol, beaded handbag, voluminous lace shawl, and broad-brimmed, flower-and-feather-topped straw hat provided a very effective barrier against any man's aspirations to her daughters' fortunes and virtues.

"Come along, my dears. We've got lots to do today." Mrs. Folsom's voice still rang musically across the pier.

"Like what?" Alice asked. "That's what we've got maids for."

"The carriage has finally arrived, and your father will be furious if we keep the horses waiting in this heat," Mrs. Folsom continued.

"He'll be even more furious if we keep *him* waiting," Alice added.

"Hush," Eleanor whispered, nudging her sister's shoulder so that she began to move across the pier. "I *told* you not to stay. . . ."

Mrs. Folsom shepherded her daughters to the carriage waiting on the clean gravel drive.

"I'm angry enough with you already," Eleanor whispered to her sister.

"What did I do?" Alice's eyes were wide with innocence, but Eleanor wasn't fooled—not for one second.

"You made me insult that . . . that nice man." That was the only word she could think of to describe him that wouldn't reveal what she'd actually been thinking about him. "And after he was kind enough to explain to you—"

"Explain! You call jooks and simmies and jobmacks an explanation? What in the world *are* those things?"

"What makes you think I know? Even if I did know, what makes you think I'd tell you anyway after what you've done?"

"I didn't do anything. I wasn't even thinking about him."

"That was pretty evident," Eleanor scolded, still being certain to keep her voice to an angry whisper.

"I just don't want to have to listen to Mother lecture."

"It's too late for that."

"Anyway, it's not my fault if he gets insulted too easily," Alice protested. "We'll never see him again."

Eleanor found herself strangely disappointed by her sister's statement. "That still doesn't mean I can go around hurting people's feelings."

"Do you want to tell Mother you need to go back and talk to him some more?"

"That *won't* be necessary. Unlike you, I *always* obey Rule Number One," Eleanor told her and continued walking toward the carriage. It was very difficult when what she really wanted to do was run back and at least make him understand how sorry she was.

"Pain-in-the-neck goody-goody," Alice grumbled. "No wonder you're so old and still not married."

Eleanor pursed her lips and walked in silence. Alice was right. She was too timid to do anything wild and daring. But her sister really should be grateful. If she wasn't such an old Goody Two-shoes, she'd shove her off the pier and right into the Bay.

Mrs. Folsom allowed Reed, the driver, to assist her into the carriage. Eleanor almost supposed that, in the confusion of their arrival, she and Alice had escaped her mother's thorough scolding.

But once Mrs. Folsom was comfortably settled in her seat, she turned around to her daughters. "Now, just what did you two think you were doing, talking to that man?" she demanded.

❖ 2 ❖

ELEANOR STOPPED, ONE foot on the carriage step, one foot still on the ground. She should have known they'd never escape.

"Alice wanted to know what a waterman was."

Drat Alice! She and her insatiable curiosity had gotten them into this mess. Where was her sister's unruly spunkiness now? She sat in the carriage, her hands folded demurely in her lap, looking as if butter wouldn't melt in her mouth, and Eleanor had to do all the explaining. She hoped her mother would accept what she'd just told her and move on to another complaint.

She really should have known her mother better.

"A waterman?" Mrs. Folsom repeated. "What *is* a waterman?" Before Eleanor could reply, Mrs. Folsom threw both hands in the air in a gesture of dismissal and declared, "Oh, what do I care? It shouldn't matter to Alice what a waterman is either, as she won't be seeing too many of them close up anyway. And you most likely won't be seeing *any* of them. I have other plans for you."

Eleanor settled into the carriage, with a shudder of foreboding.

"I could excuse such unladylike behavior from Alice,"

Mrs. Folsom continued. "After all, she's only thirteen. But you're twenty-two, Eleanor. *You* should know better. And you should be able to look out for your little sister better."

Eleanor settled herself in her seat and prayed her mother was finished. Hadn't she figured out by now that the entire Baltimore Police Force couldn't keep track of Alice?

Mrs. Folsom, however, continued, "On the other hand, you don't know when you've got a good thing, my dear. Why you haven't yet accepted that nice Randolph boy is beyond me. He must have proposed marriage a dozen times."

Eleanor closed her eyes and grimaced, and tried to ignore Alice poking her in the ribs with her elbow. How her mother could still be so blind not to see through all Bradley's fine words and hypocritical deeds was beyond her!

"He's handsome enough. He's obviously completely devoted to making you happy."

Then why doesn't he go away? Eleanor silently wondered. *That would make me happy.*

"He comes from a good family. He's wealthy enough now to support a wife and family in fine style—and stands to inherit a good deal more when that old curmudgeon of a father of his finally decides to shuffle off this mortal coil. Then Bradley will inherit the old man's house in Mt. Vernon Square, and you'll move in to take care of his mother. Unfortunately I have no doubts she'll still be living then, but everyone has to make some sacrifices. But you'll live only two doors down from us! Won't that be grand?"

Mrs. Folsom was practically beaming with delightful daydreams of the future.

Eleanor would have thought marriage to Bradley was torment enough, but also living with a querulous, invalid mother-in-law, only two doors away from her own mother, would be sheer torture of the most infernal kind!

"I've told you before, Mother—I don't love him,"

Eleanor tried to explain in the simplest terms of all.

Mrs. Folsom heaved a deep sigh as her daydreams were shattered, and turned around again to face the front of the carriage.

"Yes, and I suppose you modern girls must always be in love," Mrs. Folsom continued to complain. "Now, in *my* day, a young lady knew her duty to her family. In my day, a girl honored her mother and her father. In my day, a girl accomplished her responsibilities. In my day, a father knew how to command the utmost respect and the strictest obedience from all the members of his family."

Alice was nodding her head from side to side, and moving her mouth in mimicry of her mother while the rest of her face took on bizarre contortions.

Eleanor feigned a cough and held her hand over her mouth. Pressing her lips tightly together to hold in the laughter, she shot dagger-eyed glares at Alice, hoping that she'd stop. They might be Alice's shenanigans, but Eleanor knew if she laughed she'd be the one who'd be scolded.

"I still cannot believe your father took your part against me in this difference of opinion."

Mrs. Folsom heaved another deep, depressed sigh. For her part, Eleanor was never so grateful in her life for her father's unaccustomed understanding in this matter.

"But I suppose this is what I deserve. I've been far too lenient with you girls. I never should have allowed you to read all those romantic novels."

How could she complain about her daughter's choice of reading material, Eleanor silently puzzled, when her mother had never picked up one of "those romantic novels"—or any other book—in her entire life? And her father believed that any reading material that didn't pertain to matters of business was purely unnecessary and worthless.

Mrs. Folsom spun around again. Alice sat poised and pretty as their mother shook her finger under the girl's nose.

"Don't *you* think to be falling in love, miss."

Alice just laughed.

Mrs. Folsom probably wouldn't be able to tell if Alice were laughing at the ludicrous thought of falling in love at thirteen, or at her. Eleanor knew her sister most likely was laughing at the very idea that someone might dare try to control her at all.

Apparently their mother had decided that Alice, at her tender age, was laughing at the very thought that she might fall in love, and turned around, satisfied. Silently they sat waiting for Mr. Folsom in the shade of the carriage roof, but the heat was still oppressive. Eleanor's damp skin welcomed any small breeze.

She knew she shouldn't be curious about a man she'd never see again, but she couldn't help regretting how rude she must have seemed when he had talked so nicely to her and Alice. She tried to spare a glance back at the stranger. She could still see his broad back bent over a puzzling tangle of ropes and cables and pulleys.

Whatever a waterman was, this one was awfully handsome. And she'd never gotten to apologize, or even learned his name.

However regretful she might be, she reluctantly conceded, her mother must be right. People like him—the watermen—rarely came to her side of the island except to work. And the very idea that she might go to the other side was positively ludicrous! Slowly she turned her back on him and waited for her father.

"Hello-o-o!"

The sound pierced the air above the rumbling of engines and the flapping of the sails—even above the hoot of the whistle of the steamboat that ferried to the island those who couldn't afford their own personal transportation from Baltimore.

"Hello-o-o!"

Eleanor saw Mrs. McGruder waving her handkerchief furiously over her head and bustling toward them across the well-tended lawn.

"Oh, my gracious!" Mrs. Folsom grumbled. "I only hope she didn't notice us until *after* you two had finished *disgracing* yourselves by talking with that island person."

"Oh, now, Mother," Eleanor tried to console her.

Mrs. Folsom shook her head furiously. "Don't 'now, Mother' me, young lady. Clementine McGruder can't hold her tongue about any news. You two just can't seem to comprehend—we have a reputation to uphold in this community."

No, Mother, Eleanor thought with just a tinge of bitterness. *I understand it all too well.*

"Hello! Oh, I just couldn't wait until you all arrived," Mrs. McGruder chirped.

The plump woman's speaking voice was still in the same octave as her horrible, screeched greeting.

"It's been so lonesome on this godforsaken island! I tried to tell the mister, I said, 'Horace, why do you want to go to the cottage so early—a full week ahead—when you know perfectly well no one else will be there until the first week of July?' Well, no one except—" Her voice lowered just slightly in volume. "Except the *island people*." She wrinkled her pug nose, then continued her tirade. "I said, 'Horace, I will absolutely die of boredom! You have your fishing and your watching birds and your bug collection, but what am I supposed to do there all by myself?' But do you think I could get any kind of sensible answer from him? Oh, no. Not Horace. He's too involved with his lures and poles and—"

"Poor dear," Mrs. Folsom interrupted her friend's lament.

Eleanor couldn't decide if she felt sorrier for the bored Mrs. McGruder, or the beleaguered Mr. McGruder.

"Who else has arrived?" Mrs. Folsom asked.

Quickly forgetting her own miseries, Mrs. McGruder counted the summer socialites off on her pudgy fingers.

"The Hamiltons. They've brought Clothilda Mertz, his sister—an invalid, I hear, so we won't see too much of her—and her three children—of whom we might see more than we care to. The Stewarts came alone this year, but they may have the Hollands come by for two weeks in August. Oh, let me think who else."

Eleanor's fingers tightened into hard little fists in her lap as she desperately waited to hear the name she dreaded— Bradley Randolph.

"I doubt the Ridgelys will be here," Mrs. Folsom offered, "as his mother passed away this April."

"Oh, no, they're here."

Mrs. Folsom's blue eyes grew larger at the shocking news.

"Oh, come now, Violet. It shouldn't come as any surprise," Mrs. McGruder said, waving her handkerchief about. "Cora Ridgely never did like the old lady. Do you think she'll let her barely lamented passing interfere with her making the social rounds?"

Mrs. Folsom nodded. "No, I suppose not."

"Come, come, enough of this idle chatter," Mr. Folsom ordered as he climbed into the carriage and settled himself regally beside his wife. With a brief nod and a tip of his broad-brimmed straw hat, he acknowledged his wife's friend. "Mrs. McGruder, we shall see you again at the Reception, I'm sure."

He tapped Reed on the shoulder with his silver-knobbed cane, and the carriage took a left turn onto Folsom Drive, heading for the Folsom summer cottage.

Eleanor finally began to relax.

Joshua Claybourne could see the rear of the carriage turning left onto Folsom Drive, away from the Yachting

Club. Just before the carriage disappeared completely behind a stand of maples and white-trunked birch trees, he caught one last glimpse of the haughty young woman.

"Well, I see you've met Mrs. Folsom," Edgar Miller called.

Josh turned around. His cousin was strolling up to him across the pier.

"So that's who that was?" Josh asked, trying to show as little interest as possible. He just kept rolling up the ropes. His cousin hadn't changed much in the twenty-nine years he'd known him. Whenever Edgar found something he could tease a person about, he'd wring every last drop from it.

"If there's anyone on this island you don't want to rile, it's one of them Folsoms," Edgar warned. He reached up to scratch his balding head.

"I didn't rile her," Josh protested, hanging up a coil. "I didn't even say a word to her."

"And that's just the way she likes it. Her and all them rich summer folks from the city."

"Well, the little one seemed pretty talkative."

He figured he'd start with her first, then work the older daughter into the conversation sort of like an afterthought. Maybe then his questions about her wouldn't attract too much attention from his nosy cousin.

"Yeah, that Alice is a real terror." Edgar chuckled.

"Not like the older daughter, huh?"

"Who? Miss Eleanor?"

Eleanor. "Yeah, I guess."

Josh reached for another rope, trying to show much more interest in it than in any city girl come here for the summer. Why should he be interested? She might seem shy and quiet, and maybe she was the prettiest girl he'd seen in a month of Sundays, but she was just as condescending as all the rest of those city folk.

"She ain't pretty none."

"Yeah, I guess," Josh repeated.

"Yeah, but heck! She's so quiet—wouldn't say boo to a goose."

And when she does say something, Josh thought, *it comes out as an insult.* He began coiling another rope over his arm, a little more quickly this time.

"She's more like her parents?" he asked aloud.

"Guess so. Leastwise, she don't talk to *me*." Edgar gave another little chuckle that shook his potbelly.

"I get the feeling she doesn't talk to most people."

"I'll admit I was surprised to see her talking to you. Must be that Claybourne sugar talk, huh?"

"Yeah, sure." Josh tossed the coil of rope onto the pile.

"Every storekeeper on the island has dreaded that little one showing up every summer since she was eight years old. She liked to drove the crews crazy couple o' years ago when she was younger and kept escaping from her nanny."

"I didn't see any nanny with her this time," Josh remarked. He'd only seen her with her older sister—Eleanor—who didn't seem able to control her any better than any nanny could.

"Seems that Alice don't care who she talks to—as long as she's talking." He tapped the side of his head. "It's like there ain't no gate between her brain and her mouth, and whatever she's thinking just comes popping out."

"I never noticed—"

"You wouldn't, either. You're always out before sunup on that bugeye of yours and stay out practically all day."

"I've got to be. How else can I support Bill and the girls, and still put by enough money to hire someone, maybe buy another bugeye, or even one of those new skipjacks . . . ?"

Edgar gave another little chuckle, but this one seemed to hold more ridicule than humor. "You sure got grand plans there, Josh."

Everybody on Silchester knew Josh had big dreams for the future. The only trouble was, not too many people believed he'd ever make them come true. Just his little brother, Bill, and his sisters, Maddie and Winnie. Most of all, himself. A deep feeling in his gut told him that one day he'd succeed.

"Yeah," was all Josh said.

"Well, you just keep making them big plans, Cuz. You just keep dreaming."

He wouldn't impress Edgar if he told him those were only the beginnings of his grand plans.

"Hey, thanks for getting me the extra work here at the yachting club."

"Any time, Cuz." Edgar slapped him heartily on the back. "Say, there's a big shindig coming up in a few days—Mr. Folsom's annual welcoming party. The fellow in charge of the clubhouse told me they're going to need extra waiters and all. I could put in a good word for you. Think you'd mind spending a few hours handing out fancy food and drinks to rich folks?"

"Yeah, sure. I'm not such a fool I'd turn down the chance to make some extra money."

"Some of these summer folks sometimes even take it into their heads to tip—even to tip generously."

"Thanks again, Ed."

"Hey, what's family for?"

Being harbormaster was a big job, Josh knew, but his cousin knew enough about all kinds of boats to handle it.

"You know, I'm still looking for a good number two man."

"I know."

"Ain't found anybody knows as much as you do, except maybe me."

"You always were too modest, Ed," Josh replied. "Thanks, but no. You know I don't mind picking up temporary work for somebody, but when it comes to making a living, I don't want to work for any man. I need to be my own boss.''

''Yeah, yeah. I know,'' Ed said with a laugh as he moved on down the pier. ''You're as stubborn as your old man ever was.''

Josh continued to roll the ropes into large coils, waiting for the next yacht coming into the club.

''You there!'' Josh heard the noise of someone clearing his throat just to gain attention. ''Yes, you.''

Josh turned to the imperative call. Another one of the rich summer folks, he decided as he watched the man who was holding one finger raised in the air, as if testing the wind direction—or else he'd tried to pick his nose and missed. Josh tried to suppress a chuckle just looking at this little dandy prancing up to him.

He hadn't arrived with the Folsoms. Nobody else had docked recently. Whose yacht had he come from? When was he sailing back?

Josh noted the beads of perspiration across the man's forehead and upper lip, as if he'd been exerting himself. He also heard the hoot of the ferry whistle as it pulled out again. So that was probably where he'd come from, but why? Why would someone dressed so fancy be riding the ferry with the mail, canned goods, and ordinary folks?

''You there,'' the man repeated. He pointed his finger directly at Josh as he approached. ''Would that be the Folsom yacht there?''

''Yeah.''

''Ah.'' The man looked immensely pleased. ''I take it Mr. and Mrs. Folsom have arrived.''

No, the boat came gliding in all by itself. Josh bit his tongue and instead replied, ''Yeah.''

''And their two lovely daughters?''

More slowly Josh answered, ''Yeah.''

The man's smile widened.

Did this man have business with Mr. Folsom? Josh wondered. Then why did he want to know about the daughters? He was too old to give a hang about the little one—unless he was some sort of pervert. What was his concern with the older one—with Eleanor? And why should Josh be concerned?

❖ 3 ❖

Why should Josh care who Eleanor Folsom saw anyway? The fellow looked like just the sort Eleanor would think *was* worth talking to. He'd have bet Mrs. Folsom didn't have a rule against her daughters associating with the likes of this fellow. Or if there was a rule, Eleanor wouldn't be so insistent on obeying it.

Was that it? Josh speculated. Was Miss Eleanor-Ice-Princess-Stick-With-Your-Own-Kind Folsom having some kind of secret assignation with this fellow that her parents disapproved of? Obviously there was more to this young woman than the cool surface showed.

Then the man looked around. "I suppose they've already departed for their cottage."

"Huh?" Josh roused from his speculations. "Yeah." He nodded toward the turn that Folsom Drive made away from the club. "They went that way." Then he went back to studying his rope.

The man breathed a deep sigh of apparent relief.

"Maybe if you hurry up and run you can catch up to them."

The man glared venomously at Josh. "Surely you jest!"

Josh resisted the urge to tell this fellow to take a right turn into the Bay.

"I am also in need of lodgings."

Josh nodded toward the clubhouse. "I guess they might put you up there. I couldn't really recommend it, though. I never stayed there myself."

"No, no, no. You don't understand," the man protested.

Not much of a joker, was he? Josh decided. He wouldn't have thought so, anyway.

"I want something a bit more—"

"Cheap?" Josh offered.

From the looks of this fellow, he knew that couldn't possibly be the man's problem, but some ornery streak left over from boyhood prodded him to say that—or some nettle itching him from just knowing the man was the kind Miss Folsom would take an interest in. Another snob—perpetuating generations of little snobs.

And here he was, scrimping and saving to buy Winnie a second-hand piano he'd spotted in Easton, ten cents on the dollar.

"No, no, no," the man protested. "I knew you wouldn't understand."

The man's face was growing redder with frustration. Josh just grinned and tried to look helpful.

"I want something a bit more . . . private . . . out of the way of the . . . usual accommodations."

Josh nodded. "Then you'll probably be wanting Bodine's Boardinghouse."

He pointed. The man craned his neck, trying to look up the only other road leading away from the town dock.

"It's the only boardinghouse on the island," Josh said. "Up Mallard Street to your right, between the barbershop and Moore's General Store. You can't miss it."

The man reached into the inside breast pocket of his jacket and pulled out his billfold. "I'd like to hire a carriage to transport myself and my baggage there."

Josh shook his head. "Can't do that."

"Why not?" he demanded indignantly. "My money's as good as—"

"Don't have a carriage."

"No carriage?" the man exclaimed. "Abominable! How do you manage?"

Josh shrugged.

"Well, then, perhaps someone else . . ."

"There isn't one. Most of us just walk around here. The island's not that big, you know."

No, the man probably didn't know, Josh thought. If he'd ever been here before, certainly he'd only been to the side of the island where the wealthy stayed.

The man took off his straw hat and fanned himself with it. "Drat!" he muttered to himself, but he was loud enough that Josh could hear. "I knew I should have come a bit more prepared."

"Only the folks who come here in the summer have carriages." Josh grinned to himself. "You could go ask if they'll hire out."

The man replaced his hat.

"Well, then, I'm prepared to pay *you* to carry my baggage for me." He pushed a five-dollar bill toward Josh.

Josh tried not to let his eyes pop out of his head.

"It's only two suitcases, and you look like a fine, strapping specimen of young manhood."

Josh stared at the stranger a moment, unsmiling, one eyebrow raised. He looked at the money, then back at the man. *He sure must want to get to Bodine's in a bad way.* The man was dressed so fancy; now he was telling Josh how strong he looked.

All right, he needed the money and he'd carry the suitcases to Bodine's, he decided as he pocketed the bill. But if this fellow thought to invite him upstairs, he'd whale the tar out of him!

"Yeah. Where're the suitcases?" Josh asked.

The man turned, as if expecting Josh to follow him without question. "I left them down by the dock. I paid some grimy little urchin a quarter to watch them. I'll be lucky if they're still there."

"They'll be there," Josh assured him as he followed along. "Whatever else people might think about us 'island people,' we don't steal."

As they neared the town dock, Josh started to grin. Nobody could miss the only two suitcases left there. He couldn't miss his own little brother, Bill, perched atop them, either. His brown bare feet drummed against the side.

"You there! Stop that," the man called.

"Guarding them with your life?" Josh asked.

Bill jumped up and stood ramrod straight in front of his charge. "Yes. No. I mean, who'd want these things? Ain't got no use for them here."

"Don't say *ain't*," Josh quickly corrected.

"Well, I suppose you did your job after all, young fellow," the man said, tossing Bill another quarter. "Here, just as I promised."

"See, I told you no one would steal them," Josh told the man. "And the grimy little urchin guarding them is my brother."

"Really?" The man paused a moment, gave Bill a cursory glance, and Josh a brief nod. "My apologies."

Josh pressed his lips together and lifted the two suitcases.

"Bodine's is this way." He jerked his head, indicating the man should follow him, then started to walk up the road.

He didn't usually walk this fast through town, especially not carrying two pretty heavy suitcases, but he just wanted to see if the man could keep up with him.

Any man who thought that Bill—who, like every kid on Silchester, spent most of his life in the water and took a bath every Saturday night—was a "grimy little urchin" must have some pretty high standards. Any man who dressed and spoke so fancy, was friends with the Folsoms, and tossed quarters and five-dollar bills around so easily must be used to some pretty soft living. He'd never be able to keep up.

Josh heard the crushed oyster shells crunching under his work shoes as he walked up Mallard Street. He knew Bill's bare feet were brown and tough. He could also hear the stranger's slick leather soles slipping occasionally on unsure footing as the crushed shells rearranged themselves under his weight. Josh just kept walking.

By the time they reached Chuck Hawley's Feed and Grain Store, the stranger was beginning to huff and puff.

"It's not much farther now," Josh assured him, glancing back.

Chuck stuck his head out the doorway.

"Hey, Josh!"

"Hey, Chuck!"

"How y'doing?"

"Can't complain."

"That there fellow following you or what?"

Josh jerked his head backward. "Who? Him?"

"Yeah."

"Taking him to Bodine's."

Chuck eyed the puffing, perspiring man. "Him? At Bodine's?"

"Yeah."

Chuck reached up and scratched his head. "What's this world coming to?"

Josh just shrugged.

"Don't look like he's going to make it to Bodine's," Chuck observed.

Josh glanced back. "Oh, he's tougher than he looks."

"Have to be," Chuck muttered as he went back into his store.

By the time they reached Wally Freeman's barbershop, the stranger was tugging as his tight collar.

"Hey, Josh."

"Hey, Wally."

"How y'doing?"

"Not too bad lately."

"Catching some big ones?"

"Oh, yeah."

"Suckers?"

Josh shrugged. "You could say that."

"Keep up the good work."

"Will if I can," Josh assured him.

"Say, you're starting to look like you need a trim around the edges."

Josh would have reached up if he hadn't had both hands full of suitcases. "Might be."

"Stop on in anytime, and I'll fix you right up."

"Thanks, Wally. Will if I can." Josh moved on.

Maddie had been trimming the edges for some time now. Since when did he have time to sit leisurely in a barber chair with hot towels and barbisol?

By the time they got to the front porch of Bodine's Boardinghouse, the man had to lean against the wall to catch his breath before going inside. For himself, why, Josh felt barely winded.

So much for the kind of man Miss Eleanor Folsom would seem to prefer, Josh thought with just a bit of smug satisfaction.

He nudged the front door open with his toe, carried the two suitcases inside, and set them down in the middle of the parlor.

"Aunt Audrey!" he called up the steps. Going to a doorway that led to the back of the house, he called again, "Aunt Audrey, I got you a new boarder."

"Joshua Claybourne, shame on you," Miss Zang scolded

from her chair by the front window. She laid the book she was reading in her lap and clucked her tongue. She shook a thin, crooked, birdlike finger at him. "We're using our outside voice inside, and nice, polite young men don't do that."

"Sorry, Miss Zang. I didn't see you sitting there."

She was wearing the same thing she always wore. Summer or winter, school classroom or Sunday services, Josh couldn't remember seeing her in anything else. He would've bet this year's catch that if someone opened her wardrobe, he wouldn't find anything hanging there but black skirts and white blouses.

The fragile-looking old lady continued to shake her head. "You never were very observant, Joshua. If you were, you'd have done much better in mathematics."

"I've been out of school a long time, ma'am," Josh reminded her with a little chuckle.

"There's no need to remind me, young man," Miss Zang asserted proudly. "I'm not so old that my memory is failing. You graduated in seventy-six, the Centennial year. Your sister Madeline graduated in seventy-two, along with Aiden Darty and Nelly White, the same year we had that big snowstorm. Audrey graduated in twenty-four, the year I began teaching. William here stands to graduate in ninety-one—*if* he changes his ways and becomes more attentive in class. Just like you," she added with another shake of her head. "You could have been my prize student—but you were always making such careless mistakes—and all simply due to inattentiveness."

"Well, Josh is doing just fine now, Miss Zang, with his own business and everything," Aunt Audrey, bustling through the doorway from the kitchen, said in his defense. She wiped her hands down the front of her blue gingham apron. "Fresh bread for dinner tonight."

In spite of the flour that puffed up from her apron when

she moved, Josh leaned forward to give her a hug. His round little aunt looked so much like his late mother, with her red-blond hair and green eyes, no one could have missed the Miller family resemblance. For himself, most folks said he favored his father's people.

"I never said you were stupid or incapable, Joshua," Miss Zang continued. "Just careless."

"Sorry, ma'am," Josh answered, although why he should be apologizing for mistakes he'd made thirteen years ago was beyond him. But *no one* was rude to Miss Zang.

"Now, if you'll excuse me, please." Audrey turned to the stranger. "So you're my new boarder?"

He backed up, as if afraid Audrey would try to give him a hug, too.

"It appears I have no choice in the matter," he replied.

"How long do you think you'll be staying?"

"I haven't decided," he answered with such finality Josh knew his aunt was smart enough not to pursue the matter.

"It'll cost you a dollar a day. Bathroom's right next door to your room. You'll have to share with Miss Zang, but she don't make much mess. Baths are two bits, hot baths four."

Then, with a firm voice and a deep frown, Aunt Audrey laid down the law. "I don't allow no smoking, no hard liquor, no foul language, no work on Sundays. No cooking in the room, no ladies in your room—this ain't that kind of place."

Then she shot him a beaming smile. "So, would you like to see the room first?"

"Since there are no other accommodations available on the island, I'd say that would be pretty pointless. I'll take the room, regardless."

"Most folks like to check out the accommodations before they sign in and pay."

"I won't be staying here that long."

Audrey shrugged her sloping shoulders. "Suit yourself."

She turned the register around to face him. With a cough and a flourish, the man signed and blotted his name. He threw several silver dollars on the counter. Audrey scooped them up and stuck them in her apron pocket before the last one stopped spinning.

"All righty, then," Audrey said as she headed for the stairs. "Just follow me, and I'll show you your room, Mr. Randolph."

❖ 4 ❖

"It's in the back," Audrey explained as she huffed her way up the stairs. "Miss Zang's occupied the two front rooms since before the late Mr. Bodine—Lord rest his soul—inherited the place from his parents. We used to joke that she's always been here. They just built the house around her."

It was Aunt Audrey's perennial joke about Miss Zang, but Josh laughed anyway each time he heard it. Mr. Randolph didn't make a sound. Josh could've told Aunt Audrey this fellow didn't have a sense of humor.

"But she's a quiet old soul and won't bother you much," Audrey continued. "She likes the two front rooms so she can look out over Mallard Street and keep track of what everyone else is doing."

Audrey pushed the door inward.

"Now, the furniture's kind of old, but that's a brand-new mattress on the bed. I change the sheets weekly, and you won't find any patches in them. You can have an extra pillow—for just a little extra."

"Of course," Mr. Randolph responded with a wry twist of his lips. He walked over and pushed down on the mattress. Apparently it bounced back to his specifications. He moved along to the dresser.

"If you got any shirts or things that need doing, I can take care of that for you, too—for just a little extra."

"Of course."

He ran his finger across the top of the dresser, then examined his fingertips as he rubbed them together. He grimaced and looked around, as if searching for something to wipe his hand on.

Josh grimaced, too. Aunt Audrey kept her place spotless. This man was just looking for faults.

Josh set the two suitcases down at the foot of the bed and wished he could have set them on Mr. Randolph's feet instead.

Randolph eyed the little pictures Aunt Audrey had hung on the walls. There was a real nice *Jesus in the Garden* and a couple of *Guardian Angels*. Over by the window was a sampler she'd done when she was about five.

"I serve breakfast from six to eight every morning. First come, first served. Dinner's noon to two. Supper's six to eight every evening," Audrey continued to explain as she made her way to the single window. "Nothing fancy, but nobody's ever left my table hungry."

She pulled the chintz curtain back and raised the shade to show him the view.

"It's not Mallard Street, but maybe you'll be happier with the peace and quiet after all, Mr. Randolph. I hope you like the color green, 'cause you got a real nice view of the woods here. It's real pretty in the fall, too, if you'd care to come back."

"I doubt it."

Audrey shrugged off the insult. "In the winter we can see clear through to the rich folks' homes."

"You can?" Mr. Randolph asked. His voice was full of nonchalance, but Josh noticed how quickly he stopped grimacing at the imaginary dirt on his finger and headed for the window.

"Of course, they're all closed up then, but we can still see them." She pointed out the window. "I think right through there is that big Folsom house, ain't it, Josh?"

She turned to him, awaiting his corroboration.

"I guess, Aunt Audrey." Josh shrugged. "I've never really paid much attention."

But apparently Mr. Randolph was paying a lot of attention to the location of the Folsom cottage. The way he was peering out the window, Josh was surprised he didn't stick his head and half his body right out—or jump down two stories and start running in that direction.

"Through these woods, you say?" Mr. Randolph asked.

If he thought he was doing anything now to keep the blatant eagerness out of his voice, he was failing miserably.

Audrey waved her hand around the window. "Thereabouts."

"Can they see through to us?"

"Don't see as how they'd want to—"

"But if they did?"

"Probably in the winter, when all the leaves are gone. But in the winter there isn't anybody there. In the summer I doubt it."

Mr. Randolph looked clearly relieved.

Josh couldn't help frowning, wondering why this man was so evidently interested in the Folsoms, and yet everything he did seemed to indicate he didn't want them noticing him—at least, not yet.

The man hadn't done anything yet, least of all anything that warranted talking to Chief Groves about. But maybe this character ought to be watched, Josh decided. Maybe he was just the fellow to do it, too.

"Of course, not too many people go wandering through those woods." Josh shook his head emphatically. "Nope. Anybody with a lick of sense stays away from the snakes."

"Snakes?" Mr. Randolph asked. Both of his eyebrows

rose. Josh was surprised the fool didn't make a jump for the apparent safety of the top of the dresser.

"Cottonheads," Josh specified.

Aunt Audrey gave Josh a curious look with a tiny lift of one eyebrow, but said nothing.

"Cottonheads?" Mr. Randolph repeated anxiously. Then he drew himself up and pronounced, "I never heard of them. That's preposterous!"

"Well, no. You city folks wouldn't know. Seems like our little island is so nice, somehow a cottonmouth and a copperhead sort of got friendly with each other, and out hatches these little snakes, so we call them cottonheads."

Mr. Randolph stared wide-eyed at Josh.

"However, they're not too friendly with anyone else. They got a double dose of the venom of both parents, a triple dose of nastiness, and, in spite of their name, they're as black as pitch, so they're really hard to see."

Mr. Randolph's mouth started to hang open.

"Fortunately you can always tell when you've stepped in a nest of them. Feels kind of squishy, just like you're walking on big wads of fluffy cotton."

"That's good," Mr. Randolph said eagerly.

Josh just shrugged. "*Unfortunately* by that time, well, it's just too late to . . ."

Josh heaved the biggest, most forlorn sigh he could muster. Miss Zang, directing her school pageants, would have been proud of his dramatic talents.

"Oh, Josh, shame on you!" Aunt Audrey scolded him, giving him a poke in the ribs with her elbow.

For just a moment Josh was afraid his aunt would break down and tell the truth. Oh, well, he'd at least had this much fun with the pompous little dandy.

"Shame on you, scaring our guest." Aunt Audrey turned to her new boarder and assured him, "Now, don't you worry none, Mr. Randolph. They *never* come inside."

"No, never," Josh agreed with a perfectly straight face and silently blessed his agreeable Aunt Audrey.

"Why not?"

"Too smooth," Audrey answered. When Randolph just stared at her in puzzlement, she added, "The floor's too smooth. They can't get their bellyhooks into it, so they can't move. So, see. You're perfectly safe in here."

"Oh, that's just fine," Mr. Randolph said, completely disgruntled. "But what if I want to go outside?"

"Oh, you can still protect yourself," Audrey said.

"I *can*? How?" he demanded eagerly.

Josh looked at his aunt. He didn't have a clue what to tell the man now. *Oh, you've done it this time, Aunt Audrey,* he thought.

"Wool," she readily pronounced.

"Wool?"

"Definitely. See, they're cottonheads. So anything else is just going to drive them away."

"Obviously," Josh said, picking up on the fun.

Mr. Randolph frowned a moment, as if thinking this through. Any minute Josh expected him to start laughing along with them.

"I guess that makes sense," the man said, nodding.

"Of course it does," Josh heartily agreed. "We islanders've been bitten so many times, it doesn't bother us. But you city folks haven't."

"So what you have to do is," Aunt Audrey continued, "anytime you go outside, you need to wear something made of wool."

"I don't think I brought anything. Do you think linen would do?"

"Oh, no, no. It's got to be wool," Aunt Audrey stated emphatically.

"It doesn't have to be anything big," Josh said.

He wouldn't want to suffer a guilty conscience if this

fellow wrapped himself in wool blankets, collapsed in the middle of Mallard Street, and died of heat prostration. Worse yet, he didn't want to get stuck with the cost of burying the fellow.

"Just . . . just maybe a scarf or something."

"But I didn't bring anything." The man looked very concerned.

"Oh, *that's* not a problem," Audrey said. "Josh can lend you one, can't you, Josh?"

"Yeah, I guess so." He was churning with laughter inside. "Of course, mine tend to smell like dead fish."

Audrey waved her hand. "Oh, a good airing will clear that up . . . mostly. Just put on some more of that fancy men's toilet water stuff you city fellows wear."

"So, if I wear a scarf I can go about the island freely?" Mr. Randolph asked. "Anywhere I want?"

"Almost," Josh answered with a little less humor. He could just see this Randolph fellow crashing clumsily through the woods on his way to the Folsoms. And what would he do when he got there?

"Well, then, yes, yes. This room will do nicely. Thank you, Mrs. Bodine." Mr. Randolph took Audrey by the elbow and began leading her toward the door. Then the man turned to Josh, who got swept up in the evacuation. "And I'll be waiting for that scarf."

Before Josh could advise Randolph not to hold his breath, he and Aunt Audrey were standing in the hall, and Randolph had shut the door in their faces.

Then they began to laugh.

"Why, Eleanor, you look absolutely radiant tonight!" Mrs. McGruder exclaimed in greeting. The enormous bustle of her gold lace gown waddled behind her.

She reached up and began fidgeting with the white lace on one of the large puffed sleeves of Eleanor's pale blue gown.

"All the other young ladies will be positively pea-green with envy."

"How kind of you to say so, Mrs. McGruder. You look very elegant yourself, as usual," Eleanor responded politely.

Mrs. McGruder's hand moved along to rearrange one of the small pearl clips tucked into Eleanor's long dark curls.

"I wouldn't be the least bit surprised if several arguments didn't break out over who was going to be the first to dance with you."

"Oh, I hope not. Michael Stewart is my escort this evening, so obviously he gets the first dance."

She tried very hard to continue smiling when, deep inside, she dreaded the very thought of any man ever again telling another he couldn't dance with her, talk to her, or even look her way. She'd already had enough of that to last a lifetime.

"Ah, well, Mr. Stewart's a pleasant enough young man, even if he is a bit too corpulent at so young an age," Mrs. McGruder commented. She gave a little giggle. "My gracious, it's a good thing the boy has money to recommend him to the ladies, because he can't dance a step. He's about as graceful as a goose." She giggled again. "I do hope you'll heed your mother's wise advice and make some sort of attachment this summer. She so longs for grandchildren."

After dropping that not-so-subtle hint, and without waiting for a response, the lady moved on.

Eleanor grimaced. Mother had been longing for grandchildren since the day Eleanor turned sixteen. But Eleanor had never had any intention of being wed at that age, as her mother had been. Even now, she felt perfectly comfortable with the prospect of leading a single life. If only everyone else would stop urging her to marry. If only, she thought with just a slightly wistful sigh, she would find a man she could truly love.

She looked out the wide windows of the clubhouse. The sun was just setting into the waters of the Chesapeake Bay. Along with the hundreds of candles already lit in the chandeliers and in the sconces along the walls, the sun cast its amber glow throughout the lounge, turning everything to gold.

It threw the trunks of the trees, the tall grasses at the edge of the water, and the ducks flying like dotted Vs into sharp silhouette against the orange sky streaked with rose and purple layers of clouds. It sent golden fingers reaching out across the surface of the dark waters. The silhouettes sparkled with the winking yellow glow of thousands of fireflies.

Looking at such beauty, she was reluctant to turn again to the beautiful, yet completely artificial, decorations of the clubhouse.

"I don't want to dampen your fun," Isabelle Hamilton whispered into her ear, "but I just overheard Mrs. McGruder pay almost the very same compliment to Jemima Ridgely, the same one she paid to me."

Eleanor laughed as she turned to her best friend. "Yes. And I'll bet you next year's Christmas presents that Mrs. McGruder is just about to pay the same compliment to Dorothy Stewart, *and* rearrange all her lace and hair ornaments."

"You, too?"

Eleanor nodded.

"Do you see Dorothy?" Isabelle asked.

"I saw her earlier." Eleanor bobbed her head to see better through the throng of people gathered in the lounge, waiting to go in to dinner. "But I'm certain she's somewhere around here."

"Of course she is," Isabelle insisted. "She's got her cap

set for Albert Ridgely, and she's not about to let him out of her sight until she snares him.''

"Ah, yes. There she is.''

"Where?'' Isabelle had to stand on tiptoe to see through the crowd.

"She's talking to Mrs. Ridgely, there. By the statue of Neptune—the one Father got when he and Mother went to Greece last autumn.''

"Yes, I see her now. Undoubtedly offering words of consolation to someone who needs no consoling whatsoever.''

"Hush, Belle,'' Eleanor said. "No one's supposed to actually *know* she and the old lady didn't get along.''

"I hear she doesn't think too highly of Dorothy, either.'' Isabelle gave a wicked little chuckle.

"I hear the feeling is mutual.''

"Do you think Dorothy would be talking to Mrs. Ridgely if she weren't looking to marry Albert?''

"It appears as if history would repeat itself,'' Eleanor speculated. Then she spotted the gold lace waddling toward the young lady. "Wait, here comes Mrs. McGruder. What perfect timing.''

Isabelle giggled. "What a shame we can't read her lips to know what she's saying.''

"Why, Dorothy, you look absolutely radiant tonight,'' Eleanor mimicked in a whisper. She pretended to pick at the lace on Isabelle's sleeve. "All the other young ladies will be positively pea-green with envy. I wouldn't be the least bit surprised if several arguments didn't break out over who was going to be the first to dance with you.''

Isabelle had clamped her gloved hand over her mouth to keep from laughing too loudly.

"Honestly,'' she scolded in a whisper. Then she giggled. "Now that's my old Ellie back again. People would think you were so polite and proper, but deep down inside, you're just as mischievous as your sister.''

"Oh, heaven forbid!" Eleanor exclaimed, throwing her hands up in mock horror.

"Of course, that was before—"

Eleanor shot her a worried glance.

"No, no. Never mind."

Eleanor searched for their target again. "Oh, wait. She's moving on."

"Who's she attacking now?" Isabelle asked.

Eleanor stood on tiptoe and lifted her head, searching the wide lounge for Mrs. McGruder and her next victim.

Eleanor caught her breath and dropped down flat-footed again. "Oh, my goodness!"

❖ 5 ❖

ELEANOR HAD ONLY seen his head above the crowd, but she'd recognize him anywhere.

"The fisherman—the waterman. What's he doing here? I didn't think he'd be here now."

"Eleanor, control yourself. You're babbling. You know how I hate it when you babble."

"I'm *not* babbling. RoseEllen Peabody babbles."

"Then what is it?" Isabelle demanded, holding her friend's arm as if to support her. "Oh, Ellie, you're not going to faint, are you? You're not going to create a scene, are you? I really hate scenes."

"No, no, it's nothing that serious," she told her friend as she regained her usual composure. She gave a little laugh. "Nothing that warrants a scene." At least, she hoped not.

"It's not that Bradley Randolph, is it?" Isabelle demanded. "You know, ever since he started trying to court you last autumn, you've been acting strangely—more withdrawn, timid. You're acting even more strange this evening."

"I am not," she insisted, although she had a sneaking suspicion she was.

"Is there something going on between you and Bradley that you're not telling anyone?" Isabelle demanded outright.

"No, no, no. Of . . . of course not!" Eleanor knew she didn't sound very convincing.

"You *would* tell me if there was, wouldn't you?"

"Of course, Belle. We've been friends for ages."

"When we were little, we promised to be each other's maid-of-honor," Isabelle reminded her. "I'm not about to let you go off and do something incredibly stupid. At least, not without me."

"No, no. I wouldn't. Especially not with Bradley."

"You know if he's here, your father will have him thrown out. That *would* create quite a stir."

"No. It's not him."

"Oh, thank goodness." Isabelle's eyebrows lowered in puzzlement. "But then, who is it?"

"I don't know."

Isabelle's eyebrows rose. "What do you mean, you don't know? How can someone bother you if you don't know who he is?"

Eleanor wasn't sure, either. All she knew was, not knowing the man's name, or anything else about him, didn't necessarily mean he didn't have some kind of effect on her.

"The man, he . . . he works here," Eleanor reluctantly admitted.

"Works? Here?"

"Oh, don't say it that way," Eleanor pleaded. "You sound like Alice and my mother."

Isabelle placed her hands on her hips and glared up at Eleanor. Her foot was tapping an impatient tattoo on the carpet. "Since when are we consorting with workmen? You're not going to be like Adelaide Gittings and run off with the coachman, are you?"

"Of course not." Eleanor shook her head.

"I'd have a really hard time being your maid-of-honor if that happened."

"I told you—"

"I mean, what sort of gown goes best with a coachman's whip?"

"Oh, Isabelle!" Eleanor giggled with exasperation. "I . . . we—Alice and I—met him when we docked. He . . . he was kind enough to answer a few of Alice's innumerable questions. You *know* how Alice can be."

"She's a little terror," Isabelle stated bluntly. "No offense."

"And . . . and Mother came by—"

"Oh, no."

"And . . ."

"And!" Isabelle's expression was a mixture of eagerness and censure.

"They . . . we were quite rude to him. I never got to apologize."

"Is that all?" Isabelle was clearly disappointed. "I thought you were going to tell me your mother hit him with her parasol or something."

"I still would have liked to have apologized—for Alice's rudeness . . . and my own."

Isabelle drew herself up to her full height, which still only brought the top of her head level with Eleanor's nose. "My dear, since when do *we* apologize to the islanders?"

The clear crystal sound of a bell rang through the lounge.

"Ladies and gentlemen, dinner is served," the maitre d' announced.

Michael Stewart seemed to appear magically at Eleanor's side. She graciously took his proffered elbow. All the while she couldn't help thinking it would have been so much better—so much more *proportional*—if they had paired him with Isabelle. But then, who would she have gone in to dinner with? She almost shuddered to think, but then,

Bradley wasn't here, was he? With a lighter step, she headed toward the dining room.

Still, Eleanor stopped and gave the room a wide, sweeping glance before she dared enter. The long table, surrounded by mahogany chairs, was covered with a crisp, pressed linen cloth and vases of fresh flowers. China, crystal, and silver shimmered in the light of glowing candles in branched candelabra.

Bradley was nowhere to be seen. She breathed with relief.

Then she noticed the waterman standing directly to her left, just inside the dining room doorway. Her throat tightened with nervousness. He was so close she could have leaned over and rubbed his chest with her bare shoulder.

She turned to look directly at him. He was already watching her very closely. She swallowed hard. What horrible things was he thinking about her? She couldn't tell. His face was devoid of any expression.

He looked so different this evening. Instead of the denim pants and cotton workshirt she'd seen him in earlier, he wore dark trousers and a crisp white shirt under a short white jacket with red and blue trim. White gloves covered his bronzed and callused hands. His sun-bleached hair wasn't tousled by the wind, but combed neatly back. He even smelled like bay rum.

Should she smile? Should she nod? Could she do anything that wouldn't be remarked—and gossiped about?

No. Not here, not now, not at this gathering.

"Is something wrong?" Michael asked.

She'd paused too long at the door. She could hear the gentlemen behind her coughing impatiently. Drat! It wouldn't hurt a one of them to be a few seconds late for a meal. Some of them, it wouldn't hurt to miss a meal entirely.

"No, not at all," she replied, and took a step into the

room. "It's just . . . why, the dining room is even more beautiful than I remembered it."

"So are you, Miss Folsom."

"Oh, Mr. Stewart, you're such a flatterer!"

She smiled at him and moved on, pretending to search the length of the table diligently for her place card, and trying hard not to show she was aware of the waterman in the room.

"Here you are," Michael told her as he pointed out the pink porcelain rose that supported a cream-colored card that bore her name in elegant, embossed gold script. "Right beside me."

Through the taking of their seats and the pleasant chatter going round the table as the guests awaited the first course, Eleanor tried very hard to keep smiling.

Through her father's long speech welcoming back to the island families who had been coming here for years, Eleanor even managed not to take a little catnap. At last a toast was drunk to the success of the summer season, and dinner was begun.

"Cold crabmeat in fresh tomatoes, miss." The dish was held before her. The voice was the waterman's.

"What are you doing here?" Eleanor whispered as he picked up the silver slotted spoon and placed a small tomato on her plate.

"Working," he whispered back.

"Why?"

"Because the only things my father left me were a house, two sisters, a brother, and a boat."

"But . . ."

The waterman moved on to serve Michael, then around the table with the other waiters, offering the first course to each guest.

She watched him, barely hearing a word Michael said, barely eating a thing as she waited for him to bring round the next dish. Everyone else seemed to be enjoying this delicacy. But the juice of the tomato stung her lips, and the crabmeat felt slimy in her mouth.

"Terrapin soup, miss."

"Yes, please," she answered, although she was afraid she wouldn't be able to eat any more of this than she had the first course.

He ladled a portion into her soup bowl. She watched him. Perhaps she should take the chance to talk to him a bit more. Perhaps this time he would listen.

"I wanted to thank you for—"

"No need, miss. I'm just doing my job," he replied without showing any emotion, and carried the soup tureen around the table.

Eleanor couldn't taste the soup. All she knew was that it was brown and felt like gravel going down her throat.

"Planked shad, miss. Potatoes duchesse, spring peas."

He placed a serving on her plate. On an impulse, Eleanor reached up and placed her hand on his arm to stop him from moving on.

"Now, see here, I've had about enough of your politeness," she whispered hoarsely. "Will you just stop and listen to me?"

"I'm sorry, miss." His tone was flat. "Is something wrong with your meal?"

"No, with the service," she told him bluntly.

"I'm sorry, miss—"

"I never got to thank you properly for putting up with my sister's silliness the other day," she said as quickly as possible.

"Yes, you did."

She was suddenly very aware that eyes were beginning to turn in her direction. He looked on the verge of moving on. But she had to continue. Her fingers tightened around his wrist.

"What's worse, I never got to apologize for my rudeness to you. And I . . ." She summoned the courage to look directly into his eyes. "I never got to ask your name."

He straightened, moving away so that she had to release his arm or spill the platter of fish into her lap. His face was still a sun-browned, impassive mask.

"Josh," he replied, then moved on to continue the service of the meal. Suddenly he stopped and turned back to her. Bending closer, he whispered, "Apology accepted."

Eleanor lowered her head to concentrate on the open-fire roasted filet of shad surrounded by creamy potatoes and little green peas on her plate. She couldn't let anyone at the table see how she smiled to herself.

The fish was white and flaky, and very delicious—even without any of the savory sauces offered with it. Even the little peas stayed on her fork and didn't roll off so she had to chase them around her plate and mash them until they stuck to the bottom of the tines.

The next course of roast chicken was done to perfection. The applesauce was the sweetest she had ever tasted. The ice cream, served with sliced fresh peaches, was absolutely delicious.

Eleanor left the table feeling that she had at last redeemed herself, morally, if not socially. Lighthearted, she and Michael joined the rest of the party in the ballroom.

The sun had now set completely. The night was only illumined by the half moon, the stars, and the brilliant chandeliers overhead. Crickets outside chirped in time to the eight-piece orchestra her father had hired just for this evening. A nightbird's cry added a plaintive descant to the tune.

Michael bowed as gallantly as his rotund middle would allow. "Miss Folsom, may I have the honor of this dance?"

Taken up with the spirit of fun, Eleanor held her skirt

out to the side and curtsied gracefully, just as her mother had taught her.

"Why, of course, kind sir," she replied with a little laugh.

"Oh, no. I believe this dance is mine."

The words were so low, only Eleanor and Michael could possibly have heard them. The tone wasn't threatening, but rather held a deep and abiding passion. But the words rang in Eleanor's ears like a death knell.

Her blood froze in her veins. The meal she'd just eaten churned in her stomach. She feared she'd vomit, and at the same time believed she'd fall into a dead faint.

"Bradley. Oh, no," she murmured, shaking her head. "What are you doing here?"

"My family is a member of the club," he answered. "I just walked in."

She tried to cling to Michael's arm for support. She closed her eyes and prayed that when she opened them, her vision would be clear, she wouldn't feel so dizzy—and Bradley would be gone. It would all be some horrible figment of her imagination, some horrendous hallucination brought on by a crab gone bad, a piece of underdone chicken, or an indigestible pea.

Eleanor opened her eyes. He still stood in front of her, like some mean, ugly troll barring her from crossing the bridge to happiness.

"Bradley, what are you doing here?" she repeated.

"Crossing the Chesapeake is no barrier to me," he boasted. "Especially when it comes to being with the woman I love."

Since when was there a bridge across the Chesapeake Bay for a troll to hide under? Eleanor silently demanded.

"Don't you know I'd follow you to the ends of the earth, my sweet?"

For once, Eleanor wished Christopher Columbus had

been wrong—that the earth was indeed flat, that there really were ends to the earth, and that Bradley would sail to one of them and fall off!

"I'm *not* your love," she protested. "And I don't want to dance with you."

"But don't you know every dance is mine?" Bradley asked. "Just as you are mine."

"No, Bradley, you're very mistaken."

"The only one who's mistaken is anyone who won't believe how very much I love you," he told her.

"Then *I* am mistaken," she admitted.

"Impossible! How can you doubt my love for you?" he pleaded.

"I can't believe you would claim to love me and then torment me so."

He placed his hand over his heart. "But it's the torments and tortures of Perdition for me without you!"

He reached out and tried to wrest her hand from Michael, but Eleanor clung to the pudgy fellow as if her life depended upon it. To her way of thinking, indeed it did.

"Dance, Michael," she ordered.

"Dance?"

Did he have to be as thick-skulled as he was thick around the middle?

"You know. One, two, one, two." She gave him a little push to get him started. "Dance!"

Before Bradley could make another move toward her, she propelled Michael onto the dance floor and began twirling around with the crowd of other couples.

She didn't care where Michael led her, or where she was leading him, which was actually the reality of it. She didn't care who she bumped into—although she was constantly begging everyone's pardon. She almost didn't care when plump little Michael began to huff and puff. She'd dance with him until he collapsed, and then she'd find another partner.

Eleanor feared she'd have to dance all night just to stay away from Bradley. She didn't think she had the stamina, but she knew she didn't want to be near that horrible man, not at all!

The orchestra ended one set and began another. Eleanor suddenly realized with a feeling of sinking dread that, sooner or later, the orchestra would have to take a break. Then how would she avoid Bradley?

"Now, surely," Bradley said from behind her, "*this* must be my dance."

"How did you follow me?" she demanded, still dizzy from the whirling steps.

"I've told you before, my love, I would follow you to the ends of the earth," Bradley proclaimed. He extended his hand to her. "Shall we?"

"No, no. Sorry. This dance belongs to Mr. Hamilton." She quickly seized the hand of the closest man passing by.

Isabelle's father smiled benignly at her and gave several gruff chuckles.

"Why, why, m'dear. How flattering," he mumbled.

Through his bushy, graying whiskers, Eleanor could barely see the hint of a blush.

"Why, why, I haven't been accosted in this manner by a lady of your age and beauty since . . . since sixty-four, in Washington, on Fifteenth Street." He chuckled again. "But then, that's not a story for your tender ears."

"Then let's dance instead," Eleanor urged.

Mr. Hamilton didn't need the prodding that Michael had. Although he traveled around the dance floor much more slowly, he also did so with much more grace.

This time she was not surprised when Bradley appeared behind Mr. Hamilton, ready to take her in his arms as soon as the elderly gentleman moved out of the way.

"At last I shall dance—"

"Oh, no, no. This dance belongs to . . . Mr. Ridgely," Eleanor said as, without looking, she grabbed the hand of a passing male.

But it wasn't Albert Ridgely she'd snared. It was Mr. Ridgely, Senior, who, still in mourning, was not prepared to dance.

"So sorry, Miss Folsom," Mr. Ridgely said, bowing deeply. "You do understand."

"Oh, indeed. My error, certainly," she mumbled. "I beg your pardon." Mr. Ridgely couldn't be any more sorry than she was.

Bradley wrested her hand from Mr. Ridgely's arm. His moist hands surrounded hers, kneading her flesh as if she were a piece of dough. He began to pull her toward a secluded corner.

"Bradley, I thought you wanted to dance," she said.

"We must talk."

If she tried to pull away, if she made any kind of protest, everyone would notice. She couldn't make a scene, not at the Welcoming Reception, her father's most important day of the summer season. Reluctantly, almost painfully—like a condemned prisoner going to her execution—she slowly followed Bradley.

Josh stood in the doorway of the ballroom, trying not to look too conspicuous and get tossed out. Heck, he'd been tossed out of lots of places when he was younger and rowdier. But he was getting paid for this, and he needed the money.

He tried to watch all the dancers so he could go home and tell his sisters about the ladies' gowns. If only he could afford to buy Maddie the material to make herself one— and take her someplace special on the mainland to wear it. She worked so hard and deserved a special treat.

He tried to remember the tunes the orchestra played so he could go home and repeat them on his mouth organ. Of course, then Winnie would start pleading once more to learn to play the piano, and he just couldn't afford to buy one right now.

Most of all, he tried to find Eleanor in the crowd. She was every bit as beautiful by glowing candlelight as she was in the beaming light of day. She'd actually thanked him several times. She'd actually made a specific point of apologizing to him. And she'd gone out of her way to pin him down and ask his name. Maybe she wasn't as cold-hearted as he'd first believed.

Well, even if she wasn't, she wasn't for him. He knew that darn good and well. But he could still watch. And he could still daydream. If he could just find her!

Suddenly he noticed a couple not dancing. They stood in a secluded corner, behind some potted palms. He wasn't a Peeping Tom, but there was something about this couple that made him curious.

He inched his way along the wall, hoping to remain inconspicuous as he moved farther into the room. Everyone was laughing, drinking, dancing—they'd never pay any attention to him.

He drew closer to the palm.

Well, well, he thought as he recognized the figures. Miss Eleanor Folsom and Mr. Bradley Randolph, holding hands and talking intently in a dark, secluded corner. He'd been right about the secret romance after all, he thought. But somehow, this time, he didn't find much satisfaction in being right.

Ordinarily Josh did not consider himself a nosy man. He did his job, minded his own business, and expected others to do the same. But there was something—like a little voice in the back of his head, or better yet, like a little devil perched on his shoulder.

Move closer, the little devil urged him. *Eavesdropping is so educational. Not to mention fun!*

Josh also knew he'd never been a man to seek out trouble or temptation. So when it came his way, he figured it was meant to be, and he might just as well give in.

He moved closer, keeping the potted palm between them, until he could clearly hear all they had to say. He kept his back to them, so that if anyone caught him standing there, they'd just assume he'd been watching the dancers. But every now and then, through the fronds of the palm, he could watch Eleanor and Mr. Randolph. He didn't like what he was seeing—but that little devil on his shoulder kept tempting him to watch.

She looked so beautiful in that gown—all blue like a spring sky over the salt marshes, with little bits of lace, like the wisps of white clouds. Her dark hair was a little messy, as if she'd been bouncing around or something. Her skin was as fair and flawless as a snowy egret's feather.

If there was a devil on his shoulder, there certainly was an angel standing right before his eyes.

Mr. Randolph was clinging to her hands. Josh had seen oystermen, facing drowning in the icy waters of the Chesapeake, cling to a life preserver with less fervor.

"I've done all the talking I can to you," Eleanor said.

She tried to pull her hands away. Randolph held them tightly. Josh never would've thought such a dandified little fellow could be so strong. But then, Eleanor was so delicate.

"Why won't you ever listen to me?" she pleaded in a low voice.

"Of course I listen to you, my dear," he protested. "Why, I'm prepared to devote my whole life to you. Haven't I shown you already I'm prepared to follow you anywhere?"

"That's the point, Bradley. I don't want you following me everywhere."

"Well, of course, not everywhere. You'll always have a certain amount of freedom—to go to church, to visit your family, to attend functions of ladies' charitable societies—"

"That's not freedom!" she argued passionately.

Josh wondered why she should react so strongly against this fellow. Randolph must've been bothering her for a long time to make her react like this to him.

"It's still slavery—or indentured servitude," Eleanor said. "It's as though I still have to have a special pass to move from one area to another."

"Oh, my sweet, you're exaggerating."

"No matter where I go, I never know when you'll just show up anyway and claim all my attention, like some old lady's spoiled terrier."

"But I need you. I need you in my home." Randolph's voice rose with urgency. "I need to know that when I return each evening, I'll find you there, always waiting for me."

"By the door with your pipe and slippers? You can buy a dog who'll do that for you! A dog will go fetch your newspaper, too. I don't think I could carry it in my mouth."

Randolph gave a condescending laugh. "Oh, you can be such a jester! But I love you. I can't bear to be away from you for a day, an hour."

"Try to learn, Bradley. You've got to stop following me around and sending me gifts and things. It's very . . . improper!"

This sure didn't sound like courting talk to him, Josh decided. It didn't even sound like a cute little lovers' spat. It sounded more to him as if the lady was trying to get rid of this fellow—and he was being a whole lot more than just a stubborn cuss about it.

"We can make proper all these improprieties, my love. You know how—"

"No!" She tried to pull her hands from his grasp with more force, but Randolph was much too strong for her.

Suddenly the man dropped to one knee and declared, "Marry me, my dearest, and you'll never want for anything!"

"I already don't want for anything. My father's very rich. Now, get up!"

But Randolph remained on one knee and scooted closer to her. "Marry me, my love, and I'll shower you with attention."

Eleanor took a step backward, coming closer to the potted palm. She had her back to Josh, but Randolph might spot him through the greenery, Josh speculated. But as he watched the growing fires of obsession in Randolph's eyes, he knew the man was intent only on staring at Eleanor.

"You already shower me with attention—too much attention," Eleanor protested. "And it's *very* annoying!"

Randolph scooted so close to her that the next step backward would send Eleanor toppling into the potted palm, or into Josh's arms if he was quick enough. He made up his mind—he *would* be quick enough.

"Marry me, my darling, or I shall kill myself!"

"Oh, Bradley, don't be ridiculous!" she scolded. "Now, get up. You're messing the knees of your trousers. Where do you think you'll find a good tailor on this island?"

"I cannot bear to live. My life has no meaning without you!"

"Bradley, you could get a job writing very bad scripts for very bad melodramas, and you'd be even worse acting in them. Now just stop this silliness and let me get back to the party."

"It's not silliness."

"Let me go, Bradley," she told him, trying to pull back

her hand. "My mother and father will be wondering where I am."

He held on fast.

"Let me go."

She tried again and failed.

"Leave me alone. Go away and never come back!"

She might be trying to sound harsh, but Josh could detect in her voice the tears of frustration—and perhaps even fear—that were beginning to well in her throat.

The man was more than a little annoyance in her life. How long had this been going on for her to be so afraid of him?

Eleanor gave one strong tug against Randolph's iron grip. She would have toppled to the floor if it weren't for Josh's speed. He caught her quickly and set her upright upon her feet. Randolph immediately sprang up.

"You! You, from the docks! What the dickens are you doing here?"

"I think the lady said she wanted you to leave," Josh told him.

He glanced back to make sure Eleanor was all right. She was rubbing her bruised wrists, and staring at him with what he might have called awestruck admiration—if he weren't such a humble man.

"What business is it of yours?" Randolph sneered. "You just work here. For *us*, I might remind you!"

"That's right. I was hired to serve the guests. *All* the guests, which includes Miss Folsom."

Josh wouldn't want her accusing him, as she had Randolph, of playing bad melodrama, but he still placed himself between her and the stubborn, angry man. He refrained from standing legs astride, fists on his hips, squared jaw lifted defiantly, like some sort of stage-prop hero.

"Appears to me as if, right now, she needs me a lot."

"She doesn't need the likes of you." Randolph's sneer

deepened. "Go off and pour some drinks, you plebeian scum. Leave the quality to their own affairs."

Josh shook his head. "Can't do that."

"What do you mean?"

"Well, see, anyone could tell Miss Folsom is true quality. And I'll proudly admit any day that I'm a quality working man. But you?" Josh jabbed his finger in Randolph's direction, just so the man would be sure to know Josh was talking specifically about him. "You're not quality. I wash scum like you off my culling board every day. You're about as annoying as any pesky mosquito from any bog—and deserve just about the same treatment."

"I shall call the harbormaster and have you evicted from the premises."

"He won't do it," Josh responded with certainty.

"Why not?"

"He's my cousin."

Randolph coughed, then threatened, "I'll call Mr. Folsom and have you ejected."

Josh shook his head. "No, you won't. See, my guess is, since you're staying at my aunt's boardinghouse instead of with one of the city families, or at this fancy clubhouse, that Mr. Folsom wouldn't be too happy to see you here at all."

Randolph glared at Josh and raised his fists, prepared to fight.

Josh just reached up to scratch his head and grinned at the man.

"Looks like I kind of hit a sore spot with that one, huh?"

"Sir, I'll warn you," Bradley pronounced with exaggerated dignity. "I am prepared to remove you myself from this private property."

"You want to fight me?" Josh asked.

"Yes!" Randolph boldly declared. "I'll fight you for the lady's honor."

Josh watched him coldly. "I'm tempted to laugh at your foolishness, Randolph, but a lady's honor is nothing to laugh about. I really don't see it doing much good for a lady's honor to fight about it, either."

"Oh, no," Eleanor pleaded. "Not now. Not *here*."

Josh felt her soft hand rest, trembling, on his shoulder as she peeked out from behind him. She was still too frightened to face Randolph alone. He remembered the pain on her face as she tried to escape his grasp. What could he do, short of whaling the tar out of this idiot, to get him to leave Eleanor in peace?

"You might be able to force Miss Folsom to stay and listen to your bilge, but you can't fight me. Heck, you couldn't even walk halfway up Mallard Street without breaking into a sweat. And it's not even that steep a hill."

He gave Randolph a glare of ridicule.

"I'll fight you any way you want, you common clod. Marquis of Queensbury be damned!"

Josh clucked his tongue. "Now, now, I don't think she'd like to hear you talking about her that way."

"Who?"

"This Queen of Marksberry. . . ."

Randolph barked a sharp laugh. "You brainless oaf! The Marquis of Queensbury isn't a woman!"

"Sorry. Guess I don't know the fellow as well as you—"

"You can't be that stupid. Are you too cowardly to fight me?"

Josh gave the man a contemptuous glare. "No man who faces the wind and icy water of a Chesapeake winter could ever be called a coward." He shrugged. "A dang fool, maybe, but never a coward."

"Then you're twice the fool—for daring to antagonize me," Randolph declared. The man continued to hold up his fists and prance a fancy two-step around Josh.

"You know, there are a lot of really pretty, fragile things around here we wouldn't want to break."

"Since when does a barbarian like you care about nice things?"

Josh ignored the question—for now. He sidled toward the long French doors that led out onto the clubhouse lawn. He opened the door in invitation.

"There are a lot of guests here tonight, too, that know the lady and you."

"Of course."

"Then I'd say, especially for the sake of the lady's reputation, we take this outside."

"That's the first sensible thing you've said all evening," Randolph agreed.

Still keeping his fists raised, Randolph moved through the doorway, all the while never turning his back on Josh.

As he moved to close the door behind him, Josh felt an unexpected resistance. He looked back to see Eleanor holding the door, ready to follow him.

Her eyes were filled with worry. Was she concerned about her reputation? Or, in spite of their argument, did she really care for this strutting little banty rooster? Was Josh just about to make the biggest mistake of his life?

❖ 6 ❖

"I'M REAL SORRY about it coming to this, Miss Folsom," Josh said.

"So am I."

"I could just apologize . . . call it off . . ."

She couldn't tell him to do that. He'd done nothing to Bradley to have to apologize for. He'd be labeled a coward, and a man must have his honor.

Besides, even though he had offered to quit, she could tell from the tone of his voice that he wasn't a man to leave a job half done. It was pretty obvious he didn't consider this job anywhere near completed.

"If there were some other way . . ." she murmured.

"But if I did," he continued, "I don't know what would happen to you with that . . . um, gentleman."

Eleanor knew very well what the rest of her life would be like—until she either gave in to Bradley or died. She didn't know how to explain it to Josh, though. Could she really be selfish enough to sacrifice this gallant stranger—without even having him know what he was sacrificing himself for? Josh was the only man of her acquaintance—besides her father—who had ever stood up to Bradley for her. What alternative did she have?

"No," she answered. "We have to do what we have to."

He started to head toward Bradley again.

"Josh," she called nervously.

She wasn't used to such familiarity with a man she'd only just met. Should she call him *Mr.* Josh? That sounded like some man who ran a dressmaker's shop. But she didn't know his last name. What did it matter? She was too nervous to worry about the refinements now.

He stopped and turned back to her. He watched her, waiting.

She'd called him. Now she had to say *something*. At a time like this she might as well tell him what was really on her mind.

"Be careful, Josh. Please. Be very, very careful."

"I'm always *real* careful, Miss Folsom."

"Bradley—Mr. Randolph—he's . . . he's awfully strong," she warned.

Perhaps if she kept calling him back about one thing or another, there would never be a fight. Maybe Bradley would get tired of holding his fists up like that and just go away.

"He told me he boxes every other day at his club."

"Well, Miss Folsom, hauling in crabs and oysters isn't exactly boxing," Josh stated modestly, "but *I* do it *every* day, all year long—except Sundays and Christmas, of course. I guess I can take care of myself."

I certainly hope so, she thought as she stood there watching him. She didn't trust Bradley one bit not to do something sneaky and very harmful to this innocent man.

"What are you waiting for, you coward?" Bradley taunted across the lawn. "You and I have business to finish."

"I guess I better go quiet him down before he wakes up the neighbors."

The light was so dim. Could she be sure, as he moved away, that Josh had given her a little wink?

As she watched him striding down the gentle slope of lawn, illuminated with the eerie light of the rows of small lanterns along the paths, she certainly hoped he could take care of himself.

Bradley danced closer to Josh, bouncing lightly up and down, making fake jabs to his head, shoulders, and stomach. Eleanor's heart pounded in her throat. She was just thankful Bradley never actually landed a punch.

What if he really did hit Josh? she worried.

Josh's shoulders might be broad, and his hands large and calloused from hard work. But what chance did this poor workingman stand against a man trained and practiced in all the skills of boxing?

She could feel her stomach churning at the thought of his tanned skin marred by cuts and his blue-green eyes swollen shut with bruises. What if Bradley knocked out one of his teeth? The ferry wouldn't be here again until tomorrow around noon. She didn't know how long it would take her father's yacht to cross the Bay in the dark, or even how to explain to Father how they'd come to need it for an injured waterman.

Dr. Arnold wasn't spending the summer with the Stewarts as he had last year, and she didn't know what other kind of medical care was available on the island. Probably not much, and what there was probably wasn't very adequate. She couldn't bear to think of Josh bleeding to death for her before they could even get him to a doctor.

Behind her, Eleanor could hear people coming through the doorway. She turned, dreading to see all her family and friends lined up behind her, prepared to witness her disgrace.

At least now everyone would see what a fool Bradley was. Perhaps now they would finally believe what a horrible terror he had been to her these many past months, stalking her every move. On the other hand, now everyone might think she was some sort of loose woman, having two men coming to fisticuffs in public over her!

Mrs. McGruder might even be taking notes, so she'd be sure to get the story correct for all her gossiping friends back in Baltimore. On second thought, Mrs. McGruder never was much for strict accuracy. Eleanor could only hope that, by the time they returned in September, some new scandal would have taken this one's place.

She turned around. It wasn't her people after all who stood behind her, whispering amongst themselves. All the men who worked as waiters, all the women who scrubbed the thousands of dirty dishes in the kitchen, all the children who'd been busy running errands for the chef all evening, were lined up behind her.

She saw only one face she recognized, her friend Isabelle. But even Isabelle hung back with the crowd, leaving her to stand by herself—a lone figure of disgrace and pity.

Then she actually listened to what they were shouting.

"Sock him, Josh!"

"Don't take no guff off none of them summer folks!"

"What'd this one do to rile Josh?"

"Don't know."

"Must've been something. Josh don't rile none too easy."

"Ten dollars says the city fellow don't lay a hand on him."

"No takers on a sure thing, Pete!"

"Shouldn't we stop 'em before somebody gets hurt?"

"Heck, no! Ain't been this kind of excitement 'round here since Ruthie got her head stuck in the pump organ."

"Dang thing ain't been right since."

"What? Ruthie or the organ?"

"Wallop him one good one, Josh!"

They weren't paying her one bit of attention. As a matter of fact, she felt almost as if she ought to move to the side to get out of their way so they could see the fight better. They certainly were cheering Josh on.

The men and women were yelling with equal enthusiasm. Well, if they hoped to see blood, they were in for a disappointment, Eleanor thought. It was much too dark to discern colors. And there really wasn't much fighting going on anyway—for now. She was very grateful.

"All right, we're outside," Bradley said to Josh. "You wanted to fight me for the lady's honor, so come on. What are you waiting for?"

"I'm waiting for you to stop jumping around like a grasshopper so we can talk this over like men."

"What?" Bradley stopped bouncing for just a second, apparently while the insult sank in. Then he started prancing again. "Why, I'll have you know this is the epitome of the pugilistic techniques practiced at Gentleman John's Boxing Club."

Josh scratched his head and chuckled. "Well, I've seen fighting and I've seen dancing. . . . And this looks more like dancing to me."

Bradley gave a snicker of ridicule. "That shows what you know."

Josh rubbed his chin and silently watched Bradley for a moment. "Pugilist, huh?"

"Yes. In case you don't know—and I doubt that you would—it means one skilled in the fine art of boxing."

Josh just nodded. "Epitome, huh?"

"Yes, indeed. That means—"

"The height."

Bradley blinked with surprise. Quickly he regained his composure and grudgingly shrugged off Josh's knowledge. "More or less," he commented.

Josh watched his opponent's movements very carefully

for a while. "Well, maybe you can demand your money back."

Bradley scowled angrily.

"Come now! Enough of this foolish chatter." He took another jab at Josh's shoulder, but missed again. "Are you going to fight me or not?"

Josh sidled around, seeming to retreat. "I don't want to fight you. You were the one who started it."

"That's right."

Bradley jabbed at Josh again. They had all been little glancing blows that Eleanor realized weren't really meant to do any harm, but were merely meant to annoy. He was trying to goad Josh into this battle.

But the blows weren't even landing, and that had nothing to do with Bradley's pugilistic skills.

Each time Bradley took a punch, Josh deftly sidled away. No one could have accused him of running away. He always kept the same distance between Bradley and himself. He just never let the man touch him.

"I'd be the one to put an end to it, too, but you're a coward who won't fight," Bradley accused.

"I'm not a coward. I just don't fight," Josh replied. He didn't seem all that insulted or annoyed. "There's a difference, you know."

Bradley just watched him for a moment. Apparently he didn't know there was a difference. Then he demanded, "How can a real man not fight?"

"Oh, I used to," Josh answered, leading his opponent in what appeared to Eleanor to be an ever-widening circle around the lawn.

It also seemed to her that, although Bradley was the one who was always advancing and attacking, and Josh had the apparent disadvantage of walking backward, Bradley was doing all the work and Josh was really the one in control. He was leading where they were going, and he was gradually moving away from the clubhouse. He hadn't actually been hit yet. He hadn't thrown a single punch. As a matter of fact, he had yet to even raise his fists.

But Bradley was already perspiring heavily, and beginning to huff and puff, almost as bad as Michael Stewart trying to dance.

"I used to get all lickered up on a Friday night, sail on down to Crisfield, and drink and fight all weekend," Josh continued his tale. "I wouldn't sober up until Sunday morning when Aunt Audrey would haul me out of bed by the ear, soak me down with cold water, and drag me to church."

Eleanor could see a faint gleam of fond memories in Josh's eyes.

"Is that what you mean by a real man?" he asked Bradley with a wide grin.

Bradley didn't answer. He just tried to take another annoying jab at Josh's shoulder. He missed again.

Eleanor could see the anger and frustration growing in the redness of his face. He was swinging harder with each jab he took, but each jab was straying farther from the mark.

"But one day, when I really sobered up, I just couldn't see any sense in fighting anymore," Josh continued. "I haven't fought since. I don't intend to now."

"That's a fool's tale and a coward's reasoning," Bradley declared. "I've had enough of your excuses and evasions."

His fist shot out. Josh quickly sidestepped, and Bradley went sprawling facedown into the grass. The crowd laughed to see Bradley so quickly and easily downed.

Before he could rise again, Josh stooped down. He seized the collar of Bradley's jacket and the belt at the back of his pants. With no more effort than if he were lifting a coil of rope on the dock, he brought Bradley to his feet, and then just a little higher, so that Bradley had to stand on tiptoe.

"Stop, stop! Put me down, you insolent fool!"

"Can't do that," Josh said.

"Yes, you can."

"Nope. I don't trust you not to get back up and try to whale the tar out of me again. And I've told you before, I *don't* intend to fight."

"So you pick me up instead? This is preposterous!"

Bradley's arms were flailing in the air, still trying to throw punches at Josh, and still missing. The little part of the soles of his shoes that touched the grass kept slipping on the dampness.

"Put me down!"

"Nope. See, the way I see it, it's just too darn hot, and you're just way too hot under the collar about all this foolishness. Aunt Audrey always says that's not good for your bowels."

"What does your Aunt Audrey have to do with the workings of my internal organs?" Bradley demanded sharply.

"Well, seeing as you're staying at her place, sleeping on her sheets, I'd say she had some right for concern. So I want to make sure you're *really* cooled down before you leave here."

Without another word Josh hustled Bradley down the gentle slope of the lawn. Bradley's feet kicked up the stones with a rattling noise as they crossed the gravel drive and headed down toward the edge of the pier.

"No! Oh, no!" Bradley yelled. He tried even harder to dig his feet into the sandy ground, but Josh had him lifted just high enough so he couldn't get a toehold.

"Throw him in!" someone in the crowd demanded.

"Throw him in!" the others began to cry.

"Toss him in the drink!"

"The crabs're getting hungry! Throw him in!"

Eleanor blinked with surprise as she heard her father's booming voice over the din. She spun around. He was right beside her.

"Father?"

He wasn't scowling at her in disapproval, the way that only Father could. He was watching Josh and Bradley intently.

Not only was her father witnessing this fiasco, but so were all the other guests. Maybe they'd heard the racket outside. Or maybe they'd noticed all the waiters were missing. Those who hadn't the nerve to come outside were lined up against the large windows, pressing their aristocratic noses against the panes of glass, trying to see better.

Oh, she was done for now! She might as well go home and pack and head for Alaska or Timbuktu. Maybe, in some remote village somewhere, in some dirt hovel, huddled over a charcoal fire, eating roasted mouse, there was one person who wouldn't have heard the gossip that was sure to be spread all around.

"Seeing as this involves you and Bradley, I have a fairly good idea what this is about," her father leaned over and said. "I'll let you explain to me later what this other fellow has to do with it."

Maybe her father's presence beside her would indicate to the crowd that he wasn't censuring her for these scandalous shenanigans—at least not in public. She didn't feel so lonesome or abandoned anymore, but she was still awfully agitated.

"If you throw me in, I'll have every lawyer in Baltimore prosecuting you." Bradley's voice was loud and harsh with anger.

"Can't do that."

"Why? Are they all your cousins, too?" Bradley asked wryly.

"Nope. I'm just employed here." Josh jerked his head

back toward the clubhouse. "I'm just following my instructions this evening. Are you going to sue the whole club?"

"My uncle is a judge. By the time you're done serving the sentence he'll give you, your own mother won't even remember you!"

Eleanor gave her father a desperate glance and clung to his arm. "Oh, please, Father. You won't . . . you've got to . . ."

"Don't worry, Eleanor. Judge Randolph and I play billiards together frequently," her father whispered. "And I owe him a box of Havanas. He never did like the boy, anyway. He always says his sister-in-law spoils him far too much." He placed his hand atop hers and gave her several consoling pats. "Don't worry. We'll keep this gallant, if somewhat rustic, young champion of yours out of jail."

Gallant? Rustic? Eleanor silently repeated. Champion of *hers*?

A lady usually expected a knight in shining armor, doing battle with fire-breathing dragons—not a waterman temporarily serving as a waiter, throwing annoying men into the Bay.

Josh just kept marching Bradley down to the end of the pier.

"Even you must have realized by now, I come from a very wealthy, socially prominent, influential family," Bradley still threatened as he tried to stop his headlong flight.

"Good." Josh balanced on the edge and dangled Bradley out over the water. "Then they won't have any trouble getting their friends together to fish you out of the Bay."

"No, no! I'll pay you!" Bradley pleaded. He flailed his arms around, trying to reach into his breast pocket for his wallet. "Just name your price."

"Well . . ." Josh paused.

"Come on. Every man has his price. What's yours?"

"I could use the money." He paused. "I'll admit it's mighty tempting."

He could feel Bradley's body begin to relax with the thought of a reprieve. He could almost see the slick smile on the man's face.

"Throw him in!" the crowd insisted. Watermen and financiers, housewives and society matrons, even a few debutantes cried, "Throw him in!"

"Nope, I don't need the money that bad."

With one giant heave, Josh sent Bradley sailing into the salty water of the Bay.

A loud cheer went up from the crowd and echoed across the marshes.

Eleanor disentangled her hand from her father's arm and impulsively ran down to meet Josh.

"Are you all right?" she asked, skidding to a stop in front of him. The grass was damp and trampled, making it even more slippery. She almost collided with him.

Before Josh had the chance to reply, the crowd from the kitchen descended upon him. Eleanor was smashed up close to him as everyone tried to shake his hand or clap him on the back.

As the crowd jostled them, she felt Josh's arm move around her, giving her support and balance, and protecting her from the onslaught of eager people. His arms felt as strong as they looked, and gave her a sense of comfort and security in the midst of this joyous mob.

"Are *you* all right?" he asked.

"Of course." What could possibly be wrong now?

She enjoyed the feeling of bumping up against his muscular body as the crowd continued to mill around them. Even as they seemed to toss her easily from side to side, Josh was steady as a rock.

She could look up into his eyes and watch the twinkle as he acknowledged each of his friends' congratulations.

She could silently give thanks that Bradley hadn't even touched him, much less left any scars or bruises.

If Bradley had left any mark at all on Josh, it was a small droplet of water that had splashed up and landed on Josh's cheek. Her fingers ached to reach up and wipe it away. It would be the one small kindness she could do for Josh to erase any trace of his obnoxious encounter. It would be close to offering him some sort of comfort after his battle— even if he hadn't actually been fighting.

So tempting. Eleanor began to move her hand slowly upward, ready to feel the smooth skin of his tanned cheek, ready to feel the rough stubble of his beard as she brushed aside the water.

"I take it that's *the* waterman," Isabelle whispered as she jostled into place behind her.

Eleanor started and dropped her hand. "Yes, yes," she murmured to her friend.

"It appears to me as if he's a little more than 'nothing.'"

"No, no, not really." Eleanor shook her head.

"I must say, he's not a bad choice!" Isabelle giggled.

"Choice? Isabelle, what are you talking about?"

"Maybe you and Adelaide Gittings will have a lot to talk about soon."

Before Eleanor could deny her friend's wild suppositions, Isabelle flitted away, still giggling. But Eleanor certainly didn't think any of this had been that funny.

"Eleanor," her father pronounced sternly. He'd cut a wide path through the dancing, jostling throng, but it closed up quickly behind him.

"Yes, Father."

She tore herself from Josh's protective embrace and turned to face her father. She could feel her face warming with embarrassment. What would her father suppose after seeing her in Josh's arms?

She grimaced and held her breath, waiting.

Her father turned to Josh instead.

"Sir, since we're already indirectly connected by this little 'incident,' allow me to formally make your acquaintance. I'm Winston Stanford Folsom III. This is my daughter, Eleanor."

"Miss Folsom." Josh smiled at her. His eyes were warm and inviting. He turned a very different, much more businesslike smile on her father. "We've met."

"And you, sir, are . . . ?"

"The name's Claybourne," he replied smoothly, extending his hand. "Joshua Claybourne. Around here, just about anyone who owns a boat is called 'captain,' but I don't think that matters much here—"

"Nonsense, nonsense."

Mr. Folsom clasped Josh's hand with both of his and shook it heartily. With a little surprise and a great relief, Eleanor released the breath she'd been holding.

"You should be quite proud, Captain. Individual enterprise is the cornerstone of our American way of life. Why, back in thirty-one, my father started with a small mercantile. . . ."

"Oh, please, Father. Not another lecture on economics," Eleanor pleaded. "Not now."

Mr. Folsom chuckled. "My daughter's right. I must admit, Captain Claybourne, that was quite an exhibition."

"Well, I really didn't intend for it to be so public—for the lady's sake."

"I appreciate your consideration."

Mr. Folsom nodded toward the crowd, still milling around, recounting the event, and probably still getting a dozen different versions of the truth.

"I might even go so far as to say, this may be one of the best things to happen—"

"I'm not done with you yet!" came the cry up the sandy shore.

Bradley was hauling himself out of the water. Dripping, and dragging clumps of seaweed with him as he came, he crossed the gravel drive and lumbered up the lawn. He was wringing the sodden edges of his jacket. The water poured out onto his shoes.

He stepped directly up to Eleanor. "I'm not done with you yet, my love."

Mr. Folsom placed his arm protectively around Eleanor. "Leave my daughter alone," he ordered.

Bradley confronted Josh. "I'm not done with you yet, either, you pitiful example of a human being."

"What do you mean by that, Randolph?" Josh demanded.

"I'm warning you to mind your own business, fisherman. She's mine!" Bradley declared.

"I'm not a piece of property!" Eleanor protested over Josh's shoulder.

"I've loved you since the first time I saw you, and I knew I had to make you mine." He kept trying to move around to get to Eleanor. Josh kept stepping between them.

"I *will* make you mine, my dearest, my only love!"

"No! Go away. Leave me alone!" Eleanor cried.

"I'm Bradley Butler Randolph, son of Wellington Randolph of the Baltimore Randolphs, and Marie Butler of the Philadelphia Butlers," he declared proudly. "I can have anything I want. You can't dismiss me like a bad servant."

"Go away!"

"Move along, Randolph," Josh told him. "Unless you want *another* bath. At my aunt's you'd pay two bits. At least this one was free."

"Oh, no, Claybourne."

"That's *Captain* Claybourne to you," Josh corrected.

"No, Claybourne," Bradley repeated, backing up

slightly. He pointed his index finger threateningly. "You have absolutely no idea how very costly to you this little dunk of mine is going to be."

He reached into his pocket, pulled out a long strip of gray material, and wrung it out.

"What's he doing? What's he got now?" Eleanor could hear the people in the crowd asking each other. Apparently no one had the audacity to ask Bradley outright. She, too, wondered what he was up to, but the farther she stayed from Bradley, the better. She wasn't about to ask.

Mr. Folsom's bushy gray eyebrows folded into a frown. "What in heaven's name is that thing, Randolph? A dead fish?"

Bradley hesitated, then pronounced proudly, "My scarf."

"Well, actually, it's *my* scarf," Josh said, chuckling.

"You'd be wise to wear one, too," Bradley warned. With his index finger, he stabbed at the crowd. "Each and every one of you."

"In this heat? You must be mad!" Mr. Folsom exclaimed. "Just as I've always suspected."

"I'm going back to my room and dry out, for this evening," Bradley announced. He slung the damp scarf around his neck, flinging droplets on everyone within his radius. "I'm sure Mrs. Bodine has a slight extra charge for that, too."

"What's he doing with your scarf in his pocket anyway?" Eleanor asked. "Why in the world is he wearing it in this heat?"

"It's a long story," Josh said. "Maybe someday I'll have the chance to tell you."

Eleanor certainly hoped she'd hear about his scarf, and anything else he had in mind to say. She watched him with admiration. There was a lot to Josh Claybourne that she'd never imagined.

"Indeed, you will have the opportunity, Captain," Mr. Folsom declared. "I'd like to repay you somehow—"

"Oh, no, really," Josh modestly refused. "I just did it for Miss Folsom when it looked like she really needed help."

"Although I think monetary payment for something like this would be extremely crass—"

"Well, now, I wouldn't think it was all *that* crass," Josh hedged. He really could use the money, but, after all, he didn't want to look too mercenary.

"Please, be our guest at dinner tomorrow evening," Mr. Folsom invited.

"Yes, please come," Eleanor urged.

In the soft glow of the little lanterns Eleanor's skin looked as pale as moonlight, and just as delicate. Her green eyes gazed up at him with pure admiration. It would be mighty hard to say no to a lady who looked like her.

"Shall we say eight?" Mr. Folsom continued, as if Josh's refusing was completely out of the question.

Josh guessed with these rich, influential people, maybe it really was.

Well, dinner for himself alone wouldn't put food on his own table, he decided. But at least it would leave more of what they had there for Maddie, Winnie, and Bill.

He nodded. "Eight will be fine."

He had very mixed feelings about the whole thing. He was a little disappointed about not getting that monetary reward. On the other hand, money had nothing at all to do with why he had stepped in to protect Eleanor.

Why *had* he stepped in? It had nothing to do with hoping for a reward. It had nothing to do with following instructions from the clubhouse about keeping out "undesirables." It certainly couldn't have been because Eleanor had been so darn nice to him at their first meeting.

He was used to just doing things. Thinking too hard

about why he was doing them just made him edgy. Oh, just put it down to the way his parents had raised him, and his own silly notion of helping out a lady in distress, he decided.

He was very happy with the prospect of having dinner with her—and especially of not being at the serving end of the line this time. At the same time he'd seen how the rich people dressed and acted. He might be able to imitate them for a while, but where would he get the clothes?

"And afterward"—Mr. Folsom clapped a hand on his shoulder and grumbled confidentially—"I have a small proposition I'd like to discuss with you."

Josh had the sneaking suspicion that he was going to regret agreeing to this more than anything else.

❖ 7 ❖

BRADLEY TUGGED AT the warm scarf chafing his neck. He didn't want to go in to see the chief of police on Silchester Island all hot and perspiring.

On the other hand, if he took the chance and removed the scarf, he didn't want his last earthly memory, as he lay sprawled on the jailhouse floor, dying from the poisonous bite of the cottonhead snake, to be a glimpse up the nose of the chief of police.

Before he stepped off the front porch of Bodine's, he bent over and peered under the porch.

"Did you lose something, son? Can I help you look for it?" he heard the man asking.

"I'm looking for snakes," Bradley answered without glancing up. He wasn't about to relax his guard and have one of those snakes jump out and puncture an artery or two.

The man chuckled. "For or ag'in 'em?"

"For what?"

"I said, you looking *for* 'em—or you looking to *avoid* 'em?"

"Well, I certainly don't want to find any cottonheads." Satisfied that there were no cottonheads under Bodine's porch, Bradley looked up and stepped off the porch.

The old man was grinning at him with teeth so white and even they couldn't have come from Nature's hand. They matched the color of his thick wild hair, which stood on end as if blown from underneath. How did he manage to get it to stay that way? His pale blue eyes squinted against the sun.

"Cottonheads, huh?" The corners of his mouth were twitching, and his little paunch was shaking.

"Yes."

The old man nodded. "Pesky critters, ain't they?"

"I hope never to find out."

"Yeah, I reckon Josh knows more about them critters than anybody else on this island. But the rest of us are learning, real fast. So where y'going, son?"

"I need to speak to the chief of police. I assume you have one here."

"Oh, yeah. Thataway." The old man stretched out his arm, indicating a house across and at the far end of the street.

"Perhaps you could tell me, Mr. . . . Mr.—"

"Unk."

"Unk?"

"Yeah."

"Mr. Unk—"

"Just Unk."

"Mr. Claybourne and Mrs. Bodine said the cottonheads were in the woods, but they didn't tell me whether the snakes hid elsewhere, such as slithering under the shells that seem to be some sort of rustic local equivalent to actual street pavement."

Bradley picked up one foot and then the other, just in case he might be near a snake, even as they spoke.

Unk reached up and rubbed his chin. "Well now, in the summer of fifty-four we had a visitor here who had the brazen audacity not to believe us—of course Josh wasn't born then, but there's been others knowed all about these cottonheads—when we tried to tell him 'bout the scarf and all. He was sitting in the necessary, answering Nature's call, and I guess he'd been taken kinda suddenlike, 'cause he didn't have no scarf, when—''

"I'd really like to see the chief of police before the summer's over." He touched the brim of his hat and walked away.

"Watch them there cottonheads," Unk called. "They might be poisonous, but at least they ain't rude about it." He chuckled a little harder as he added, "They're liable to be anywhere."

Bradley stepped more carefully across the street.

He passed the hardware store and the bookstore. He noted the exact location of the door handles, just in case he spotted a cottonhead and needed to duck inside quickly.

He was pretty surprised to see a bookstore at all on this island. Then again, they probably only carried McGuffy's Readers—that was probably about as far advanced as their reading abilities went. He snorted when he noticed copies of *Little Women* and *Moby Dick* displayed in the window. A little behind in current literature, he scoffed, but then having *any* literature here surprised him.

Just what these people needed to read, he thought with another snort. *Moby Dick*.

No, those books had been there for a long time and would probably stay there forever.

He passed Darty's Tavern. Well, at least now he knew where he could get lots of whiskey for a snakebite remedy. Unless the barkeeper was a cousin of Claybourne's, Bradley speculated. Then he'd probably just let him die.

He noticed a dirt road, little more than a path, leading off from Mallard Street. There wasn't even a sign indicating the name of the road. It probably didn't have one.

Small irregular houses sat at irregular intervals on either side of the road. He saw women hanging out their laundry and could hear them calling to one another and laughing. Squealing, barefoot children and barking dogs scampered all over the street, so he couldn't have told who belonged to whom if his life depended on it.

Was this the kind of place where Claybourne lived? he wondered. His lip curled in a distasteful sneer. Probably. No wonder the man fought so sneakily, living in such decay and degeneration.

Did Eleanor know how Claybourne lived? he speculated. His eyes narrowed as he thought. If she could see this, she wouldn't think he was so heroic anymore.

Her parents kept her carefully sheltered from this side of the island. It was certain Claybourne wouldn't bring her here. After last night's unfortunate little incident, how could he manage to convince her to come with *him* to see this squalor?

Bradley moved on to the next large house facing Mallard Street. He was glad to see a small white shingle with crisp black lettering hanging on the door. Harrison Whitaker, M.D. Probably not even as good as a horse doctor, Bradley thought with contempt. But the man apparently was the only medical help available on the island. In case of snakebite, or in case Claybourne actually did injure him, he knew where to come before going to his lawyer.

He passed a small shed that housed what looked like an ancient pump engine. Did this godforsaken place actually have a volunteer fire company? That was pretty hard to believe. From the looks of those rickety houses, if any of them caught fire, the neighbors could all pitch in and just push it into the water.

He'd bet the islanders wouldn't come running if any of the summer cottages caught fire. Of course, that antiquated pump wouldn't do any good anyway.

At last, on the other side of the small shed, he found the jailhouse.

With his hand on the knob he gratefully acknowledged that, once inside, he could take off the irritating scarf.

He entered the cool dimness of the jailhouse. Rapidly he whipped the scarf from his neck, wadded it up, and shoved it into his coat pocket.

"Are you the chief of police?" Bradley demanded.

The slender man behind the desk looked up slowly from the thick volume he'd been reading. The book, a small pad of paper, and a pencil were the only things on top of the immaculate desk.

The hair on the sides of the man's balding head was combed back neatly. His pale blue shirt was still crisp and starchy, in spite of the heat. Even the lenses of his spectacles were clean.

He pushed the spectacles back up onto the bridge of his nose.

"Morning, friend. You're one of the summer visitors, I see. What can I do for you on this fine morning?"

"Wait. How could you tell?"

The man pointed his pencil at Bradley's head. "You're not as sun-browned." He lowered the aim of his pencil. "You're much too well dressed." He lowered the pencil still further. "You're wearing shoes."

With a supremely self-confident smile, the man put down the pencil and folded his hands on top of the book.

"Besides, I keep track of everyone who's living—or dead, come to think of it—on this island. Although I must admit the dead ones are easier to keep account of." He gave a brief chuckle. "I'm sorry, my friend, but I don't recognize you."

Bradley pursed his lips. Oh, how he hated people who liked to show off—especially when he wanted to be the center of attention—like now!

"My name is Bradley Butler Randolph, of the Baltimore Randolphs and the Philadelphia Butlers," he pronounced.

The policeman just blinked through his thick spectacles. Bradley wasn't surprised. Of course, those illustrious names would mean nothing to a common workingman with no concept of the importance of social standing.

"I presume you're the chief of police here."

"Indeed, I am, sir."

Bradley almost expected the man to salute. But he rose from his desk and extended a hand. His nails were clean. Even his dark blue trousers were pressed.

"Beauregard Groves, at your service."

He seated himself again behind his desk. He crossed his hands in front of him. Without a protruding paunch to rest them on, he merely placed them on the desk. He held himself ramrod straight, Bradley noticed, as if he'd been in the military. Ha! Groves wasn't the only observant person around here, Bradley thought smugly.

Bradley looked around the room. Several wanted posters were hung on the walls in regimental order—almost as if this place were some strange combination of art gallery and army barracks. Even the beds in the jail cells were neatly made. This man probably spent so much time cleaning his office that he never had time to catch any criminals.

Chief Groves motioned to the chair in front of the desk for Bradley to sit down. "Now, what can I be doing for you, Mr. Randolph?" he asked.

"You can arrest Joshua Claybourne."

The chief's eyebrows rose with surprise, but otherwise the expression on his face didn't change one bit. "I'm sorry. I can not do that, sir."

"Why? Are *you* some relation to him, too?"

"No. Leastwise, not real close."

"Then, Officer, do your duty."

"Can't do that," he repeated.

"Why not?"

"Josh hasn't done anything wrong."

"He threw me in the water!"

Chief Groves's eyebrows rose as he coughed. The corners of his mouth were twitching. Was this some strange disease the island people contracted?

"Well, now, Mr. Randolph—" He stopped and coughed again. "You've got to understand. Around here, that's just horsing around. We don't go throwing folks into jail for just horsing around."

"We weren't horsing around. We were *fighting*!" Bradley hammered his fist down on the top of the desk.

Chief Groves didn't bat an eyelid.

"Well, now, Mr. Randolph, in my many years as a lawman, I've noticed that if you have a dozen different people telling a story, you'll get a dozen different versions. This morning alone I must've already heard them all. But one thing becomes apparent to me in every case."

"What's that?"

"That *you* were the one who was throwing the punches. Seems to me that *you* were the one who was doing all the fighting. Stands to reason, then, that I should be putting *you* in jail for public fighting, not Josh."

"What? Why—why—that's preposterous! I'm a law-abiding citizen."

"So is Josh. And I've known him to be law-abiding for a lot longer than I've known you."

"But he assaulted me!"

"No one saw him hit you. No one even saw him throw any punches."

"He grabbed me up—"

"Grabbed you?"

Chief Groves leaned forward just a bit. Now, at last, Bradley thought with relief, the officer was showing some hint of performing his sworn duty. Now, at last, he had some hopes for justice—and revenge.

"Yes, indeed. And lifted me—"

"Grabbed *and* lifted?" He took his pencil and wrote the two words in big, bold letters on his pad.

"Yes, indeed." Bradley nodded his head emphatically. Maybe the man was effective after all.

"Oh, well, now we have something entirely different here." Chief Groves began to thumb through the pages of the thick book lying on the desk in front of him.

"Well, at last!" Bradley leaned back in his chair with relief. "I'm glad to see that finally I'll have some justice!"

Chief Groves pored over the fine print in double columns through several pages. At last he stopped, held his place with his fingertip and slowly read down the column.

Bradley waited and waited. Finally he began to suspect that the man was only pretending to be able to read until he could think up some plausible lie to exonerate Claybourne.

"Ah, see! Just as I suspected." His fingertip jabbed at the line that answered all his questions. "Grabbing and lifting does *not* fall under the definition of public fighting."

"It doesn't?"

Chief Groves shook his head.

"Then what is it?"

"Public *wrestling*," he pronounced with great gravity as he closed the book with a loud slam. "And I cannot find any city, state, county, or federal law, statute, or ordinance against public wrestling."

"What!"

"No crime has been committed here," he decreed. "I'm afraid I can't arrest Josh and, as much as I might like to, I can't even arrest you for wasting my time." He pointed his pencil directly at Bradley.

"This is absolutely, positively, the most preposterous miscarriage of justice—a veritable travesty of police procedures," Bradley fumed as he rose. "My uncle, the judge, will certainly hear about this. You'll find yourself seeking a new job, I'll guarantee!"

He strode angrily to the door and pulled it open. Before he left, he dug into his pocket, yanked out his scarf, and wrapped it around his neck.

"Excuse me, Mr. Randolph. Don't leave just yet, if you please," Chief Groves called.

Bradley stopped in his tracks. Yes, the mention of his uncle the judge did it every time. He didn't care if the old man didn't like him a bit. He'd certainly made enough opportunities for himself just by mentioning the man's name.

Turning, he smiled smugly at the policeman. "I'm glad you're beginning to see things my way, Chief Groves."

"If you don't mind my asking, Mr. Randolph, why are you wearing that scarf?"

"What does that have to do with anything?" Bradley demanded.

Chief Groves held up one hand as if to soothe the angry man. "Don't go getting all riled, Mr. Randolph. I was just asking."

"Mrs. Bodine told me it would protect me from the cottonheads."

"Cottonheads?"

"Snakes."

"Oh, yes. Cottonheads. Of course. I'm just going a little deaf in this ear—from the cannon during the war, you know."

He thumped the heel of his hand against the side of his head, just to indicate how truly deaf he was in that ear.

"Yes, cottonheads. Dangerous—very dangerous critters."

Chief Groves raised his hand to his mouth and coughed several times.

"Wool scarf for protection. Wise move. Very wise

move. Especially since this time of year is their courting season, and they're even more rambunctious than usual.''

"Really?" Bradley wrapped the scarf around his neck even more tightly. "I must say, I'm learning more and more about these cottonheads every time I talk to someone on this island."

Chief Groves coughed again. Bradley could see the man's eyes were beginning to water.

"Excuse me, I *really* need . . . a drink of . . . water!"

Even as Bradley slammed the door closed behind him, he could hear the chief of police still coughing.

"Captain Claybourne." Eleanor greeted him at the beginning of the white gravel drive that led from Folsom Drive to their summer cottage.

She knew Captain Claybourne was the proper name to call him, but she still longed to return to calling him just Josh.

"I've been waiting for you. I'm so glad you could come tonight."

"Miss Folsom. Thank you . . . and your father for inviting me. I . . . I'm glad to be here."

He was speaking so much more formally than usual, and it sounded very forced. And he didn't *sound* at all glad to be here, she thought with foreboding. Were his new shoes too tight? Was he nervous about dining with people he barely knew? Considering all the trouble she'd already made for him, was he dreading being with her again?

"I'm glad you weren't hurt in the fight. . . .''

He chuckled. "Oh, that was no big deal. It wasn't even much of a fight, was it?"

"Well, I haven't seen too many, so I couldn't really tell. But, I mean, I was marveling all the while, and I kept wondering how you'd never taken boxing, but you kept dodging his punches and . . .''

She was babbling. Isabelle was right. RoseEllen Peabody wasn't the only one who babbled.

She knew she wasn't being too successful at keeping the blatant admiration for this man out of her eyes, but did her tongue have to go careening along, out of control?

"Well, Miss Folsom, when you're out on a boat in a gale, you learn to be quick on your feet and to duck the booms when the sails are coming round."

"I see."

"I didn't expect to see you here," he told her.

"I live here—at least in July and August. Where else would I be?" She laughed.

Suddenly it occurred to her that that was a terrible mistake. Supposed he mistook that she was laughing *at* him? She'd already managed to apologize for insulting him once. She didn't need to go doing it again.

He shoved his hands into his pants pockets and shrugged. "Oh, London. Paris. Rome. Wherever all you rich folks like to gather."

"I'm happy right here," she protested. "Paris and Rome are miserable in the summer."

"I figured a lady like you had been to those places. I just never expected to find you waiting here, in the driveway—for me."

Only because my parents would keel over dead if I'd gone to your house to bring you here, she thought to herself. She could hardly speak this truth to him, but she hadn't thought she'd have to think up an excuse.

"Since this is your first time here, I . . . I wanted to. . . . to show you some of the grounds before you were overwhelmed by the guests at the cottage," she managed to sputter. Hospitality was always a good excuse.

She gestured toward the house at the end of the drive and began walking toward it. Josh remained standing where he was, staring at the house.

She turned back and called, "Are you coming? Or should we arrange to have dinner brought out here to you?"

"Oh, sorry. I'm coming."

He hurried to catch up to her. His long, muscular legs brought him quickly and easily to her side.

"Cottage, huh?" he asked, still looking at the house. "Is that what you call it?"

"Yes."

His head was moving around, and he kept stepping from side to side, trying to see the building from different angles.

"Why in the world do you call it a cottage?"

"Because it's smaller than our house in Mt. Vernon Place."

Josh gave an uneasy chuckle. "It's bigger than my house and any two of my neighbors' houses all put together."

"You should see some of the summer cottages on Long Island," she told him.

"There are so many little turrets and porches shooting off from all sides," he observed. "No offense, but it looks as if the architect played with a set of darts on the blueprint and just built the next addition wherever the dart landed."

Eleanor stopped and pondered the building awhile with him.

"My father hired the best architect—"

"Oh, don't get me wrong. He must've been a great architect. It's just, he must've been a really bad dart player."

She nodded. "You've got a good point there."

Josh groaned. "That's a bad pun."

"Is there any such thing as a *good* pun?" she replied. Again she motioned for him to come with her.

He followed. "It's a wonder you don't get lost in that 'cottage.' How many of you are there?"

"It depends."

"Why? Are there so many of you that you lose count?"

"No, no. In my family, I just have my parents and my

younger sister. We also have a butler, a cook, two maids, a coachman, and a gardener, but the coachman and gardener don't live in the cottage. They have rooms over the stable.''

''Are the servants all really fat, maybe, that you need so much room?''

''No, no.'' She tried to explain through her laughter. ''My parents entertain a lot. We have guests all summer, always coming and going, but on the whole they usually only stay for about two weeks at a time.''

Josh gave a disgruntled chuckle. ''Yeah, we had my cousin Archie stay with us back in the summer of eighty-three while they rebuilt his house after lightning struck it. Two weeks of him sleeping on my couch was about all I could stand.'' He grimaced. ''But we were still stuck with him for two and a half months.''

Eleanor nodded. ''That could get . . . tedious.''

''Yeah, especially since *I* usually sleep on the couch and ended up on the floor.''

He lowered his voice and moved his head slightly closer to her, as if ready to exchange a great confidence. She could smell the bay rum cologne again and his shaving soap, but all she could think about was Josh, with his broad shoulders and long muscular legs, trying to stretch out on a tiny couch.

''I still think his house would've been finished in three weeks, but he kept fooling around just so he could stay with us and get free food.''

She could feel his warm breath on her ear. It didn't matter if he talked about his couch or his cousins. She wanted to keep him right there, talking to her—close to her.

''Is . . . is everyone on this island your cousin?'' she asked.

''No. Some of them are my aunts and uncles.''

He drew back from her as he laughed. Eleanor felt her

heart sag in disappointment. Well, she could hardly grab him just to keep him near—no matter how much she might want to.

"If . . . if you're all related, how . . . how do you find a wife?"

Merciful heavens, she was turning into Alice! Horrified, she wanted to slap herself for blurting out that rudely probing question. She hoped he wouldn't think she was being too personal. She really hoped he wouldn't think that, with one man out of the way, she already had her eye on another prospect for the future.

"Oh, some of the men came back from the war with wives from mainland families. So there are always a few families that aren't related yet," Josh explained.

He didn't sound angry or insulted. Maybe he hadn't taken her question personally. Maybe, while her luck was still holding, she ought to change the subject.

"I would've thought, living on this island, that you'd already seen all of these houses."

"I've seen them through the trees or sailing around the island. They don't look that big from a distance. But I've never seen them up close. We don't trespass on other people's property."

Eleanor nodded. She hadn't paid much attention before to how much the Silchester people obeyed their own sort of laws, written and unwritten. She'd never paid much attention to the people at all, until now.

"So you've never seen all this before."

"Not for a while. And not like this."

"Oh, I thought you just said . . . When were you here?"

"When I was just a little kid, this was all woods and salt marsh." He raised his arm to shoulder height and swung a wide circle, indicating how much had been changed. "We'd run through here looking for rabbits and muskrats, sometimes we'd spot a deer or a mink—"

"You're joking!"

Josh shook his head.

"There are still lots of wood ducks and egrets, and there are *always* crows and seagulls. We'd catch minnows for bait. And there was a clump of honey locust, and this big old walnut tree . . ."

Eleanor looked around at the neatly trimmed lawn and the carefully pruned elm trees lined up in neat procession down the drive.

"I'm trying to imagine . . ."

"You can't." His answer was short and clipped. "That was before your father and his friends bought this side of the island, and drained and filled in the marshes, just so they could build—"

He stopped abruptly, then continued in a gentler tone. "Sorry. You probably couldn't picture what it used to be like unless you'd actually seen it—in the wild, in all the seasons. Maybe someday . . ." His voice held a dreamlike quality that he suddenly shook off. "No. Never mind. I'm sorry."

"No, really. Please continue."

"It's really nothing, miss."

He motioned for her to continue down the walk, as if leaving the place where they were standing would allow him to leave his thoughts as well.

"No. You were going to ask me if I'd like to go out and see some of the wild places, weren't you?" she persisted.

"Yeah, but . . . well, it's kind of swampy . . . and hot . . . and muggy. There are lots of mosquitoes. Frogs. Snakes."

"I can see you trying to sneer, Captain Claybourne," she told him. "But I can also see in your eyes how much you really like all those frogs and snakes—"

"I still hate the mosquitoes."

"If you're trying to discourage me, it won't work."

"But it's not a place for a lady like you."

"I'd really like to go. Please say you'll take me."

Her mother would have told her to stop whining. But how else was she going to convince him to take her?

"After all, you already invited me," she reminded him.

"I did?" He grinned and shook his head. "Oh, no, Miss Folsom. I can guarantee, if I'd asked a lady like you out, I'd remember."

"Well, it wasn't me precisely. You invited my sister and me to come see the sookies and jimmies and some other kinds of things with bizarre names."

"Oh, son of a gun, if I didn't!" His face brightened with the recollection.

She placed her hand on his arm and peered directly into his eyes, to hold his attention. For a moment, gazing into his eyes, she almost forgot what she was saying. Then, seeing the blue-green eyes, the color of tidal pools, she grinned and said, "In your bugeye."

He looked at her and gave a surprised laugh.

"You might have puzzled Alice, but at least *I* figured the bugeye was some type of boat."

Josh nodded his approval.

"But I have absolutely no idea what those other things were," she admitted.

"Like what?"

"Sooks. Jimmies."

"Oh, those're just names for female and male crabs."

She looked at him in surprise. "But they all look alike. You can tell the difference?"

"Sure. It's really easy. Someday I'll have to show you."

"What about spongers?"

"That's just a female full of eggs."

"Oh. Mobjacks? Manninoses?"

Josh shrugged. "Different kinds of oysters and clams."

"There are different kinds?"

"Yeah. And they don't all look alike, even once you've got them out of the shell. A good waterman can tell you what kind of oyster it is and where it came from just by looking at it. Some are whiter, some are more pink."

"My, I thought I was being so clever, figuring out a bugeye is a boat, and there's so much more I don't know."

"That's all right. I still think you're pretty smart."

She released his arm and shrugged. "For a girl?"

"What do you mean, for a girl?"

"My father doesn't like *clever* women. He doesn't hold with feminine education—giving women things to think about only gives them ambitions above their station, and is planting the seeds of the destruction of the family, a moral society, and the American way of life, which contributes to his enormous bank account. Mother just thinks all a lady needs to worry about is what to serve and who *not* to sit next to whom at a dinner party."

"Well, if it keeps them happy . . ." Josh offered awkwardly. He paused a moment. "Oh, all right then. If it keeps you happy, too. I'll take you on my boat."

"Oh, thank you!"

Her father owned one of the biggest yachts at the club. Why should she be so excited about a trip in a little fishing boat? Something called a bugeye at that! It probably leaked like a sieve. Maybe because Josh was offering to show her things she'd never seen before—some things she'd never even heard of before. The Bay was a beautiful, interesting place. She was looking forward to exploring it with this very intriguing man.

"On one condition."

"Oh?" Suddenly she didn't feel quite so elated anymore.

"That I take *you*, and Alice stays home. She can find somebody else to tell her what a mobjack is."

He was still gazing into her eyes. Beyond the blue-green depths she could see that he was as eager to take her as she was to go. He just wasn't the kind of man to let the world see everything he was thinking. Josh Claybourne was becoming more intriguing all the time.

"I'll try to arrange it." After a brief pause she added, "I promise." Finding herself growing increasingly bolder as she gazed into his eyes, she added, "I'm really looking forward to it."

Josh chuckled. "You think so now, but just wait until the mosquitoes start eating you alive—which won't take long," he warned. "Then you'll be pleading for me to take you back home."

"Oh, no, I won't," she asserted bravely. "I'm not afraid of a little mosquito."

"I'm not talking about the little ones," he said ominously. "They just bite. The ones I'm talking about—well, maybe a little thing like you ought to tie weights to your feet so they don't carry you away."

He was watching her, sizing up her body. He'd called her a little thing. She'd never thought much before about her height—after all, she was taller than Isabelle. But standing beside Josh, her head only reached his shoulder. His arms were twice around the size of hers. She felt very small, but very protected.

"Maybe if they get too rambunctious, you'll hold me down—" she started to suggest.

She stopped in midsentence, her mouth still hanging open like a hooked fish. The image of her lying on her back, with Josh's strong body canopied above her, his stormy eyes gazing down on her, erased any other thoughts from her brain.

She could feel her face blazing already.

When she gathered up enough nerve to look at Josh, his face seemed slightly flushed as well. His eyes looked a little glazed, and she could have sworn she saw a slight flare to his nostrils, as if he'd been breathing hard.

He'd been gazing at her, too, but when their eyes met, he quickly turned away.

He looked out over the water as the sun approached the horizon.

"Speaking of mosquitoes, I think we ought to be getting to the house." His voice was unusually gruff. "We're going to be late for dinner or we're going to *be* dinner."

"They won't start without you," she assured him. Did her voice sound too lighthearted as she tried to return to normal after their shared imaginings? "*You're* the guest of honor."

"Oh, jiminy, don't put it that way," he protested. "Do I have to make a grand entrance like some sort of Russian grand duke?"

"Of course. I warn you, you're going to be wined and dined and feted tonight." She laid her hand on his arm to reassure him. "But there's nothing to be nervous about."

"Wined and dined is good," Josh told her, nodding. Then he glared at her skeptically. "But I've never been feted before."

She noticed the merry twinkle in his eye—the same one she'd seen that first day, when he was teasing Alice.

"I see you like to play with words, too, Captain."

Josh grinned and held her eyes with his gaze. "Unlike your father, I like a clever woman—one who appreciates good jokes and bad puns. I don't think Miss Zang ever did."

"Miss Zang?" Was this one of the women he *wasn't* related to—yet?

"Silchester's schoolteacher," he explained.

Schoolteacher? Smart, clever, young, pretty? Eleanor jolted herself away from such potentially dangerous musings. Josh—Captain Claybourne—had merely tossed Bradley into the water for her. She had no right to take such an interest in his personal life. But she did.

"Just one teacher on the island?"

"There's not enough kids to warrant several. I guess we all couldn't afford too many, anyway. Miss Zang boards at my aunt's house, same place as Mr. Randolph—sorry to bring him into this conversation."

Eleanor grimaced. "Just tell me more about Miss Zang," she urged. Oh, she was a glutton for punishment! Why didn't they just invite Bradley here, too, and spill red wine and brown gravy down the front of her new pink silk dress, and make her misery complete?

"Not much to tell, but she's got to be more interesting than what's-his-name."

Oh, horrors! He thought Miss Zang was *interesting*! Would she have to spend the entire evening listening to him extol the virtues of the very *interesting* Miss Zang?

Josh was grinning at her.

"My aunt and uncle had this joke—they always said Miss Zang's been here so long, they just built the boardinghouse around her. The kids in school always used to say she's been here so long, God built the island around her."

Eleanor had to laugh, not just at Josh's words, but at her own foolishness. Suddenly her image of Miss Zang changed to crooked spectacles, a tight gray bun at the nape of her neck, and a hickory stick for naughty students.

"But as we got older, we realized we'd been wrong."

"Oh?"

With a reverent nod of his head Josh pronounced, "God built this island for Augusta Moore."

"Who?" She gave a little laugh. This time she had no illusions that Augusta Moore might be tall and blond and witty.

"Augusta Moore and her husband own the General Store. Everybody calls him the mayor of Silchester, even though we've never had a real election. But everybody knows it's Miz Augusta who really runs the show.''

Eleanor laughed again.

"Miss Zang's been everybody's teacher—except maybe Unk Moore."

"Unk?" she repeated.

"Short for Uncle."

She nodded. "I remember you mentioning him now. He's the one with all the stories."

"Oh, most everyone around here is full of stories—and sometimes a lot more. But, yes, that's Unk."

"Is that Augusta's husband?"

"No, her husband's uncle. I forget his first name."

"Augusta's husband's name?"

"No. He's Charles. But Unk's been called just Unk for so long, I forget his real name. Most likely everybody else has, too. Himself included. He's the one you hear blowing the trumpet for the raising and the lowering of the flag in Evering Square every morning and every evening."

"So that's him." Eleanor laughed with recognition of the sound, even if she'd never met the man.

"He's even more regular than the ferry, because he doesn't have to worry about the tides and the weather, and he doesn't have as far to go."

"I remember the first morning I heard him. We had just arrived the evening before, and I was just barely awake. I jumped out of bed and ran for my parents. I thought it was Gabriel at the Last Judgment."

Josh shook his head. "Oh, my gosh! I hope the angels can play better than Unk."

"Someday I'd like to meet these people. They sound so much more interesting—more real—than all the bankers and stockbrokers, their gossiping wives, and pretentious offspring that my father invites to our houses."

"Well, I've got to admit, they've got their boring moments, too. And some of them do tend to gossip a bit too much. And one or two of them can try to get pretentious once in a while, but we can usually manage to tease them out of it. Mostly they're pretty decent people."

"Yes, indeed. I'd like to meet them. Do you think—"

"Oh, no, Miss Folsom."

She hadn't even said the words that waited on the tip of her tongue, but Josh was already firmly shaking his head.

"No, no, no. You've already sugar-talked me into giving you a boat ride that would probably give your parents conniption fits. You're *not* talking me into helping you break your mother's Rule Number One any further."

He sounded very insistent about this. And she was truly having fun talking with Josh. She felt more at ease strolling with him than she'd felt around any other man since Bradley started making a nuisance of himself. Wasn't that darned Rule Number One what had gotten her in trouble with him in the first place? That and Alice. She decided to let the visit to the town drop—for a while.

They stood at the doorway to the summer cottage. Josh was seized with the sudden urge to say, "It's been great talking to you, gotta go," and head down the path at a run.

He'd been taught to open doors for ladies. What if he just never opened this one? Would they stand out here and talk all night? That could be nice—very nice. Of course, sooner or later, everyone inside would start wondering where Eleanor was, at least.

What if he did open this door for her and, after she was inside, shut it tight and make a run for it? Then he'd be out a dinner, he'd have borrowed all these fancy clothes from his cousins for nothing, and he'd probably never see Eleanor again until she boarded her father's yacht for the trip back to Baltimore at the end of August.

Before he could finally make up his mind to open the door and take his chances on the inside, the door swung open by itself.

Josh wondered if he should he take this as a sign from God.

❖ 8 ❖

JOSH REALIZED THE butler was standing on the inside, holding open the door. Even before he crossed the threshold, he could hear voices drifting out to him.

"I realize it's *your* house, Winston." He recognized Mrs. Folsom's voice immediately.

A man's deep mumbled reply was incoherent, but it must have been Mr. Folsom, Josh figured. He didn't think anybody else but her husband would have the nerve to talk back to Mrs. Folsom that way.

"I realize you can invite whomever you wish to it."

Josh still couldn't make out the man's mumbled reply.

"No, I did *not* see what he did for Eleanor. I positively refuse to watch such vulgar displays—especially when my own daughter is involved."

Another mumbled reply.

"Well, yes, if it had been someone else's daughter, of course I would have watched—just to make sure I got all the information correct, you understand. I do so hate misinformation."

Another mumble.

"*You* may think it did her good. *I* do not."

More mumbling.

"It was a curious coincidence that threw them together *momentarily*," she insisted. "You could have just given the man a few dollars, and he'd be gone. Trust me, that's the only thing these people know or appreciate. Of course, then he probably would have squandered it on the drink, but that's none of our concern."

The mumbling turned into grumbling. Mrs. Folsom's voice grew louder, too. Was she getting angrier, or were they drawing closer to the door?

Josh wondered if he still had time to make a run for it.

"But, no. *You* had to invite him for a dinner and make life absolutely unbearable for me. Arranging a party on such short notice! And I had positively *no* idea whom to invite. Pleading Eleanor's friendship with Isabelle, and promising to work this winter on that ineffectual charity committee of Louella's, was the only way I could persuade the Hamiltons to come."

Mrs. Folsom must not have even drawn a breath between sentences, allowing Mr. Folsom no time to make any more mumbled replies. Either that, or he'd decided just to give up and remain silent.

"Even then, I never thought they'd bring his sister. Oh, Perdition! How I despise Clothilda Mertz! I'd bet the price of my next hat her husband died young because he couldn't stand her whining anymore. Isn't she supposed to be an invalid? Although what sickness she has, no doctor has ever been able to tell. But she manages to haul herself out of her sickbed, as well as drag along those three incorrigible brats of hers, just to get a free meal. Well, at least the little monsters might be some company for Alice. Certainly, with those three around, she'll look good for a change just by comparison. But, I ask you, who wouldn't be totally affronted by being invited to dine under these circumstances? I refuse to allow my daughter to continue to associate with a mere *fisherman*!"

"Excuse me," Josh said.

He strode boldly past the startled butler and an equally startled Eleanor, straight up to Mr. and Mrs. Folsom, still arguing as they entered the vestibule.

"I'm not a fisherman. I'm a waterman. I'd have thought your daughter would've explained the difference to you by now. Or, since I'm your guest, you'd have remembered."

"Oh, well, yes, of course." Now Mrs. Folsom was the one who was mumbling.

"Welcome, Captain Claybourne," Mr. Folsom said. "We've been eagerly awaiting your arrival."

He extended his arm, inviting Josh into the parlor.

As they followed him, Josh turned to Eleanor and whispered, "How was that for a grand entrance?"

"Shame on you!" she whispered back. "I thought you said you hated making an entrance like a Russian grand duke."

"I do."

"You made that entrance like a Russian Cossack!"

Josh shrugged. "I can't help if I do it so well."

"For shame!" she scolded, then gave a little laugh.

Mr. Folsom had told him everyone had been waiting eagerly. From the way they were all looking at him, Josh decided it was the same kind of eagerness with which a vulture awaited the death of prey in the desert.

Mrs. Folsom, however, could better be described as anxious.

She certainly had an anxious enough look on her face as he met each guest in turn. Her eyebrows were so turned down at the outer edges, they looked like a giant inverted "V."

"I do hope you don't mind all the children," Mrs. Folsom said. She was probably trying to sound apologetic, Josh figured, even if she didn't mean it.

It was hard *not* to notice these children as they ran past

him, tugging on his coattail and hurling pillows at his head.

"I have a little brother and two sisters myself," Josh said. "I don't mind children at all." If he and his brother and sisters had acted like this in company, his pa would've given them a licking they wouldn't soon forget.

"I thought it would be so much more . . . familylike."

"It's . . . sort of like family," Josh tried to agree. A family of wild baboons at the zoo, maybe!

Mrs. Folsom still looked very worried as he took his seat at the long mahogany dining room table directly to her right. She looked as if she'd positively swoon with concern when he picked up the crystal goblet of wine.

When he picked up the silverware and began eating from the fine china, would she fall over in a dead faint? Hiding an ornery grin, he silently pondered, if he picked up his bowl and slurped his soup, why, she might be comatose for years!

The butler wheeled out a cart. While he stood by watching with hawk eyes, the maid served everyone a plate of stewed eels.

He could eat just to be polite, Josh thought as he surveyed the dish. But he and his friends usually used these things for bait.

The child seated next to him had other uses for them.

"Louella, my dear, please see to it that the children eat properly," Clothilda languidly requested from her seat at the far end from the children. She was as pale as her dress, and just about as lifeless. "I just can't seem to manage. . . ." Without finishing her sentence, she lapsed back into her chair and picked at her food.

When Mrs. Mertz did raise her eyes, Josh noted she watched him with about the same expression he'd once seen on Dr. Whitaker's face when he'd helped hold Edgar down while the doc lanced a boil on his cousin's butt.

On the other hand, he wasn't sure if Eleanor's friend's

expression was an improvement. He recognized Isabelle Hamilton from the incident at the club. She definitely remembered him. She kept staring at him as if she were expecting him to suddenly spring up from his chair, draw his sword, and slay a few dragons—or at least an evil troll or two.

"Roger, eat your delicious eels," Mrs. Hamilton told the little boy who was bouncing in the chair next to Josh. "Don't play with them."

Roger was taking the individual pieces of eel out of the dish and lining them up on the tablecloth in front of him in an attempt to reconstruct the entire eel. The sauce was seeping into the pure white tablecloth. Maybe a year or two of scrubbing with lye soap would get out the stain.

"Don't do that, Roger," Mrs. Hamilton scolded gently. She might as well talk to the chandelier, and the boy's mother did nothing to discipline him.

"It won't fit," Roger complained peevishly.

"You may not have all the pieces of the same eel," Alice, seated to his other side, pointed out to him.

"No?" he cried in dismay, thumping his fists on the tabletop. "Where are they? Give me some of yours."

Without even a "please," he dipped his hand into her plate, pulled out several chunks, and tried to add them to the dismantled beast.

"Oh, buggers! They don't fit, either!" He flung the pieces across the table at one of his brothers. "Gimme yours, Rudy."

He stood up on the chair, knelt on the table, knocked over the flower arrangement into Mrs. Hamilton's lap, and stole some of his brother's eels.

"Ye gods, Violet! Can't you do something to restrain the child?" Mr. Folsom demanded.

Mrs. Folsom merely shrugged.

"Oh, I have tried," Mrs. Mertz said with a languid sigh.

"Why the Almighty, in His infinite wisdom, blessed an invalid such as myself with three healthy boys and then saw fit to take my husband is a mystery to me."

Alice leaned behind Roger's chair and whispered to Josh, "Mr. Mertz died because he *wanted* to."

"Yeah! These'll fit nice," Roger declared as he seated himself with a plop.

"No, they won't," Alice quickly contradicted.

He glared at her, but Alice smiled pleasantly at him.

Much too pleasant for Alice, Josh thought. Was she up to something? Of course she was. Now if he could just figure out what it was—and stay out of her way.

"Alice, what are you saying?" Mrs. Folsom demanded in her sugary-sweet voice with the underlying threat that even Josh was beginning to recognize.

"I just wanted to tell him that I was in the kitchen this afternoon when the cook was making these. I saw the maid dip out the exact pieces that match his in Mrs. Mertz's dish."

Before anyone could protest, Roger had climbed up on the table, knocked over a candlestick that ignited the tablecloth before Mr. Folsom could douse it with the water in his goblet, and was fishing through his mother's dish.

"Got it!" he cried triumphantly, raising a long piece that splattered sauce on the front of Mrs. Mertz's dress.

"Now sit down and put it all together," Alice encouraged.

Why would Alice be helping this little spawn of Satan? Josh wondered. Then, just before Roger's rump hit the upholstery, Josh noticed the slick sauce smeared on the fabric, which quickly attached itself to the seat of Roger's white pants.

Josh looked up at Alice. Alice looked at him, smiled sweetly, and returned to pushing what was left of her eels around in her plate.

Josh's plate was still practically untouched when the maid removed it.

"Oh, dear," Mrs. Folsom murmured solicitously. "You didn't like the eels, Captain Claybourne?"

"I . . . uh, I had eels at lunchtime," Josh answered.

He didn't elaborate that he'd actually eaten several cheese sandwiches and a peach, and had washed them down with a bottle of sarsaparilla, and that the eels had stayed in his bait pail.

"Oh, dear. I'm so sorry, but how was I to know?" Mrs. Folsom glanced frantically around the table.

Was she looking for sympathy?

"I mean, how was I supposed to know?" she cried. "What. . . . what do *those* people usually eat?"

Josh watched Eleanor cringe at the far end of the table and send him an apologetic look.

"Oh, bread, meat, corn—just about like everyone else, I guess," he answered quickly. He glanced around the table as Mrs. Folsom had. "I mean, I don't know," he mimicked as he leaned closer to her for confidentiality. "What . . . what do *these* people usually eat?"

Eleanor giggled.

As if in answer to his question, the maid began to place portions of sturgeon and various side dishes in front of everyone.

"Say there, Captain Claybourne," Mr. Hamilton called cheerfully to him from down the table. "Do you see anyone you recognize?"

Josh pretended to give a quick glance to everyone's plate. "No, sir, I can't say as I do," he replied.

"I guess it'd be easier to recognize one of these whole fellows than it would be to single anyone out of those chunks of eels."

"I guess so." Josh had never paid much attention to singling out eels anyway.

"Just like after Antietam," Mr. Hamilton continued. "It was a lot easier to identify the whole bodies lying around than it was to pick up a loose arm or leg and say, 'Oh, hey, that belongs to John Smith.' "

"Willard, please!" Mrs. Hamilton cried while the other ladies gasped.

Josh cut in abruptly. "Oh, well, for a minute there I thought Roger had a fish I once caught."

Everyone else at the table just stared at him. He was grateful to hear Eleanor laugh.

"Actually, Mr. Hamilton, I try very hard not to mix business with my personal life."

Mr. Hamilton laughed, his gray whiskers wiggling up and down. "Myself, I'm always very careful about that, too. I remember once, in the winter of sixty-four, down on Thirteenth Street in our nation's capital, I saw my commanding officer entering a house of somewhat dubious repute—"

"Willard!" his wife exclaimed again. Her face was growing red. She was fanning herself furiously.

Josh wondered what upset her more—dead bodies or houses of ill repute?

"Oh, Mr. Hamilton, I do think I should prefer to discuss . . . anything else," Mrs. Hamilton stated.

"His piece is bigger than mine," Roger complained. He made the mistake of standing up, reaching over, and spearing his brother's piece, and then tossing him his rejected fish.

"Are you sure?" Alice asked, tilting her head this way and that as she compared the two fish.

Roger repeated the entire process until he'd finally settled on one fish. By the time he sat down, Alice had added a good mound of mashed potatoes and asparagus tips—indirectly by way of the chair—to the seat of Roger's pants.

Josh thought he was going to choke with laughter before he got to eat a single bite.

"It's very kind of you to help Roger," Josh told her.

"We just call the three boys Roger, Rudy, and Russell."

"Why?" he asked cautiously. He wasn't sure yet whether to take Alice seriously or not.

"It's easier to pronounce than their real names."

"Which are—?"

"Beelzebub, Molloch, and Asmodeus."

Josh nodded and went back to eating his sturgeon.

"So, you're a waterman, Captain Claybourne," Mr. Folsom said. "I take it you own your own boat."

"Yes, I do. But I have a younger brother and two sisters to support. So I'd like to be able to buy a few more boats someday, and hire the men to work them for me."

"Admirable, Captain," Mr. Folsom pronounced. "Admirable ambition. Unbridled ambition is the cornerstone of our American economy. Just look where it's gotten me, sir, and follow my example."

"I . . . why, I could only aspire . . ." Josh gasped, speechless with what he hoped Mr. Folsom took for admiration.

As much as he needed it, he couldn't run roughshod over anyone for the sake of mere money. He couldn't plow under the marshes he loved for any amount of money.

He glanced over at Eleanor. If only he'd been able to sit beside her, instead of between Mrs. Folsom and Roger, alias Beelzebub.

If only all these other people would just disappear. Then, in a quiet, candlelit room, he could continue to talk to Eleanor alone about the way it used to be on the island. Maybe he could tell her more about the people on the island, people he knew and loved in spite of, or maybe because of, all their eccentricities. He'd tell her about his own family.

As things stood, the best he could hope for was to get a good meal out of this arrangement before they all decided they were tired of him and threw him out.

At last Mrs. Folsom rose, announcing that coffee would be served in the parlor.

Josh took a little more time than usual in rising from his chair. He lingered just a little longer, pretending an interest in the vases set atop the marble mantelpiece. He was waiting for Eleanor to come by.

"Are you enjoying yourself?" she asked as she came to stand beside him.

"Yes." He wouldn't want her to think he didn't appreciate the invitation. He especially didn't want her to think he wasn't glad to be with her. "The food was good."

"I'm just sorry you were constantly reminded that you'd probably caught it this morning. We'd better be joining the rest," Eleanor suggested.

"I guess that's part of the invitation, too. First they fatten up the calf for slaughter—"

"Oh, hush." She gave him a playful little swat on the arm.

Before she could move her hand away, he'd clasped her hand under his.

"My, you're . . . you're quicker than I'd supposed."

"No. You're just not as tough as Bradley." He paused a moment, still holding her soft hand. "I like it that way."

He knew his hands were rough and calloused from working all his life, and she was so soft he was afraid he might scratch her skin. But from the gentle gleam in her eyes, Josh could tell she liked having him hold her hand.

He heard the low clatter of china against china as the maids began clearing the dining room table.

Eleanor pulled her hand away. "Come on. Mother has coffee in the parlor."

"Your version of a parlor is something like your version of a cottage," he said as he followed her.

At the door to the parlor, he stopped.

"Any fool could tell he'd just gotten a haircut," Mrs. Mertz's voice rang from the room.

"I wonder if it's his usual day to get a haircut or did he get it especially for this evening," Mrs. Hamilton said.

"Do you have to ask?" Mrs. Mertz declared sarcastically. "It's pretty obvious by that awful white line all around the edge of his hair, where it's not brown like some sort of wild Indian, that the man only gets a haircut for special occasions."

Eleanor looked at him. He'd had his lips pressed tightly together. He tried not to look so mean and harsh when he turned to her.

"I'm sorry they're so rude," she said.

"At least they don't insult me to my face," he said. "Gossip is just . . . gossip." He shrugged.

"I . . . I don't mind your haircut," she told him. "I . . . I . . . no, never mind."

"No fair," Josh said. "You made me finish my thought."

"Then I'll tell you," she said. There was a mischievous twinkle in her pale green eyes as she added, "When you take me on your boat."

"I'll hold you to that, Miss Folsom," he told her.

He'd like to hold her to a lot of other things, too, like his arms, his chest . . . *No time to daydream now, Josh, he warned himself. Stay on your toes with these treacherous people. They're more dangerous than Rocky Point.*

"And where in the world did he get those clothes?" Mrs. Mertz continued her demands.

"Hush, Clothilda!" Mrs. Folsom said. "Since when did you become an arbiter of fashion?"

"Just look at him! I haven't seen anyone else wear a

vest like that since Grandfather died.''

"It's black. It's an entirely appropriate color,'' Isabelle came to his defense.

"Oh, hush, child," Mrs. Hamilton told her. "When you're a little older, you'll understand the impropriety of these things better.''

"He's dirty, too. His shoes were practically white from the gravel.''

Josh and Eleanor both looked at his shoes.

"Well, the dust must have shaken off,'' Eleanor told him. "They look perfectly black to me.''

"They're practically brand-new,'' Josh told her.

"I watched him when he came in,'' Mrs. Mertz said, "stopping every couple of steps, shifting from one foot to the other, trying to wipe the dust off the tips of the toes on the back of his pants legs.''

Josh grimaced to himself. He had done exactly that. He didn't like the idea that some of them had been watching him even then.

Mrs. Mertz laughed, a deep throaty, vicious laugh. "He isn't very graceful, either.''

"That's all right,'' Josh said, striding into the parlor.

Eleanor followed quickly behind him. So far, he'd seemed very capable of handling every problem that came his way. But he wasn't as sophisticated as some of these people. Mrs. Hamilton and Mrs. Mertz had tongues of stainless steel. She wanted to be with him, in case he needed any help.

"I can take dancing lessons, but you'll still be rude.''

"I'm not rude. I'm truthful.''

Josh just stared coldly at her. "Someday, when you're a *little* older, and a whole lot wiser, you need to ask yourself what the truth really is.''

Clothilda lounged back against the sofa cushions. "Oh,

merciful heavens! Save me from another waterlogged philosopher!''

Josh approached Mr. Folsom and extended his hand. ''Thank you for being so nice. Mrs. Folsom, I thank you for the meal. Miss Folsom.''

He turned to her, but couldn't think of anything to say to her with all these people standing around. What he wanted to do was to be alone with her for just a few moments. From the looks of things right now—and from what he knew of the way of the world in general—it didn't look as if anything like that would happen at all.

''Miss Folsom, I wish you the best in the future.'' He nodded to her, then headed for the door.

''Wait, wait, Captain Claybourne,'' Mr. Folsom called. ''You're not leaving already, are you?''

''Yes, indeed, I am.''

''But . . . but . . .''

''You don't have to pretend to protest, sir,'' Josh told him.

''But we have business yet to discuss.''

''You've already repaid me more than enough for getting rid of Randolph. I can't imagine what further business we could have.''

''But you've done so well protecting her from Mr. Randolph, I was hoping you'd consent to be my daughter's bodyguard.''

''No, sir,'' Josh answered abruptly.

''But you can see for yourself—why, I only just realized—how much she truly needs one.''

''I know, sir, but it's not me.''

''It'll just be for the time we're on the island this summer.''

''No, sir.''

''But you're big, and strong—and just what we need to keep undesirables away!''

"Until you decide to consider me an undesirable."

"What? No, no, Captain Claybourne! You'll be a valued employee."

"I already have a job I like very much. Thank you anyway."

"With what I'll pay you this summer alone, you can buy those boats you dream of a lot faster," Mr. Folsom hinted.

Josh shrugged. "I'll just have to find some other way."

"We might even consider some sort of . . . partnership."

Josh shook his head firmly. "No. I work for myself. I don't like to be beholden to any man. I need to stand on my own."

"But I'll pay you *very* well," Mr. Folsom offered.

"I don't like to be paid any more than exactly what I'm worth."

"It's worth it to me to have my daughter looked after."

Josh nodded back toward the people in the parlor. "I think your daughter is already well taken care of."

"But . . . but . . ."

Clearly a man like Winston Stanford Folsom III was not used to being refused. But Josh had already decided, whether it was as an employee or as a guest, he didn't want to spend any more time around these people. Josh wasn't a man who was used to changing his mind.

"Thank you for inviting me this evening," Josh repeated. "But you only invited me for a dinner, and I will tell you, sir, I've had a bellyful. Good-bye."

Eleanor watched Josh stride toward the front door. The butler was standing at attention, ready to open it. She hurried to follow after him.

"Captain Claybourne," she called. "Captain Claybourne. Josh!"

"Eleanor, come back here immediately," Mrs. Folsom commanded. "We have guests."

Eleanor stopped. She was breathing hard and trying not

to let the tears well up in her eyes. She wanted to follow Josh. She *needed* to follow him.

He was fun. He was clever and witty—and liked her when she was clever and witty, too. He was brave and didn't take abuse from anyone—not even the so-called ladies who made up the company this evening. He was prepared to show her a world from which her parents had kept her sheltered.

She was ready to follow him. But was he ready to accept her? What would she do if he didn't? Once she'd traveled in his world, would her parents take her back?

She swallowed the lump that was tightening in her throat and turned back to the parlor.

She heard the front door shut with a loud noise that cracked her heart in two.

❖ 9 ❖

JOSH WALKED THROUGH the grass to get to the end of the driveway, so he wouldn't mess up his cousin's shoes on the gravel. Dan had only worn them once, to his wife's funeral last year. They'd been in his closet ever since.

He hadn't noticed any dust or scuff marks on the shiny black leather. On the other hand, he'd been pretty occupied with Eleanor, and then with defending his life from those saber-toothed matrons.

When he reached Folsom Road, he stopped, leaned against the fence, and took off his cousin's shoes and his own socks.

His feet were as tough as his brother Bill's. He had no trouble crossing Folsom Drive, or finding his way in the moonlight through the shortcut in the woods to the back of Aunt Audrey's house.

Was Randolph standing in his upstairs window, looking down, watching him? he wondered as he walked through the backyard. Was the little weasel laughing at him on a full stomach?

Josh had eaten at the Folsoms' table, but it wasn't the kind of food he was used to. It wasn't even the kind of food he *could* get used to. He'd match Aunt Audrey's chicken and dumplings and roasted corn against that fancy city eel-cooker any day!

Across the street from Aunt Audrey's, Darty's Tavern was still open. The kerosene lamps that hung on either side of the door burned a bright welcome.

Jack Darty was a good listener, the perfect kind of fellow to own a tavern. Dan would probably be there, too. Since Katie died last year, he didn't really have any other place to go.

He pushed open the front door.

"Hey, Josh!" Jack Darty called to him from behind the long mahogany bar.

"Hey, Jack." Josh returned the greetings of the men seated at the bar—his cousins Edgar and Dan, Red Taylor, Shadrach Nicholson, and Eric Langenfelder, the owner of the chandlery.

Jack set a glass of beer on the bar in front of Josh.

"Thanks, Jack. You know I'm not much of a drinking man anymore," Josh protested.

"Have one on the house," Jack said. "I never expected to see you here tonight."

"Yeah. We thought you were hobnobbing with those summer folks," Red said.

"I've had those summer folks up to here," Josh replied, bringing the back of his hand up to the bottom of his chin. "I think right now, after what I've been through, I could really use this."

"I thought you were going up there for a meal," Jack said. "Didn't they feed you? Did you come here to drink your supper?"

He picked up the glass of beer and downed it in a few gulps. With a deep sigh of satisfaction, he set the empty glass down on the bar.

"Had to wash the taste of this evening out of my gullet. Not even the seagulls would eat that food."

"Gee, what happened?" Edgar asked.

"Yeah. Have another one on me," Red said. "And tell us all about it."

"No, no. I really shouldn't," Josh protested.

"Come on. It's only a beer," Red encouraged. "It's not like you come in here that often."

"It's not like you're ever going to go out fighting again."

"Well, okay."

Josh picked up the refilled glass Jack had set in front of him. This time, feeling a little more relaxed among friends and family, he sat down on the stool next to Dan and slowly sipped his beer.

"Don't know how those summer folks can stand each other," Josh complained. "Can't imagine one of those steel-edged women pulling in her claws long enough for any man to—"

"Had a little trouble with the beautiful Miss Folsom?" Edgar teased. "I thought that Folsom gal was sweet on you."

"No. Not her. It's her ma—must've invited some of the nastiest people on the face of the earth. Miss Folsom must be adopted or something."

"I thought her pa was right impressed with you," Dan said.

"Yeah. Right. They're the biggest bunch of gossiping, back-stabbing, pretentious, hypocritical snobs ever to walk the face of this green earth."

"Gee, just say what you think, Josh," Eric encouraged.

"Oh, they can be so nice to you if they want something from you—if you're doing something for them. If you're doing their dirty work for them—something unsavory they don't want to get their lily-white hands dirty doing. They think they can throw you a few crusts of bread, a few stewed eels, and you'll be happy with it."

"Yeah, life's tough," Red commented.

"But you're not bitter," Jack said.

"Have another beer on me," Red offered.

Josh plopped the shoes on top the bar in front of Dan.

"Didn't even scuff the soles. Thanks for the loan."

"Any time."

"Won't be a next time."

Josh shrugged out of his coat, then removed the vest he'd been wearing, too.

"Gee, Josh, it ain't that hot in here!" Edgar remarked. "And we ain't so drunk we'd cotton to seeing you in the altogether."

"Calm down, Ed. I'm not so drunk I'd cotton to being seen in the altogether. Here's Grandpa's vest." He offered it to his cousin. "Didn't even spill gravy on it. Thanks for the loan."

"Well, I won't say any time like Dan, 'cause you've already made it plenty clear there won't be a next time."

"Darn right. Those pernickety summer folks didn't like the shoes. They didn't like the vest." Josh screwed his face into sarcastic contortions. "They didn't like the way I walked. They didn't like my haircut."

"Not the haircut!" Eric protested. "Wally's the best barber this side of the Bay."

"You try to figure these rich folks out." Josh shrugged and downed what little was left of his beer. He raised his hand to call for another one and nearly toppled off the stool.

"Say, you ought to go easy there, Josh," Dan warned him. "I don't want to go fishing you out of the Straiten Narrows tomorrow morning, finding the crabs mistook you for bait."

"Naw, he's so sour the crabs wouldn't want him," Shad teased.

"Appreciate your concern, fellows." Josh felt his head getting heavier and heavier. It was getting harder all the time to keep it from falling onto the bar. "But I'm feeling just fine. It's touching—refreshingly touching after the less than cordial surroundings of this evening's fesitivis . . . fevisifits . . . shoot!" He downed another glass. "A man needs his friends around him."

"Look, why don't you go on home and sleep it off, Josh?" Jack suggested.

"Nope. I'm going home, fellers, and going to bed." Josh tripped as he lowered himself from the stool and had to grab hold of Edgar's shoulder to steady himself.

"You want me to walk a bit with you?" Edgar offered.

"Nope. Jiminy, it's a little island, fellers. I can't get lost. I can find my way home in the dark with my eyes closed."

"Yeah, we'll find him draped over one of the tombstones tomorrow morning."

"Or drying out in Bo's drunk tank."

"Or cuddled up next to Miss Zang."

The men all made sounds of vomiting.

"Or cuddled up next to Eleanor Folsom," Shad teased.

Josh strode crookedly toward Shad. Almost nose to nose, he poked at Shad's chest with his index finger and told him, "I'm *not* cuddling up to her. Not now, not never. Unnerstan'?"

"Sure, Josh, sure."

"Couldn't get near her no ways, no how," he grumbled.

He tried to dip into his pocket to pay for his beer. He was having a hard time. Darn it, did Maddie sew his pockets shut again? What had he done to rile her now? Did he put his pants on backward and not realize it until now? It was a wonder somebody at the Folsoms' hadn't said something about *that*, too.

"Never mind," Edgar said, tapping him on the shoulder. "I've got it." He laid a few quarters on the bar. "You just go home and sleep it off."

"Yeah, sure."

"Can you find the door?" Shad called.

"Yeah, sure."

"Can you find your house?" Red called.

"Yeah, sure."

The evening air hit him in the face like a bucket of cold raw oysters.

He walked very slowly and very carefully down the street, so no one would be able to tell he'd had a bit too much to drink at Darty's.

He could feel the beer churning in his stomach. He shouldn't have mixed good beer with the awful wine they'd served for dinner.

He never had been much for drinking wine. Heck, he wasn't much of a drinker at all anymore.

"You're out of practice, Joshua," he muttered to himself.

Why in tarnation had he stopped at Darty's anyway? Oh, yeah, to return Dan's shoes and Grandpa's vest.

"That darn food them summer folks served was too rich for you," he told himself as he walked along. "Too much for your stomach to handle. You're used to good old American cheese sandwiches, fried chicken, beef stew, fresh watermelon, peaches, and scuppernongs. Yeah. That's real food. That garbage they served you gave you a bellyache. Headache, too. It's got to be *their* food. It sure as heck wasn't Darty's good beer."

Josh blinked hard. The back of his head suddenly started hurting a whole lot worse. The ground was coming up to meet his face faster than usual. He would've held his arms out to catch himself in fall, as usual, but they seemed too heavy to lift.

It was dark at night anyway, but suddenly things were getting a whole lot darker. . . .

*   *   *

Eleanor slipped her dimity nightgown over her head and started to fasten the small pearl buttons of the bodice. She had been looking forward to spending more time with Josh. But this evening had turned into a disaster!

He'd been repaid for his kindness to her by a dinner he could barely eat. He'd been insulted by her friends and family. He'd made such a hasty exit, she wouldn't be surprised if she never saw him again. *That* was the worst disaster of all!

At least Isabelle was spending the night with her. They could sit up and chat all evening, just as they used to do when they were little girls. She really needed to talk to her best friend.

She thought she heard a scraping noise at her window.

Probably just a tree branch tapping in the wind. She didn't think it had been that windy earlier this evening, but storms blew up quickly on the Bay.

Was a nightbird fluttering at the window, trying to get in because of the light? She hoped not. Hadn't old Madame Orlov, who came around with fresh eggs each morning, said that was a bad omen? Madame Orlov was a gypsy. She ought to know.

Eleanor shivered and tried to resume fastening her nightgown.

The scraping outside continued.

Maybe it was Alice, up to some sort of weird shenanigans again—like climbing across the roof with bedsheets, just to see if she could fly. She wouldn't put anything past her wild sister.

The curtain rippled inward. Eleanor froze. No breeze moved like that. He appeared from behind the curtain, unwinding his scarf and shoving it in his pocket.

"Bradley!"

"No, no, my love. Don't scream," he pleaded as he rushed up to her.

Eleanor made a dash for the door. He was too quick. He slammed his back against the door and spread his arms out so she couldn't reach the knob unless she fell into his embrace.

She backed up, but could only go so far. She wasn't about to end up on her bed. She stood in the middle of the room, watching him, waiting for his next move. She prayed she'd still be quick enough to dodge him.

"What are you doing here?"

"I came to see you, my only love."

This was a terrible turn of events. Bradley had followed her unmercifully from party to party back in Baltimore, but he'd never had the audacity to sneak into her home and come into her bedroom before!

She could feel her insides quivering and prayed her shaking knees would continue to support her. She wasn't sure what to expect now.

"How . . . how did you get in?"

"There's a trellis outside your window."

"It's coming down tomorrow," Eleanor vowed. "If I have to chop it down myself."

"It doesn't matter. I'll still always find a way to get to you."

She knew what he said was absolutely true.

For a moment she stood in the center of her room, staring helplessly at Bradley and the door, through which there was no escape. She felt her shoulders sag in defeat. Her arms hung limply at her side. She glanced over to the window, from which the only escape meant certain death on the brick walkway below.

"I watched that obnoxious fisherman leave." Bradley gave a low chuckle. "I didn't think he'd be able to stay long. A rustic, uncouth fellow like him doesn't belong here with people like us, my dear."

Josh was the only person she truly felt safe with anymore. How dare Bradley continue to belittle him!

She swallowed hard to rid herself of the lump of frustrated tears in her throat. Her hands balled into tense fists.

"I will tell you once more to leave quietly the way you came, and then I will scream as loudly as I can," she warned.

"No, you won't." Still leaning cockily against the door, he crossed his arms over his chest.

"My parents will come running. The butler, the maids. They'll probably bring a gun and shoot you as a trespasser. Or get the big strong coachman and the gardener to throw you out."

"No, they won't."

He looked so smug, standing there, blocking her exit.

"Of course they will."

He just grinned at her and shook his head.

"Why not?"

Bradley gestured toward her, his hand moving up and down as if he were caressing her body through thin air. Even though he stood halfway across the room, just the thought that he was contemplating touching her sent a shiver of revulsion down her spine.

"There you stand, my lovely, in your nightclothes. And here I stand, a man who's already publicly avowed my affection for you—and my intention to marry you—many times over. It's simply a matter of having your family find us in this compromising situation and—"

He shrugged and grinned triumphantly, as if he knew the outcome of the situation was without contest.

"That's stupid!" She began to pace back and forth across the room. It was hard to believe that even Bradley could try something so desperately dumb. "It's reprehensible. It's another bad plot from another bad melodrama. For Pete's sake, Bradley. If you're going to be annoying, at least have some originality!"

"I don't want to be original," he declared as he left the doorway and fell to his knees at her feet. He reached up and seized her hand. "I want to be with you, my love."

"I don't want to marry you." She tried to pull her hand away. "We've been through all this over and over and over again, until I'm sick of it and sick of you. I don't want to be with you. The more you do this, the more I feel as if I don't even want to be in the same building with you."

"If you'd just stop being so nervous, you'd get used to me, my sweetness."

"No!"

"You'd learn to love me."

"Never!"

He fumbled around in his pocket. As he pulled out a small box, his scarf spilled out, too.

"See. I've come prepared to show you the depths of my affection."

"Not again, Bradley," Eleanor said with exasperation. "You know these gifts are entirely inappropriate."

"No, no. It's not inappropriate for a man to give gifts to his beloved."

"I am *not* your beloved. A nice young lady does *not* accept expensive jewelry from nice young men. Although I don't think you fall in that category, Bradley."

He lifted the lid. On the black velvet interior lay an ornately set garnet and diamond brooch.

"This is ridiculous. You know I haven't accepted any of your other gifts. I won't accept this one."

"But you must, my darling!"

"It's expensive jewelry and inappropriate."

"It's a small token of my affection for you."

"No. Now get out, before they find your dead body here in the morning! Instead of a wedding, we'll have *your* funeral."

"If I must die, then let me leave this life with your kiss on my lips," he pleaded.

She exclaimed in disgust.

He rose to his feet. Suddenly he grabbed her shoulders with both hands. His face, lips pursed, drew nearer.

She threw her arms up in front of her face. Bradley's kiss met her elbow.

"Ow!"

Bradley backed up, holding his hand to his mouth.

"Did I hit you?"

"Yes," he mumbled through his fingers.

"Good!"

She rushed to her dressing table, grabbed her brush, and turned to him. What was she going to do with this? she suddenly realized. Groom him to death?

"Get out!"

"I can't. I'm injured."

"You're going to be even more injured if I push you out the window. Climb down now, while you still can."

"Holy Hannah!" Alice cried. The door banged against the wall as she flung it open.

Isabelle followed Alice into the room.

"Close the door, quick!" Eleanor ordered.

Isabelle slammed it shut behind her.

"Where are Mother and Father?"

"Still in the parlor with my parents."

"Good." Eleanor breathed a sigh of relief.

"Do you want me to get them and tell Father to bring the gun?" Alice volunteered.

"No! There's still time to get him out of here before they see him—and something dreadful happens."

"Looks like something dreadful has already happened. He's here again," Alice complained. "I thought we'd finally gotten rid of him."

She rushed up to Bradley, trying to peer into his face,

but he still kept it covered with his hands. He backed away, but she kept advancing.

"What happened to you? Are you blowing your nose without a handkerchief? Ick! You better not rub boogers on anything."

"Of course not!" he declared.

"Did she finally get fed up and hit you? That's what I would've done a long time ago. What did she hit you with? Her brush? Puny. I'd have used the poker, and maybe stabbed you, too."

"How did he get in?" Isabelle asked.

"The window."

"The same way he's going out," Alice said.

"I'm not leaving," Bradley asserted. Apparently satisfied that his nose wasn't bleeding, he dropped his hands and turned to Eleanor. "I have witnesses now, my love." He gestured to Isabelle and Alice.

"Witnesses?" Isabelle asked.

"You've both witnessed Miss Eleanor Folsom and me in a very compromising position," he declared triumphantly.

Alice looked from one to the other. With a blatant sneer on her face, she slowly walked around Bradley.

"I don't see what's so compromising about it. You were holding your nose, and she looks like she's ready to brush her hair."

"My dear child, when you get older, you'll understand these things," Bradley said with more condescension than all the people at dinner this evening had had for Josh.

"Well, *I'm* old enough," Isabelle declared. "And I didn't see anything. I didn't witness anything." She shook her head until Eleanor thought her curls would fall off. "You won't use me in your rotten plans, Bradley Randolph!"

"If you're thinking of waiting around here until some

more compliant witnesses arrive, I'd advise you not to,'' Eleanor said.

''As a matter of fact, if you don't leave now, I'll make you go back *without* your scarf,'' Alice threatened. Dangling it in front of her, she danced backward from him.

''What? My scarf. How do you know . . . ?'' Bradley began slapping at his side pocket, searching for the wad of wool. ''It's not there. I know I had it.''

He dug into his pockets but still came up empty-handed.

''How did you get it, you little pickpocket?''

''I found it on the floor.'' Alice said. ''You know, you really ought to be more careful with something your life depends on.''

She moved over to the window and dangled the scarf outside.

Bradley started toward her.

''Don't try to grab me, or I'll drop it for sure,'' Alice warned.

He stayed in place. ''Give it to me now and . . . and I'll leave quietly.''

''Come on, Bradley. You're a bigger liar than I am,'' Alice said, moving the scarf tantalizingly back and forth. ''Do you honestly expect me to believe you?''

''I guess not.''

''Now, just climb down the trellis and leave my sister alone.''

Bradley sat on the windowsill. He threw one leg over and then the other, until he was dangling outside the window completely.

''Now, give me back my scarf.''

''Okay. It'll be waiting for you when you get to the ground.''

Alice flung the scarf out the window and slammed the sash down so hard the windowpanes rattled.

''Hey, hey.'' Bradley was still tapping on the windowpane. "Eleanor, my love, my darling, my sweetheart. I'll be back!"

Eleanor walked over and closed the curtains tightly.

Isabelle and Alice rushed to Eleanor's side. They guided her to her bed. All three sat on the edge.

"Oh, my gracious, are you all right?" Isabelle asked. "What did he do?"

"Nothing. I'm fine. Just fine. Oh, I don't know what I would do without my little sister and my best friend!" She reached out both arms, trying to embrace them both at the same time.

"Why was he so concerned about that scarf?" Isabelle asked.

Eleanor looked to her sister. "Yes, what was that all about?"

Alice just grinned. "Maybe I ought to let Josh tell you."

"What's that supposed to mean?"

Alice was still grinning. "Well, who would you rather hear about it from—me or him?"

When Eleanor made no reply, Alice started laughing.

"But how do you know?" Isabelle wondered.

"Oh, I get around this island. Why, I'm practically one of them now."

"I'll believe that the day I see you catching sooks and jimmies in a bugeye," Eleanor replied skeptically.

"Don't get flippant," Alice warned. "But one thing I do know. You do need a bodyguard. I can't be around all the time to protect you."

"Oh, Captain Claybourne would be perfect." Isabelle's eyes still glowed with admiration.

"Oh, yes, indeed," Alice agreed.

"If *he* can't keep Bradley away, I don't know who could," Isabelle declared breathlessly. "He's so strong . . . so powerful . . . so masterful!"

"Oh, shut up, Isabelle," Alice complained.

Eleanor sighed. "Josh—Captain Claybourne—will *never* be my bodyguard now."

"Not after what Clothilda the Pale, and Beelzebub, Molloch, and Satan put him through tonight," Alice agreed.

"Captain Claybourne very adamantly refused when Father asked him."

"Sure, when *Father* asked him," Alice said. "Did *you* ask him?"

"Well, no. Of course not. Josh—Captain—"

"Oh, for goodness sake, Eleanor," Isabelle scolded. "Don't you think we know by now you're kind of sweet on the man? You can call him Josh when you're with us." She heaved a deep sigh. "Oh, if only a man like that would come to my rescue!"

"You read too many fairy tales, Isabelle," Eleanor scolded in return.

"You've got to ask him," Alice insisted. "He'll do it for you."

"Yes, yes," Isabelle urged. She and Alice began laying their plans. "You must go to him tomorrow."

"You'll have to go early, before he leaves for work on his boat," Alice warned.

"You'll have to find out where he lives," Isabelle said.

Eleanor shook her head with dismay. "His aunt owns the boardinghouse where Bradley is staying."

"You can't go there. You'll have to find somebody else to ask," Alice said. "But I don't think he'll be too hard to locate."

"Yes," Eleanor finally announced decisively. "I'll find Josh tomorrow."

❖ *10* ❖

"**W**ELL, CERTAINLY YOU may walk with Isabelle to her home," Mrs. Folsom readily agreed.

She was lounging against her bed pillows, wearing a lacy pink bed jacket. She seemed to be in a better humor this morning than she had been since they'd arrived.

"An early morning walk sounds like just the thing to clear your head after last night's foolishness."

Eleanor wanted to protest that, everything having been done deliberately and with malice, it was far from foolishness, and that none of it had been on *her* part.

"I'll go with you," Alice volunteered. She tugged at Eleanor's sleeve. "Come on."

A little too readily for Alice, Eleanor pondered.

"Yes," Mrs. Folsom said. "Isabelle is such a flighty little thing. Perhaps you can all keep each other out of trouble."

Eleanor had to admit Alice had saved her neck last night. But when it came to looking out for each other, she still thought she had the harder job. And Isabelle had turned into such a flibbertigibbet, a person would think she was the one who was in love—not Eleanor.

"Come on," Alice whispered, tugging more insistently.

"I certainly hope you realized yesterday evening that I've been right all along," Mrs. Folsom continued. She shook her finger at her daughters. "I've always tried to keep you girls from associating with the island people for a very good reason, and now you see why. They simply do not fit in with our society, and we certainly do not belong in theirs."

"Yes, Mother."

If anyone didn't belong in polite society, Eleanor thought, it was Clothilda and her three demonic children.

"And Isabelle, although I'm not your mother, I know she would say to you the same thing I'm telling my daughters. So I hope you take the lesson, too."

"Yes, Mrs. Folsom."

"Come on, Eleanor," Alice said. "We've got to get Isabelle home."

Alice grabbed her sister's hand and pulled her toward the door. Isabelle hurried along after them.

Once outside, Alice said, "Thunderation! I thought you were going to stand there listening to her lecture all day. You've got to learn to escape while you can."

"I never know what I'm escaping to anymore." Eleanor looked around her. "I used to think I was at least safe inside my own home. You saw how Bradley follows me. It's getting worse instead of better."

"Well, you're going to take care of that today, aren't you?"

"I . . . yes. Are you and Isabelle coming with me?" Eleanor asked.

"No," Alice answered emphatically for both of them.

"I thought you said—"

"Do you really think Mother would let you go out all by yourself?"

"Well, no, not really," Eleanor had to admit.

"But if we tell her we're together, she won't ask you so

many questions when you get back.''

Eleanor pondered the wisdom of this for just a moment. Then she asked, ''Just do me one big favor.''

''Sure,'' Alice replied brightly, as if nothing were too difficult for her. Eleanor believed it was true—Alice didn't have difficulties; she made them for other people.

''Don't get into any trouble I'll get blamed for not getting you out of.''

''Sure,'' Alice replied. Eleanor didn't believe her for one minute.

''Good luck, Ellie,'' Isabelle said, her eyes still shining with admiration for Josh. ''Oh, I wish I could go with you.''

Isabelle was her dearest and oldest friend. Why did she suddenly feel such a strong pang of jealousy at Isabelle's admiration of Josh? She was just as bad as Isabelle herself.

Alice turned, grabbed Isabelle's arm, and took off. Looking back over her shoulder, she called, ''Good luck.''

Eleanor knew with great certainty that she was going to need it—not in finding Josh, but in avoiding Bradley. If she didn't know where to find Josh, how was she supposed to know where to find hiding places from Bradley?

She had no idea where she was going on this island. She'd spent her summers strolling up Folsom Drive to their friends' houses, or down Folsom Drive to the Yachting Club, or walking or sailing along the sandy shoreline in front of the summer cottages.

She'd never been to the Other Side of Silchester. It was like crossing the border into a different country.

Somebody at the Yachting Club probably knew where Josh lived, since he obviously worked there from time to time. But many more people at the club knew her and would note that she was asking after Josh. Then they probably wouldn't be able to wait to report the news to her parents.

She couldn't take that chance. She walked through the club as fast as she could without attracting attention.

The public dock was at her back, smelling of seaweed and oil. It was still way too early for the steamer to arrive from Baltimore. The place was fairly deserted. She'd get no help there.

The grimy white building she'd seen when she first arrived looked busy, but she was too shy to approach all those strange men hanging around outside. She knew it was silly to feel intimidated by all those ships' supplies, but she did anyway.

She moved on down the street. Josh had talked about the Moore's General Store. It shouldn't be too hard to find. Since they probably also served as the post office for this little island, she could definitely get some help from them.

She passed the blacksmith's shop. She could hear the clanging of hammer on steel. The hardware store beside it probably sold people things that the smith couldn't repair anymore. That was a fairly unusual concept to her. All her life, if something broke or wore out, her father simply bought her a new one, and the old things were simply thrown out or given to the servants. These people actually reused things. It was a wonder to her that her father didn't see this as supremely economical for his factories.

She passed two small dirt roads, little more than paths, actually. She'd glimpsed a few small white houses through the clumps of trees and bushes. But she decided she'd get lost less quickly, and find Josh more quickly, if she stayed on the main street.

Also, she figured, if she stayed on the main street, even if Bradley did accost her, there were witnesses to run to her aid, or run for the police or her parents. Of course, the best thing they could do for her would be to run and find Josh. The police she might not mind, but going for her parents was an absolute last resort!

Eleanor's eyes brightened when she saw the name of the next store—Baxter's Books. Certainly civilized people lived and worked here. She wouldn't wait until she got to the General Store. She gathered up her courage and opened the door.

The little bells hung above the door jingled softly. The light was dim, and the entire shop smelled of dusty paper, leather covers, binding glue, and the faint scent of lilacs.

She loved the scent of lilacs. It always reminded her of her great-grandmother, who had died when she was very young. Just about the only memory she had of her was white hair and the scent of lilacs.

"Good morning. What can I do for you today, miss?" the lady seated behind the counter asked.

Her skin was as dried and yellowed as the pages of an old volume. Her hair looked just as dusty as the shelves she sat amongst all day. But her dark brown eyes were as bright as any idea contained in her precious books.

"Do you work here?" Eleanor asked.

"Well, yes and no. I own the store, so I'm not really an employee, but I certainly do work here." She gave Eleanor a broad smile. "I'm Miss Baxter."

A woman who not only read, but who made her living from books and the people who loved them. *If only Father could meet her,* Eleanor thought with a chuckle. *What would that do to his theories on masculine superiority in public education and private enterprise?*

"How can I help you, miss? Are you just browsing or is there a particular book you're looking for?"

"I'm . . . I'm looking for Captain Claybourne."

"*Captain Claybourne, Captain Claybourne,*" Miss Baxter muttered.

She hopped down off her stool and began searching the shelves behind her. The scent of lilacs grew stronger as she approached Eleanor.

"I don't seem to recall the title, dear. Do you know the name of the author?"

"No, no. Captain Joshua Claybourne—a real person, who lives on this island."

"Oh!" Miss Baxter threw her hands up to her reddening cheeks and laughed. "Silly me, with my head always buried in a book so that I think everything *is* a book. So, you expected to find him here with his head in a book, too?"

"No, not really."

"Well, you might." Then Miss Baxter shook her head. "Just no time, you see, poor fellow. He works so hard. If he had more money, he'd be my best customer. Well, he and his little sister, Winnie."

"Could you tell me where he lives?"

"Certainly. Just follow Doc Street to the end. It'll be the last house on your left."

"What color is it?" Maybe that would help her find it more easily.

"White. If you fall in the water, you'll know you missed it."

"Thank you for your help."

With a little laugh, Miss Baxter added, "Of course, this is an island. If you fall in the water, you'll know you missed everything."

"Thank you very much."

Eleanor left the bookstore and stood on the steps for just a moment, getting her bearings. Dock Street must be that first little dirt path she passed on the way here, closest to the docks. She turned to her right and began walking.

She hadn't reached the end of the sidewalk by the hardware store when Miss Baxter stuck her head out the door and called out in harmony with her jingling door chimes. "Oh, miss! Where are you going?"

"Captain Claybourne's, on Dock Street. You told me."

"No, no. *Doc* Street is that way." Miss Baxter pointed in the opposite direction.

"But the dock is that way," Eleanor argued, pointing in her intended direction.

"But the Doc is *that* way," Miss Baxter countered.

"Dock?"

"D-O-C. As in doctor," the little woman explained.

"But—"

"Chandler Street lies between the chandlery and the smithy. Smith Street lies between the smithy and the hardware store. We thought it just didn't sound right having a Hardware Street, don't you?"

Eleanor gave a noncommittal shrug.

"Doc Street lies between Darty's Tavern and Doc Whitaker's house. All the doctors we've had on this island have lived on that lot, just not necessarily in that house."

Eleanor paused a moment, trying to sort it out in her head.

"School Street is between the school and the police station. Lighthouse Road is on the other side of the school, through the big trees, but that only leads to the lighthouse— nothing much of interest up there. Everything else is on Mallard Street. The rich summer folks live up on Folsom Road."

"Don't you have street signs?"

"What do we need little bitty street signs for when we've got nice big buildings to mark our places?" Miss Baxter replied.

"But—" She stopped. There was a certain logic in Miss Baxter's explanation.

"Anyway, when you've only got seven streets, it's not hard to tell them apart."

Eleanor couldn't argue with that. She sighed with resignation. "No, I suppose not. Thank you again."

"Any time."

She turned and began walking in the direction away from the dock, up Mallard Street toward the doc. Yes, she was beginning to see how Alice could feel right at home in a place like this.

Darty's Tavern. All right, Eleanor figured, she must be getting close. Yes, on the other side of the tavern was another small dirt road. Across the road she could see a big, white clapboard house with a white picket fence around it, and a hanging shingle that said Harrison Whitaker, M.D. Definitely Doc Street.

She turned to her left. Now she just needed to keep walking and make sure she didn't fall in the water before she found Josh's house.

The houses on either side of the dirt road were smaller than the houses on Mallard Street, but they were just as clean. The bushes surrounding them were well trimmed. The beds of verbena and sweet williams were weeded and well-cared for.

The only trouble was, they were *all* white. Some had red or gray or green shutters, with a door painted to match, but they were *all* white clapboard.

"I should have asked what color the door was," she muttered to herself. "Well, the only thing to do is keep walking—and don't fall in the water."

Clean white sheets flapped in the breeze. Along with the white houses and the brilliant glare of the sun, the entire island on this side seemed composed of shining white objects. The laughter of lots of children, and the friendly barking of a few dogs, drifted to her along with the scent of someone's roses. She wouldn't have been surprised to find that the dogs and the roses were all white, too.

She could see she was getting closer to the water. Josh's house should be the last one on the left.

It was a neat little white clapboard house, with zinnias and daisies growing in the front yard on either side of a brick path. It had bright blue shutters—she couldn't have missed it. Miss Baxter had been right. Any farther and she'd fall off the pier into the water.

Eleanor blinked and peered more closely into the bushes at the side of the road. There were bare feet sticking out. Long legs were attached to those feet, and a man's torso was connected, too.

"Sir, sir, are you all right?" she called loudly, in the hopes of rousing the person before she drew completely near.

No reply.

Cautiously she came nearer and nudged his side with her toe.

No response.

"Oh, merciful heavens! I've found a dead body!" she murmured to herself.

That jacket looked familiar. So did the color of his hair. She knelt down to see better. She reached out and nudged his shoulder with her hand. He groaned.

"Well, at least you're not dead," she told him with immense feelings of relief.

She pushed him harder until he rolled over with a low groan.

"Oh, my lord! It's Josh!" she gasped in horror.

Where were his new shoes? Where was his terrible old vest? Footpads, thugs, and pickpockets weren't uncommon in the rougher sections of town, but she didn't believe there were clothing thieves on this tiny island. And who would want that awful vest anyway?

"Josh, Josh!" she cried, trying to rouse him.

His eyes were still tightly closed. She placed her hands on his chest and felt it moving up and down.

"Oh, thank goodness you're still breathing! What happened to you?"

Josh groaned and threw his arm over his face.

"I've got to get help," she told him, rising to her feet. "Stay right there," she ordered.

He just groaned.

She marched up the path and knocked on the bright blue door.

A young woman answered. With hair and eyes that color, she just had to be Josh's sister. "Can I help you?"

"No. But you can help your brother."

The young woman frowned and eyed her suspiciously. "Who are you? What about my brother?"

"I'm Eleanor Folsom—"

The frown left her face as the young woman nodded. "One of the summer folks. Yeah, I'm Maddie Claybourne."

"Captain . . . Josh. He's lying in the bushes—"

Eleanor had expected Maddie to rush outside with alarm. Instead, she just nodded.

Holding up one finger, Maddie requested, "Will you excuse me a minute? Please wait right here."

"Yes." Eleanor felt too puzzled to do anything else.

Maddie disappeared into the recesses of the house. When she emerged again, she was carrying a hammered tin pitcher of water. For just a moment, Eleanor was afraid she was going to throw it on her to chase her away. Then the young woman slowly opened the screened door and made her way to the inert body in the bushes.

"Oh, Josh," she said in exasperation, shaking her head as she looked down on him. "I thought you'd stopped all this foolishness."

She knelt beside him and moved his arm away from his face. She peered closer, apparently searching for injuries. Then she waved her hand in front of her nose.

"Whew! Yeah, you've been drinking again. Gol-darn it, Josh!" Rising to her feet, she spoke to the unconscious man. "You *promised* you wouldn't do this again!"

She stamped her foot angrily on the ground. For a moment Eleanor was afraid Maddie was going to kick him.

"He stood up in church right in front of Reverend Straiten and the rest of the folks and *promised* he wouldn't do this again," Maddie ranted.

"Well, I wouldn't be too hard on him," Eleanor told her, with an apologetic frown on her face. "He had a really terrible night last night."

"How'd you find him? What do you know about this?" Maddie's eyes narrowed as she peered at Eleanor more closely. "What's someone like you doing on this side of the island anyway?"

"I . . . I'll tell you all I know. But don't you think we should get him inside?"

"Sure. Just a minute. He needs this. He *deserves* this."

Maddie dumped the entire pitcher of cold water on Josh's face.

He bent up double, uttering a variety of words both Miss Zang and the minister would undoubtedly disapprove of. Then he fell back again against the ground.

"Ow!"

He raised his hands, placed them on the top of his head, and continued to groan in pain.

"Hangover?" Maddie asked. "Serves you right."

"No, no, I . . . Oh, heck, it hurts too much to talk." He went limp against the ground. His mouth moved, but no sound came out.

"Let's just get him inside," Eleanor suggested.

Maddie reached down and braced herself to help Josh pull himself to his feet.

"He's too heavy for me alone." She ordered Eleanor, "Help him on the other side."

Eleanor quickly moved beside Josh, to help push him up. His sister quickly ducked under one arm to support him. Eleanor quickly ducked under Josh's other arm. He was clumsy on his feet, and his arms kept flailing around. She tucked herself farther under his arm, to give him more support.

He turned to Maddie. "Now, don't you scold me. It's not my fault."

"It never is."

He turned to Eleanor.

"Oh, my goodness. Miss Folsom, my little angel of mercy. *You* won't scold me, will you?"

"No." She figured Maddie was doing a good enough job already.

"But you will surely get the scolding of your life if your mother catches you here with me."

"Just hush and try to concentrate on walking," she told him. *She* was trying to concentrate on walking. Snuggled up so close to him, it was very hard to think of anything but Josh.

"But I'm awful glad to see you," he continued anyway. "I'm awful glad to have *you* come to *my* rescue for a change."

He pulled her closer to him. She didn't shy away from him. In fact, she was tempted to hold his body all the closer. His sister might have just smelled the liquor, but Eleanor could feel his muscular body struggling against itself to regain control.

His shoulder muscles tensed as he tried to hold his arms at an angle that didn't so much resemble a flailing windmill. His strong thigh muscles battled to control his rubbery legs. His soaking wet hair was dripping down on them all.

Maddie would have dumped him unceremoniously on the big old camel-back sofa, but Eleanor still held on to him a moment longer. His arm slid over her shoulder and down her arm as he eased into his seat.

"Lay down," Maddie ordered, tossing a pillow at him.

Josh complied, until the back of his head hit the pillow.

"Ow!" He sprang up again, holding the back of his head.

"What's the matter now?" Maddie demanded. She might have sounded harsh, but Eleanor could see the worry in her eyes.

Still standing close to him, Eleanor moved around to examine the back of his head. She reached up and parted the sandy-colored hair—something she'd longed to do, but under very different circumstances, and from a slightly different angle.

"My goodness! You've got a bump the size of a goose egg back there!"

"What?" Josh's fingers began busily probing the back of his head. "Ow! Ow!"

"Stop that. I can't see," Eleanor scolded as she pushed his hand out of the way. "There isn't any bleeding. Just this huge bump."

"Probably hit his head last night on the way down," Maddie said, her lips twisted in a wry grimace.

"No. I remember I fell face first," Josh said. Some of the blurriness must have been wearing off. "See."

He brushed both hands down the front of his jacket and pants. His clothes were both covered with dust the same color as the road. He tried to sit up and turn around.

"Is there any dirt on my back?"

Eleanor looked. She tried to see beyond the muscles that strained against the dark broadcloth of his jacket.

"Yes, there is," she had to answer truthfully. "A bit of dried grass, too. But I found you facedown. When I nudged you, you rolled over."

"So somebody *did* hit me on the back of the head," Josh said.

He struggled to take off the dusty jacket, but only floundered, miserably entangled in the arms, until Eleanor helped free him.

"Drinking again is bad enough," Maddie complained. "But fighting, too? It was bad enough when you'd go down to Crisfield and fight with strangers, but here you're beating up your own friends and kin."

"No, no," Josh insisted. "I wasn't fighting. Look."

He held his hands out, knuckles up. There weren't any scratches or bruises, or any indication that he'd been punching.

"That doesn't prove anything, except maybe you just slapped them silly," Maddie remarked with a wry grin that quickly disappeared. "Of course, your face doesn't look like you've taken much of a beating."

Eleanor remembered how good Josh was at ducking.

"Maybe you are telling the truth for a change," Maddie conceded.

"I remember now. I was walking home from Darty's after that terrible party—no offense," he offered quickly to Eleanor.

She shook her head. "I'm sorry. It really was terrible for me, too."

"No, no. None of it was your doing," he hurriedly assured her.

"See, I told you not to go, but you never listen to me, do you?" Maddie scolded. Both fists were resting on her hips, and her foot was tapping rapidly against the floor. "We don't belong with those kind of people, Josh. Rich, arrogant, lazy—not having to work a day in their lives."

"Hush, Maddie," Josh said, frowning. He tilted his head as much as he dared in Eleanor's direction.

"Oh, I knew who she was as soon as she told me her name was Folsom, as soon as I saw her fancy clothes," Maddie said. "I can put two and two together."

Then she turned to Eleanor.

"I really don't mean to insult you. I'm just more than a little concerned for my brother."

"I understand," Eleanor told her. "I frequently am more than just a little concerned for my sister." She turned to Josh. "I'm concerned for you now, too."

She watched him. His gaze tried to hold hers, but his eyes kept blurring out of focus, and his lids kept slipping down.

"He really should see a doctor," Eleanor suggested to Maddie.

Without comment, Maddie stuck her head out the front door and called, "Bill! Bill!"

The smiling, tousle-haired boy appeared on the doorstep like a summoned sprite.

"Go get Doc Whitaker," Maddie requested. Bill was gone before she could explain, "Josh hit his head."

"Somebody hit Josh's head," Josh corrected from his invalid couch. "And I got a darn good idea who did it."

"Who?" Maddie frowned. "Who around here doesn't like you? Besides me right now."

"No one from around here. Bradley Randolph."

"Who?"

"Friend of hers," he explained, nodding in Eleanor's direction.

"He is no friend of mine!" Eleanor protested.

His eyelids still half closed, Josh grinned at her faintly.

She liked watching him smile at her. She liked seeing him with his eyes half closed, as if he were only now rousing from sleep instead of coming to from a hangover and a bump on the head.

She could picture what he'd look like waking in the morning. Could she imagine lying at his side? Too easily, she decided. She tried to pull her gaze away, but when she really didn't want to, it was awfully hard to do.

"You know, I'm sorry. I really have been pretty rude to you up until now." The young woman wiped her hand off on her apron again and offered it to Eleanor. "I'd be more pleasant under different circumstances. See, the reason I got so upset was, Bill was born kind of late in life, and Ma died right afterward. Pa just worked himself to death. Josh was nigh onto twenty and took to drinking a good bit. Aunt Audrey finally grabbed hold of him and snapped him out of it—or rather shook him out of it. And he *promised*—'' She struck him with a riveting glare. "He *promised*—''

"Don't get started again, Maddie," Josh warned, holding a shaky hand in front of him. "I might've had a beer or two, but that was it. I'm in this shape because somebody hit me," he insisted.

The rapping on the door drew their attention.

"Well, Doc was fast today," Maddie commented as she headed toward the door. "He must not have had anybody in his office. And Suzanne Proctor's baby's not due for another month yet."

But Dr. Harrison Whitaker did not enter the room. A tall, slender old woman strode in instead. She held the stump of an unlit corncob pipe between her teeth. Her black-and-gray hair was pulled back in a tight bun. Her piercing black eyes seemed to take in everything in the room in one glance, particularly Eleanor—or was she feeling persecuted?

"Gussie, what are you doing here?" Maddie asked.

"I know you didn't see fit to send for me, but I won't hold that against you," she said. "I just had a feeling Josh needed me, and son of a gun, looks as if I was right—as usual."

She placed a large, brightly patterned handbag on the round table beside the couch. Eleanor was surprised to hear the clink of bottles and the rustle of what sounded like dried grasses from inside.

She made straight for Eleanor.

"I'm Gussie Farrell."

"Eleanor Folsom." She extended her hand.

"Good to meet you."

Instead of taking her hand in a customary shake, Gussie flipped Eleanor's hand palm up, wiggled her thumb, turned her hand over, and examined her nails.

"Eat more spinach," she advised. "Excuse me, dear." She moved between Eleanor and the couch. Eleanor moved to a side chair, but continued to watch Gussie with great interest.

"Now, let's see what we've got here," she said. She rubbed her hands together several times as if to warm them, then placed her palms just above the bump on Josh's head.

"Shouldn't we wait for Doc?" Josh asked cautiously.

"*You* can," Gussie replied. "I don't need him. Now hold still. This won't hurt a bit."

❖ *11* ❖

"THAT'S WHAT YOU said last time," Josh replied.

"And did it?" Gussie demanded, moving her hands slowly above his head.

"Well . . . not really, no."

"Only what damage you'd already done to yourself, you big dummy," Gussie scolded. She grabbed both sides of his head between her hands and peered down into his face over his shoulder. "A grown man ought to have enough sense not to go around trying to swing from a tree like a kid."

"*You* swung from a tree?" Eleanor asked.

"No, he didn't," Gussie replied instead as she straightened and continued to move her palms above his head. "That's why they had to call for me."

Eleanor tried hard not to laugh when she still didn't know how serious Josh's injury was.

"Come on, Gussie. I was just having fun—"

"With kids half your size and another half time your age. You should've known that branch wouldn't hold the weight of a full-grown man."

There was a loud knocking on the door.

"Maddie? Josh?" came a man's voice.

"Doc Whitaker," Maddie said, rushing to open the door for him.

"Too late, Doc," Gussie said without looking up at him.

"Why? Have you killed him already with your crazy herbs just like you did your last three husbands, you cantankerous old biddy?"

"Nope. He's still alive," she replied. "Which is more than I can say for your last three wives after you dosed them up with your phony pills, you old fraud."

Doc Whitaker set his little black bag on the table beside Gussie's huge colorful one. He opened it and took out his stethoscope.

"Come on, Gussie. You've had your turn. Now let's see what a man of science can do."

Gussie grinned and bowed with great ceremony as she backed away from Josh. "Be my guest, Doc. But when he's all cured, just remember—I got to him first, so don't you go trying to take credit for what I did."

"We'll see. We'll see."

Eleanor was much more familiar with what Doc Whitaker was doing than with anything Gussie had done or said. At last he stood up, folded his stethoscope, and put it away in his bag.

"Looks like you've got a bit of a concussion there, Josh."

"I agree," Gussie said with a nod.

"As your physician, I advise you to stay in bed a day or two until the headache goes away. Then take it easy for a while."

Gussie turned to the doctor. "Are you done with your prescribing?"

"Yes."

"Good. It doesn't do any good anyway." She waved her hand in the air as if she could wave away his bogus medications.

Gussie opened her bag and scrounged around inside for a while. Eleanor almost expected to see her disappear inside it—or to see her pull a white rabbit out of it.

Then Gussie pulled out a little paper packet. She sniffed it, then handed it to Maddie.

"Make a little tea out of this for him. That ought to take away the headache. If it doesn't, I'll give you another one."

She dug inside the bag again and pulled out a small, translucent lavender stone.

"Put this in the bottom of the cup. It ought to help, too."

"Yeah. Sure, Gussie."

Maddie headed for what Eleanor assumed was the kitchen. In a few moments she heard the sound of water pumping into a kettle. She wondered if Maddie was supposed to put the stone in before or after she'd brewed the tea.

"What is that stuff, Gussie?" Doc Whitaker asked, trying to lift the flap of the bag to see inside. "Dried eel grass? Shredded newspaper?"

"Your worthless old prescriptions," she shot back, batting his hand away.

"Some more of that high-woman babble and hocus-pocus?"

"Would you know what it was if I told you?" Gussie countered.

"Probably not. Probably in some cases, I wouldn't even want to know."

"Probably not, you stubborn old fool," Gussie muttered. Then she turned to Josh again. "Now, what *I* would prescribe for you is to take it easy for a couple of days."

"I believe that's what I just told him," Doc said.

"Not quite. See, I'm not finished yet. That's where your scientific gibberish fails." Gussie turned to Eleanor. "I'm prescribing *you*—to take him on a nice, slow, quiet walk down along the shore."

"Me?" Eleanor laughed. "I've never been a prescription before."

Josh smiled at her. "I kind of thought you were just what the doctor ordered."

"Please, don't go calling me no doctor!" Gussie protested. "You follow my prescription—first the tea, then a nice quiet walk down by the shore with this pretty young lady, who obviously thinks kindly of you since she's here, and ain't family, doctor, nor high woman."

"What's a high woman?" Eleanor asked.

"Me," Gussie declared proudly. She lifted her bag. "And these." The bottles tinkled, and the dried leaves rustled against each other.

Gussie turned to Doc Whitaker. "Well, have you done all the damage you can do here, you old fake?"

"Only until I have to come back to undo what you've done, you fraudulent gypsy."

"You mean all the good I've done, you meddlesome old fool."

"Want a light for that pipe, Gussie?" Doc asked as they both headed for the door.

"You know I don't smoke, you charlatan."

"Then why do you carry it around?"

"Someday I'll have to tell you, when I think you'll be able to understand."

"You know, you really should smoke occasionally," he advised. "Most doctors agree it's good for you. It makes you cough and clears your lungs of unhealthy accumulations."

"We'll see," Gussie replied. "We'll see."

"Mr. Randolph, is something wrong with the food this morning?" Mrs. Bodine asked.

"I . . . I don't think so," he replied. "I hope not."

"It doesn't look as if you've touched a thing."

He took a bite of buttered toast. She couldn't have done too much damage to plain bread and butter.

He lifted his cup and sniffed the coffee. Did he detect a slight odor of almonds? Could Mrs. Bodine have put arsenic in the coffee?

"There's not a thing wrong with this food," Miss Zang pronounced as she put down her cup. Using a blueberry muffin piled high with jelly, she scooped up a mound of scrambled eggs on her fork. "Eat up, young man. How can you hope to fuel your brain and body for the tasks they must perform today if you're poorly nourished?"

Miss Zang was drinking plenty of coffee, and she wasn't dead yet. Bradley took another sip. Suddenly he recalled hearing that people could build up a tolerance for arsenic. He almost spit out his coffee.

Miss Zang was certainly old enough to have built up a tolerance for every poison known to man. She'd still be sitting there at her place in Mrs. Bodine's dining room when he was six feet under.

Just not on this godforsaken island, please! Bradley pleaded with the Almighty. *Just don't let me be buried here.*

Bradley cut his sausage in half. He cut it into smaller pieces, then smaller and smaller until it was all out of its casing and smashed flat on his plate. He didn't think Mrs. Bodine stuffed her own sausage, but he couldn't be sure. Ground glass—that was it. She'd added ground glass to the meat and cornmeal. He'd die in agony, and no one would be able to tell from what.

"Don't play with your food, sir," Miss Zang commanded. "We are not cats or raccoons. We are human beings and ought to eat as civilized people do."

Bradley tightened his lips and said nothing. Maybe when Miss Zang went out for her morning constitutional he could sneak up behind her and smack her in the back of the head, too. Then he could eat a meal here in peace for a change!

There'd be no one to lecture him on proper table manners, eating habits, sleeping habits, or summer attire.

Miss Zang helped herself to another portion of sausage and scrambled eggs. He couldn't be sure if the old lady still had all her own teeth or not—and he really didn't think he wanted to get that close to ascertain. She certainly could down that sausage with vigor. Of course, as tough as she was, she could probably bite through oyster shells.

"Eat your meal, sir, and don't be ungrateful," Miss Zang ordered. "Mrs. Bodine did not spend the early hours of the morning cooking so you could waste food. Don't you know that children in heathen countries are starving?"

"I'll send them my sausage. Do you have their address?"

Bradley threw his napkin down on the table and stalked off.

"Such manners," he heard Miss Zang complain as he headed for the stairs. "I'll warrant he went to one of those abominable progressive schools with headmasters who wear odd gowns instead of a good old American school with one stern maiden lady and a hickory stick."

"Probably," Audrey agreed as she scraped his unwanted sausages onto her plate. "Please pass the jelly, Miss Zang."

Bradley stood in his room at the window, looking out over the woods that separated him from his beloved. He'd failed miserably last night to convince her of his continuing adoration and devotion. He'd succeeded in eliminating his rival, though, he thought smugly.

Of course, that was why Mrs. Bodine was trying to poison him. After all, Josh was her nephew. Family seemed to stick together on this island. Not like his family. He knew his uncle, the highly acclaimed judge, hated the very sight of him. His father had never been overly fond of him, either. The only one he could really rely on was his mother.

Why couldn't Eleanor be more like his mother and dote on him, too?

Ah, well, it didn't matter, anyway. Josh was clearly out of the picture now. Winning his beloved Eleanor's heart should be smooth sailing from here on.

"I don't know what Gussie puts in those teas of hers," Josh told Eleanor. He stretched his long arms out to his side comfortably and moved his head from side to side.

"You mean besides rocks?"

"They just seem to do whatever it is she tells you they'll do. And they don't taste half as bad as some of the tonics Doc prescribes. Have you ever tried Hostetter's Celebrated Stomach Bitters?" Josh's face drew up in a terrible grimace.

Eleanor shook her head.

"I see your parents have sheltered you in more ways than one."

"I think I should be glad."

Josh rose from the couch on much steadier legs.

"Where do you think you're going?" Maddie demanded as she picked up his cup. The small stone rattled in the bottom.

"I'm following the other half of my prescription."

"What?" With one hand on her hip Maddie wiggled the cup at him. "As I recall, Doc told you to stay in bed a day or two."

"As I recall, Gussie told me to take a long, slow walk along the beach with Miss Folsom."

"Go ahead, then, you hardheaded man," Maddie said, throwing up one hand in resignation. "Not listening to Doc's advice. You can take a long, slow walk off a short pier, for all I care."

Maddie turned back into the kitchen.

"Hey, Maddie," he called. "You wouldn't have any stale bread, would you?"

"It's a little late for breakfast and a little early for lunch, isn't it?" she called back.

"Oh, stop it," he called cajolingly. "You know what I want it for."

"Here." She stuck her head out of the kitchen doorway and tossed Josh half a loaf of bread.

He caught it deftly. Eleanor could hear the hard crust crunch as it compressed between his hands. Crumbs flew out over the carpet.

Maddie just raised her eyes heavenward, then disappeared back into the kitchen.

Josh held out his other hand to Eleanor.

There was no thought involved. She merely stood and placed her hand in his. It was the only right and natural thing to do.

He folded his fingers around her hand and pulled her gently toward the door.

"You don't mind if I keep holding your hand, do you?" he asked as they strolled down the brick walk.

"Oh, no. Not at all." Eleanor tried not to sound so eager. "I suppose you still need . . . a certain amount of support."

"Oh, yes. Oh, definitely."

Josh led her down the dirt road to the beginning of the wooden pier that stretched out into the water in uneven stages.

"Gosh, and you thought my summer cottage was built strangely," Eleanor said with a laugh. "It looks as if they just added onto the pier as they needed more space to tie up their boats."

"Well, that's not far from the truth," Josh admitted.

"It also looks as if the height of each section of pier depended on whether the tide was in or out when they built it."

Josh nodded. "You're probably right there, too."

"Is this still part of the Chesapeake Bay?" Eleanor asked.

"Sort of yes and no. We call this the Straiten Narrows," he told her with a hearty laugh.

"Straight and Narrow?" she repeated very slowly.

"Straiten. We had this minister awhile back—Reverend Jeremiah R. Straiten—*R* stands for 'Repentance,' he always used to say. Of course, it also stood for 'Redemption,' 'Reward,' or 'Reach Deep Down Into Your Pockets, Brothers and Sisters'—depending on what the topic of his sermon was that morning. Hellfire and brimstone preacher of the first order. Kept you awake in church. Made you really want to sing out with the choir. Who wouldn't name a place like the narrows after him?"

"I can't imagine."

There were huge pilings along both sides of the pier, and places where other boats could tie up. There just weren't any boats.

She pointed to the cluster of pines and maples growing near the shoreline, and the gentle rise, covered with larger beech and chestnut trees.

"Why aren't there any piers down that way?" she asked.

"Too dangerous."

"Dangerous?"

"That's Rocky Point."

"Can we go there?"

"Sure. But you can't get there from here. It's only dangerous to boats—or anyone stupid enough to try to swim there. That's why we put the lighthouse there. But there's really not much to see. Just a lot of rocks, and most of them are underwater—which makes it all the more dangerous."

"Which is how it got its name."

"Sure."

"I guess Gussie goes there a lot for her rocks."

"I wouldn't put it past her. See, it seems like Nature had one little spot on this island where she put all the orneriness. The tides come in, hit Rocky Point, and cause a lot of turbulence in the water as it comes through the narrows. Not much sense living around there."

She pointed to the end of the pier. "What's in that little shack?"

"My boat."

"The infamous bugeye?"

"None other. The *Lady Claire*."

"Claire?"

"My mother's name."

"I'd like to see it someday."

"Someday? Why not now?"

Eleanor shrugged. She didn't think it was a good idea to admit that not seeing the boat now would give her an excuse to see him again.

"You can give me that promised boat ride later, when you're feeling better. Right now you're supposed to be walking quietly along the shore," she reminded him. "Remember, doctor's orders."

"High woman's orders," Josh corrected.

He leaned against the pier railing. Eleanor leaned beside him, looking out over the water.

"What is a high woman? I mean, she was taller than the average woman, but—"

Josh laughed. "That's just what we call her. She's good at finding weeds and herbs that cure what ails you."

"Like what she gave you?"

"Yeah." Josh pulled off a piece of bread and dropped it into the water.

"And rocks?"

"I guess. Of course, the day she starts putting live frogs in my tea, that's the end of it."

"A turtle!" Eleanor exclaimed.

"No, I wouldn't be too happy with a turtle, either."

"No, no. A turtle in the water. Look!" Jumping up and down with excitement, she pointed downward. "He's so cute, with those little red eyes and almost like a yellow beak."

"Yeah, that's what I brought you out here to show you. Although, actually, that's a terrapin."

"You mean as in terrapin soup?"

Josh nodded.

"Oh, I don't think I'll ever eat turtle soup again!" she declared.

Josh handed her the loaf of bread. "Break off little pieces and watch what else comes to the surface for them."

Eleanor kept dropping little pieces of stale bread.

"The turtle's back. There's another one. That was a fish. There's another one. Oh, that's an ugly little character."

"It's a catfish. They don't usually come up from the bottom."

Josh watched her eyes twinkling with delight as she fed the greedy creatures. A seagull came flapping down, screeching.

"He's obvious not happy that he wasn't invited to the feast," Eleanor said.

"But he came anyway. Should we name him Bradley?"

"Oh, please! He's a nice seagull," Eleanor protested. "Don't do that to him."

She broke off a piece and tossed it to the gull. The bread landed in the water and was scooped up by a large, dark fish before the seagull had a chance. She tried again, and this time the seagull caught the bread in midair.

Other seagulls were beginning to gather, landing on the railing farther from where they were standing, or hovering overhead. They were making so much noise, Josh had to get closer to Eleanor just to hear what she was saying.

Josh decided that later he'd leave a nice big mess of cullings for the seagulls, just to thank them.

Another gull flapped by, but this one sounded as if he were laughing.

"Did you see that?"

"Where?" She turned around, trying in vain to single out one bird from the flock overhead.

"That was a laughing gull."

"He certainly sounded as though he were laughing."

"No. That's the kind of gull he is."

"I didn't know there were different kinds of seagulls. I mean, they all sort of look alike."

"Only if you don't look at them real close."

"Do they always gather like this?" Eleanor asked, looking around with some trepidation.

"Only if somebody's feeding them."

She looked to the other side. Gulls were still gathering there, too.

"I don't know why, but I have the strangest feeling I should be getting very nervous right now."

"No, they're pretty harmless," Josh assured her. "The only trouble we have with the birds around here is on wash day, when we hang out the sheets."

Eleanor continued throwing crumbs to the birds and dropping pieces in for the turtles and fishes. All too quickly, the loaf of bread was gone.

"Oh, I'm sorry. It's all gone," Eleanor called up to the gulls. She peered down into the water. "Sorry."

She held her hands out to show how empty they were. Then she brushed her hands together out over the water. The fish scrambled for one last taste of crumbs. The seagulls raised a raucous protest and flapped away.

Then she turned her hands palms up and studied them.

"Why did Gussie tell me to eat more spinach?"

He shrugged. "Who knows? I told you she liked weeds.

I guess most folks would call her remedies old wives' tales.''

"Oh, yes. Kind of like Madame Orlov."

"Who?"

"A gypsy woman who comes around our neighborhood every morning selling eggs. Whatever is wrong, she knows some peculiar way to cure it. Not with herbs and things. She does things like melting the wax of a red candle onto a chicken egg and hiding it under beds—things like that.''

"How do you know?"

Eleanor grinned. "Some friends and I went to her once and had our fortunes told.''

"Did she read your palm, too?"

"Yes, but she didn't say anything about spinach.''

Josh nodded. "What was that egg thing for? Some gypsy love potion?''

"I don't know."

"You shouldn't have used it on Bradley."

"Please! I told you not to mention his name." She held her hands to the sides of her head in desperation. "Now you've given *me* a headache.''

"Sorry, but you've given me an idea. Madame Orlov is too far away, but maybe we could ask Gussie to put a curse on Bradley." Josh laughed.

"Bradley *is* a curse," Eleanor grumbled, picking at the weathered wood of the railing.

"Come on," Josh said, pushing himself away from the railing. He offered Eleanor his hand. "I know why Gussie told you to take me on my walk.''

"Why?" Eleanor reached for his hand.

"Because you need a long, slow walk along the shore as much as I do," Josh told her. "Maybe more.''

In a slow, subtle movement he slid his hand over her shoulder and pulled her closer under his arm.

"I'm feeling a little weak," he said as he stepped down

from the pier onto the sand. "You don't mind giving me a little support, do you?"

Smiling to herself, Eleanor replied, "No, no. Not at all."

She slid her own arm around his waist. For a man with shoulders so broad, his waist was trim and firm. He walked with a steady tread off the pier and onto the sand.

"You need my support about as much as that pier does," she told him.

"Well, maybe," he hedged. "But it sure is nice to know you're there when I need you."

She nodded. "I was recently thinking the very same thing about you."

His hand slid tentatively, a very short distance up and down her shoulder. It felt good to have him near. It felt even better to have him touching her. He was warmer than sunlight against her skin. How could a man be strong and gentle at the same time?

"Now, since you've been plagued by him, and I've been smacked by him, why don't you tell me all about this Bradley Randolph so I'll know what to do next time?"

❖ 12 ❖

"At first I was rather flattered by his attentions," Eleanor admitted as she and Josh strolled slowly along the sand. "I mean, after spending most of my time with portly Michael Stewart and pimply Albert Ridgely—Bradley *is* a rather good-looking man, you must admit."

Josh shook his head. "Well, I don't think he's particularly good-looking, but then, I'm so picky."

Eleanor laughed.

She laid her head against his shoulder. Josh felt his skin tingle where her soft, dark hair touched him. He wasn't much of a poet, but it felt as if the tingle ran straight through his body into his heart, making it beat faster. He was pretty much of a realist, though, and he knew exactly where else the tingle that ran through his body ended up.

Down, boy, he told himself. *It's just your masculinity wanting to protect her.*

It's your masculinity, all right, the little devil perched on his shoulder whispered, *but I don't think* protect *is the right verb.*

She's a lady, Josh silently protested. *She's not for me. She doesn't belong here. She's only here for the summer, and then I won't see her again until next July—if I'm lucky,* if *she looks me up, if she even remembers me.*

I got her out of a tight spot with that Randolph nuisance, so right now she thinks I'm pretty much the hero. With what he thought was great nobility, he silently asserted, *I'm just not going to let my pride lead me astray.*

Astray is a lovely place to go, the little devil whispered.

"Well, all the ladies seemed to like Bradley," Eleanor said. "He was always so polite, always ready with a compliment. He's a wonderful dancer, dresses well. So I was particularly flattered when he singled me out for his attentions."

Then her fine brows drew down into a frown. She gave a forlorn sigh. Josh watched her blue eyes cloud over.

"Then I realized what it truly meant to be singled out by Bradley Randolph." Her slender shoulders shuddered with the remembered persecution.

"What did he do?"

"He called constantly at my home. Early in the morning. Late at night. He never left my side at parties our families had been invited to."

"That's some pretty strong devotion," Josh observed.

"Then he started showing up at parties that my family and I had been invited to and he had not."

"Isn't that considered really bad manners?"

"Even worse, he found out which parties I was going to by going through our mail."

"That *is* really bad manners."

"Bradley is bad *everything*. I couldn't dance with another man without him chasing off the fellow. I couldn't sit next to anyone else at a dinner party. He'd deliberately go around changing the place cards. I couldn't go for carriage rides or picnics, canoe rides or walks—or even go shopping with my girlfriends, without him showing up."

"The man has to be insane to want to tag along with a bunch of women shopping!"

She jabbed him in the ribs. Her small fingers only tickled and made his insides quiver more.

He didn't mean to be flippant or make light of her problems with Bradley. He only made those bad jokes to keep her spirits up. She'd had a miserable enough time with the man—no sense in him making recounting the tale worse for her.

"Then there was one of the absolute worst moments in my entire life."

She put one hand to her cheek, as if reliving the embarrassment. Already he could see the faint flush coloring the pale pink of her flesh. From the pained expression on her face, he knew it wasn't simple embarrassment, but complete and utter mortification.

"What happened?"

"Isabelle—you remember—"

"Who could forget Isabelle?" he interjected.

"Isabelle and Jemima Ridgely and I had gone to the dressmakers. I was being fitted for a new dress when—"

"Don't tell me."

"He actually burst into the fitting room, claiming I was in there with another man! The dressmaker called an officer on the beat and had Bradley thrown out of her establishment."

"Served him right."

"I tell you, Father had all he could do to keep my name from appearing in the newspapers because of *that* little incident. And Bradley still didn't learn his lesson."

"I didn't think he would. What else have your parents been doing about all this?"

"Mother seems to think Bradley is an excellent match for me. After all, he's handsome, comes from an old and wealthy family that is still influential in society, business, and politics. She just won't listen to me when I try to tell her how much I've grown to hate him."

"Maybe after that incident at the club she'll believe you."

"I hope so."

But from the way Eleanor looked down as she shook her head, Josh didn't think she had much hope. Considering what little he knew of Mrs. Folsom, he didn't think she did, either.

"What about your father?"

"At least he acknowledges how much I hate Bradley, and refuses to allow Mother to pressure me into marrying him."

"It's good to have someone on your side—besides me."

"His biggest effort has been trying to keep my name from being connected with Bradley's in the society columns. He has friends who'll accept certain amounts of money to do just about anything he asks."

"I sort of figured that."

"You know how rich, powerful men can be when they get together."

"No, I can't really say as I do."

"They're very clannish. They protect each other, and each other's interests. They have the money and the influence to do it." She paused. "I must admit, it hasn't been all bad when I needed a new dress or wanted to wheedle an invitation to someplace very exclusive. But in spite of all Father's money and influence, he still hasn't been able to keep Bradley away from me."

She looked into his eyes with a gaze that gleamed with pure adoration. "Until you came along." Suddenly sadness tainted the gleam. "And even that didn't work."

Josh felt the muscles of his jaws tightening. His hands were already doubling into fists. Even after throwing him in the water and making a fool of the fellow, Bradley had still come back.

"What happened? Did he hurt you?" He could hear his own voice growing rough.

"No, no. Although I thought Alice might hurt him for a moment there."

"If anyone can, it's Alice."

She gave a little laugh that was more nerves than humor. "You see, each time Bradley does something obnoxious, he tries to give me gifts so I'll forgive him. That's what he claims."

"That could be good," Josh offered jokingly.

"No, it's not," Eleanor insisted.

"Sorry."

"I don't want to forgive him." Her hands were balled up into fists at her sides. "I want him to go away and leave me alone. And the gifts are entirely inappropriate for a young, unmarried lady."

"What's an inappropriate gift? Horseshoes? A bucket? A side of beef?"

"No. Yes." Flustered, she half muttered, half laughed. "No, don't be silly." She jabbed him in the ribs again. "He tries to give me expensive jewelry—diamond brooches, garnet bracelets."

"Entirely inappropriate. I'm sure your mother was horrified."

"I've tried my best to make sure Mother never finds out about any of them."

"Oh, well, she won't hear it from me. Word of honor." He tried to raise his right hand, but that would have meant letting go of Eleanor. That was something he knew he never wanted to do.

"Of course, I never accepted any of Bradley's gifts."

"Of course not."

"The worst one was the pink silk peignoir."

Josh stopped and turned to look at Eleanor.

"Pink? Silk? Peignoir?" With each word he lifted his

eyebrows higher and higher. Then he frowned and asked, "What's a peignoir? Is it as inappropriate as horseshoes?"

Eleanor laughed and slapped playfully at his shoulder. "Silly. It's a negligee. A nightgown."

"Oh. Sorry. I'm not very informed when it comes to ladies' underthings." He nodded and hoped she'd take it for comprehension instead of what it truly was—appreciation. "Very soft? And sheer?"

Eleanor grimaced. "I guess so. I really didn't examine it too closely. I don't want Bradley to believe I might actually accept one of his gifts."

Josh shook his head and made clucking noises with his tongue. "It's a darn shame you didn't keep that one."

He didn't want to scare her off. He didn't want her to think he was anything like that scoundrel Bradley, but he knew he couldn't keep the flame from his eyes when he thought of her in soft pink silk, the curves of her smooth body partially veiled. *He* would have taken the time to examine that gift very closely.

His stomach tightened into flipflops, pulling his heart and other good parts along with it.

He stood and gazed at her for a moment.

"Eleanor."

"Josh."

"I'm a poor man."

"You're a very brave man."

Suddenly the image of Eleanor in the negligee expanded to reveal his tiny cottage. The parlor with the couch with the worn upholstery. The single fireplace that had to heat the whole house on a winter night. The kitchen with the kerosene cooker. Two bedrooms—one for Bill, one for the girls, and him on the couch. And Bill's bed needing a new mattress. The whole darn house would fit in the Folsoms' parlor. Every penny he had in the bank probably totaled up to what Mr. Folsom carried around as loose change.

No, that was no life for Eleanor.

Was there a word for the moment a man realized he'd found the woman he'd been searching for his entire life, and also realized at the same time that he had to let her go?

"As a matter of fact, that's what actually brought me to your house this morning," she admitted.

Obviously Eleanor had no idea of the turmoil he was feeling inside, nor of the pain it caused him.

"Oh?" was all he could manage to utter at the moment.

"Did you think I just sort of 'knew' you were in trouble, like Gussie?"

"No, but I kind of hoped." Realizing his expression was much too serious, much too intense, Josh forced himself to laugh.

The corners of her mouth turned up a bit, as if she were trying to laugh with him. But she still watched him with deep intensity in her green eyes.

"So why were you looking for me?" Josh asked.

She looked at him and very bluntly stated, "I need you to be my bodyguard."

A cold chill swept through Josh.

"Did your father send you here?"

"No! My parents think I'm at Isabelle's."

"You've already heard me tell your father no."

"I know. But Alice said you'd say yes if *I* asked you."

"Alice? Alice doesn't even know what a bugeye is, and now you're listening to her?"

Eleanor cringed. "So you won't?"

"No." He tried to make his voice sound less angry.

He wasn't really angry with her, anyway. And if her father didn't have anything to do with this, he could hardly be mad at him, either. Alice was a little troublemaker, as usual, but that wasn't anything to be truly angry about.

Bradley had a lot to do with this, but he'd be mad at him no matter what.

"Look, I'm sorry if I yelled." He pulled her closer to him in a consoling hug. "I just . . ."

She looked so scared and helpless standing there. He knew she truly needed his protection.

"I still won't be your bodyguard. I won't take money from your father. I definitely won't be staying with you at your house. But if you need me, I'll be there," he assured her. "I promise."

She tightened her arms around him. "Thank you, Josh."

Oh, that was the wrong thing to do, he silently lamented. If she could only know how much he wanted to hold her, she'd probably go running back home in a second.

"Come on," he said, moving away from her. "Gussie ordered me to walk along the shore, and we've hardly made it to the Smith Street pier."

There weren't any boats tied to this pier, either.

"Where'd they all go?" Eleanor asked.

"Out crabbing or fishing."

"Oh."

"They'll be back sometime in the afternoon."

Eleanor could see that the narrows was even narrower here. The opposite shore, with its thick grasses and lone tree sticking up occasionally, was easier to see. Behind the marshy grassland, a background of tall, dark green pines gave contrast to the white and brown birds that fluttered in and out of their branches.

Closer to the ground, the background appeared misty from the small swarms of minute insects buzzing in the hot summer air.

A small spit of sand jutted out into the water.

"Can we walk on that?" Eleanor asked.

"Sure. Just go slowly," he cautioned, "in case any birds

are nesting across the narrows, you don't want to disturb them.''

''Oh, I wouldn't want to do that.''

As soon as she got closer to the end of the sand spit, she heard a rush of wings, but heard no birdcall. Looking up, she spotted a long-legged bird.

''A blue heron,'' Josh told her. ''Don't go any closer. They've got a nest there.''

''I didn't hear it.''

''You won't, unless you come near mating time. Then all you get is this honking squawk. Worse than Lollie Green singing in the choir. It's a wonder they attract mates at all.''

Quickly and quietly Eleanor backed away. She collided with him. Her soft bustle nestled against his leg. The tingle went through his entire body.

He held her shoulder with one hand and pointed with the other.

''Look over there, though.''

''Where?''

''To the left of that clump of grass. There. See.''

He placed his cheek very close to hers and tried to line her eyes up with his pointing finger.

''See.''

''Oh, yes. What is it?''

''A muskrat nest.''

''With little baby muskrats?''

''Probably.''

''Will they run away, too, if we get too close?''

''Well, it's for certain they won't be flying.''

Eleanor laughed. She raised her shoulder and tilted her head slightly, resting against Josh's cheek. He pressed more closely against her.

''I think I see one—or at least the top of his nose—moving through the water.''

As she followed the movements of the little swimming

muskrat, her face turned more fully to him.

"Yeah, that's him, all right," Josh confirmed.

He followed the point of the *V* with his finger as it moved through the dark waters and disappeared behind a clump of marsh grass.

"He'll be out in a minute," Josh said. "Wait."

Go ahead, kiss her, the little devil on his shoulder prodded as they waited in silence.

I can't do that, Josh silently protested. *She's a lady. It wouldn't be right. It would be . . . disrespectful.*

It's only her cheek, the little devil tempted.

Well, you do have a point there, Josh silently conceded.

He turned his face and leaned toward her. She didn't smell like the usual flower scents ladies used—lilacs or roses or lavender. It was some special concoction—a mixture of scents he couldn't identify. Something expensive from Paris? Whatever it was, it smelled good. Rich and sweet, complex and pure. It smelled like Eleanor ought to smell.

He brushed his nose against her soft cheek. He wouldn't want her to get a burn from his beard stubble.

Just as he was about to place his lips against her cheek, Eleanor jumped up and down. Her shoulder met his jawbone with a crack.

"Oh, look! A deer!" She pointed out over the marsh to the edge of the pine woods.

"My head hurts again," he mumbled.

Slowly he opened and closed his jaw and moved the joints from side to side, just to make sure she hadn't broken anything and he'd have to spend six weeks eating nothing but Maddie's soup again.

"I've never seen a deer this close!" Eleanor exclaimed in an excited whisper.

"You've been to Paris and Rome, and yet you've never

seen a plain old Virginia white-tailed deer?'' he managed to mumble.

''Not in the wild like this. Not so close. And there's nothing plain about it!''

''What a deprived life,'' he quipped.

Not as deprived as you, the little devil on his shoulder taunted.

Shut up! Just shut up! Josh silently shouted.

''Oh, there he goes,'' Eleanor said sadly. ''And, oh, what have I done?''

''You hit me.''

''Oh, no!'' She rushed up to him. ''I was talking about my shoes.'' She looked at him and realized he was holding his jaw and grimacing. ''What have I done to you?''

Standing close, she placed her hand over his on his jaw.

''It's nothing, really.''

''Now, don't try to be such a tough guy. You can't be hurt twice in one day and say it's nothing.''

She managed to pull his hand away and was now stroking his stubbly jaw with her soft hand.

''I'm so sorry. I was so excited about all these beautiful little animals, I never realized . . . Oh, Josh. I'm so sorry.''

He placed his hand atop hers and held it to his face.

''I think I can manage to forgive you.''

He continued to hold her hand, but moved it away from his face just far enough for him to place a single kiss in the palm of her hand.

''Josh.'' Her voice was soft and breathless.

''Will you be able to forgive me?''

Still holding her hand, he pulled her to him, so that her arms entwined around his neck. He slipped his arms around her small waist and pressed her close against him.

Slowly he lowered his face to hers.

Her lips were as soft as she was, small and pink, sweet. He knew he was browned and chapped from the sun and wind. He tried not to press too hard. How could he hurt such an exquisite woman? But he'd wanted to do this almost from the very first time he'd seen her. He was usually a pretty patient man, but all his patience disappeared the minute he held Eleanor.

She responded to his kiss with a fierce longing he'd never expected to find in the Ice Princess. How could he ever have called her that? She was warm and pliant against his caress. She absorbed his strength like a parched garden seeking rain, and yielded it back to him again, making him feel a hundred times stronger than before.

"I need you, Eleanor," he murmured against her lips.

There was no little devil perched on his shoulder now, urging him on. He needed no urging. All his feelings, all his longings, came from within.

"I need you, too," she responded. "Not just as a bodyguard."

"I'll be more than delighted to guard your body."

"I need you, Josh," she repeated, with a world of meaning that only he could understand in those four words.

"I think we need to do something about this, Eleanor. Right now, I just don't know what." He gave a deep, throaty chuckle. "It's a little hard to think clearly with you in my arms."

He gently pushed her away from him. It was the hardest work he'd ever had to do.

He still held on to her hand as he suggested, "Why don't we continue our walk? I think that's probably safe."

"I don't think so," Eleanor told him with a little grimace on her face.

"Why not?"

"It's going to be a little difficult after what I've done to my shoes."

❖ 13 ❖

"I GOT SO excited when I saw the deer, I jumped up and down—" she tried to explain.

"I remember," Josh replied, rubbing his jaw where she'd accidentally hit him.

"And I jumped into the water," she finished, grinning sheepishly. "My shoes, my stockings, my feet are soaking."

"Well, there's only one remedy for that."

"What? More of Gussie's teas and rocks?"

"Nope. Take your shoes off."

"Go barefoot?"

"That's usually where taking your shoes off gets you."

"I can't go barefoot! I've never gone barefoot in my life."

"You bathe with your shoes on?" He shook his head. "I can't picture that."

"Well, no, of course not."

She felt her cheeks growing warmer at the very idea of appearing naked in Josh's thoughts. Maybe in his daydreams. She hoped she at least had a towel over her. No. There was too much in that kiss to ever include a towel. Her cheeks continued to grow warm.

"But I . . . I always have slippers waiting for me. I take them off at the edge of the bed." Oh, gosh! First he had to go bringing up the bath, and now she went and mentioned bed.

"That I can picture," Josh admitted. "Now if I just add that pink silk thing . . ."

Eleanor thought her cheeks felt like an ant that some evil child was holding a magnifying glass over in the sunlight.

"Well, just stop it," she scolded.

"Come on. You've got to take those wet shoes off. Oh, you haven't lived until you've squished through wet sand barefoot. It's better than eels," he joked.

"Anything is better than eels," she said wryly. "My mother's the only one around our house who actually likes to eat those awful things."

"It's better than peaches." He held out his hand and helped to sit on the edge of the pier.

"Better than apple pie?" she asked, reaching down to slip off her shoes.

"Better than ice cream," he vowed, kneeling at her feet.

"Better than chocolate?"

He looked up into her eyes. He was so close, she could feel his breath against her cheek, brushing warm with the cool island breeze. "Better than . . . a kiss?"

"*Nothing* could be—"

"Oh, yes, there is."

"I . . . I think I need to take my shoes off if we're going to finish this walk," she said quickly.

Josh stood up. "If that's what you really need to do."

"No, but I think it's what we *ought* to do—and you know it, too."

Josh gave her a playful grimace. "Are you always so dutiful?"

"Yes. Now turn around and don't look," she ordered.

After Josh had turned his back to her, she reached up

under her skirt, untied her garters and rolled down her hose. She rolled them all up and stuck them inside her shoes.

"Now what do I do with them?"

"We'll take them back to the house where they can dry on the porch," Josh said, turning around again. "Nobody'll bother them."

"I'm not used to that."

"Around here, where everybody knows everybody else and who has what, it's pretty hard to make off with somebody else's belongings."

She held up her shoes for him to see. "But I can't go walking around barefoot."

"When we get back to the house, you can borrow a pair of Maddie's."

"I don't think she'd like that."

"Why? What? Oh, don't let Maddie's gruff exterior fool you. She's had to take care of us since she was sixteen. She just pretends to be tough to make us all listen. She's really a pussycat at heart."

Still uncertain, Eleanor replied, "If you say so. I just don't want her sharpening her claws on me."

"Why not? Clothilda did a good job on me last night."

Eleanor carefully picked her way over the sand. It did feel warm and squishy between her toes. When they reached the dirt road, she was even more careful of small pebbles. She clung to Josh for support. The bricks were hot from baking in the summer sun. She tiptoed quickly across them, uttering "oohs" and "ouches" all the way until she reached the cool safety of the small front porch.

"Maddie," Josh called as they entered the house.

"All right," she asked as she emerged from the kitchen, drying her hands on a towel. "Who hit you now?"

Pointing without hesitation, Josh said, "She did."

"Only with my shoulder," Eleanor amended.

Maddie threw up her hands. "I don't want to hear about

it. I've got enough trouble with Winnie and Bill bickering like cats and dogs. I don't need to referee you two.'' She started to head back into the kitchen.

"Maddie, we need your shoes," Josh said.

"They won't fit you, you big lummox."

"No, for Eleanor."

Maddie eyed her, sizing her up. "They're my Sunday shoes, my only other pair."

"I'll treat them as if they were my own."

"I see what you did to your own." Maddie nodded to the soggy pair on the front porch. "I hope you treat mine better than that."

"I will," she promised.

Maddie brought out her shoes. They were worn to a comfortable softness that made them a little too large for Eleanor, but usable nevertheless. In no time at all, Eleanor and Josh were strolling casually up Doc Street toward Mallard Street.

"Are you hungry?" he asked.

"I suppose."

"Come on. I'll get you the best chicken sandwich in the state." He turned her to the right.

"Is there a restaurant on this island?"

"Well . . . not exactly."

They stood before the door of Darty's Tavern.

Eleanor's eyes grew wide with surprise. "We're going in a . . ."

"It's a friendly neighborhood tavern—only this neighborhood just happens to be a whole island. Jack Darty's president of the Silchester Methodist Men's Association. His wife's chicken sandwiches are so good, I'll bet they'd even make Clothilda pleasant."

He held the door open for her invitingly.

"That I'll believe when I see it," she replied as she stepped into the cozy amber glow of the tavern's interior.

"Hey, Josh," Jack called from behind the bar. "You look like you're feeling better today."

Jack was making strange motions with his head and eyes, looking to Eleanor, then nodding to Josh, then nodding his head vigorously up and down. Josh knew he was just dying to ask if this was *the* Eleanor Folsom who had caused all Josh's troubles, but he wouldn't dare.

Josh figured he'd just let Jack wonder a while.

"Jack, I'm feeling so good, the lady and I'll have two of your wife's famous chicken sandwiches." He held up two fingers as he led Eleanor to a small private booth near the back of the tavern. "And two sarsaparillas."

"You got 'em."

Jack quickly plunked down the two glasses of red-gold sarsaparilla.

"What are they?" Eleanor asked, pointed discreetly to a large glass jar of round pink objects in ruby liquid sitting on one corner of the bar. Beside it sat a large jar of easily identifiable pickled cucumbers.

"Pickled eggs."

"I've never had a pickled egg."

"You don't know what you're missing," Josh declared. He turned around in the booth. "Hey, Jack! Two pickled eggs for the lady."

"Coming up."

Eleanor looked at the pink eggs rolling around on the plate in front of her.

"Pick it up and eat it," Josh told her.

"With my fingers?"

"I guess. I don't know. Can you use your toes?"

She giggled, reached down, and picked up the egg. It was cool and just a little slimy, but she figured she'd eaten caviar and ought to be able to cope with this.

She lifted it. It smelled strongly of vinegar and onions. She took a bite. It was just a plain hard-cooked egg, soaked in onions and vinegar, and something else to make it pink.

"It's delicious."

"Of course it is," Josh agreed. "Haven't you figured out by now? Everything around here is delicious."

"How do they make them pink?"

"Beets."

"Well, I never would have imagined." She ate the first egg, and then a second.

In a very short time a little lady in a flowered dress with a white lace collar and a big white apron brought them two platters.

"Miz Jeanine, I'd like you to meet Miss Eleanor Folsom."

Mrs. Darty didn't seem the least bit surprised to see the daughter of the richest man on the island in her establishment. "Welcome, Miss Folsom," she said as she placed the platter in front of her. "I'm sure you'll enjoy the food."

She folded her hands across her waist and stood there beside their table, waiting.

Eleanor studied her sandwich, trying to figure out the neatest way to pick up the precariously stacked arrangement. She knew Mrs. Darty wasn't about to leave until Eleanor had tasted her cooking—and pronounced it fare fit for the gods.

Might as well get it over with. Eleanor picked up the sandwich and took a small, tentative bite. She took another, slightly larger bite.

"You're absolutely right," she declared. "This really is the best chicken sandwich—my goodness, *the* best sandwich—I've ever had."

No sense in confessing to Mrs. Darty that the only other sandwiches she'd ever had were the size of a silver dollar and had cucumbers and watercress on them.

"I've eaten in some of the best restaurants in Baltimore, London, Paris, and Rome," Eleanor continued. "I have never tasted such a wonderful chicken sandwich.''

"Do tell your friends about us," Mrs. Darty said pleasantly as she walked away. Her face was beaming with a supremely satisfied grin.

Well, except for Isabelle and Alice, none of her friends would be caught dead in a place like Darty's Tavern, Eleanor thought. Oh, maybe Michael Stewart, who would dare anything as long as it included food. Poo-poo on the rest of them, she decided. Most likely, they didn't deserve a meal this good anyway.

Eleanor was just about to start the second half of her sandwich when she looked out the front window.

Her sandwich fell to pieces on the plate.

"Are you all right? Are you choking? What can I do?" Josh was looking frantically around for some object that would help her.

She quickly ducked into the far corner of the booth. She hoped she was out of sight.

"Bradley," was all she could say.

"He's here?"

"He's outside," she whispered, even though he'd never hear her through the glass and the distance. "He's looking inside."

She tried to push herself farther into the corner.

"I'm so afraid he'll see me. He'll come in here after me." She stopped a moment and stared. "Why in the world does he still have that awful scarf on?"

"Still? Oh, jiminy, I never thought it would go on this long!" Josh looked as if he was ready to explode with laughter. He started to turn around.

"No, no. Don't look. He'll see you. He'll see me." Her words were coming faster. Her tone of voice was becoming increasingly nervous. "Oh, see. This isn't funny. I told you he follows me everywhere."

"You're with me now. I'll take care of you," Josh assured her. He tried his best not to laugh at Bradley anymore.

She didn't want him fighting with Bradley again. He should be able to see how sneaky the little weasel was. And Josh should be taking long, slow walks along the beach, not engaging in barroom brawls!

And it was all her fault!

She wasn't sure how much influence her father had with the people around here. She wasn't sure if he'd be able to keep her name, Bradley's, and Josh's out of the newspaper this time. She wondered if this little place even had a newspaper!

She watched Bradley move closer to the door. He reached out to place his hand on the doorknob.

"Oh, goodness. Hide me, please. Do something."

Josh was already on his feet. "Jack. Back door?"

Jack just nodded in that direction and continued washing glasses.

Josh seized Eleanor's hand and pulled her from the booth. Apparently he was very familiar with making quick, back-door exits. Jack was also apparently very familiar with having a clientele that frequently needed to make quick, back-door exits.

Just as they heard the doorbells jingling, indicating Bradley's entrance, Josh and Eleanor closed the back door of Darty's Tavern behind them.

Eleanor looked at the dirt road beside them.

"Didn't we just come from here?" she asked.

"Come on, quick, while he's still in there. Jack'll know to stall him until we can get away."

Josh was still holding on to Eleanor's hand. He pulled her away from the door and made a dash up the dirt road.

"I can't run. I can't run!" Eleanor cried as they hit the crushed oyster shells that paved Mallard Street. But she ran anyway.

"Sure you can. It's not that far."

Josh pulled her along, across Mallard Street, past a flagpole surrounded by white-painted bricks and forget-me-nots, and up onto the long porch that ran across the entire front of Moore's General Store.

The shoes had rubbed against her heels. Her hairpins were scattered, and her hair was beginning to fall. They were the least of her worries.

"He'll see us from here," Eleanor whispered, breathless from running.

"No, we'll hide behind the flagpole." He stepped in front of her, aligning himself with the flagpole.

"Stop kidding. This is no time for jokes. I've got to get away from him," she insisted. "I can't have you fighting him in the middle of town."

"Why not?"

"There's no water to throw him into. You'll actually have to *fight* him."

"No, I'll just run him up the flagpole in Evering Square."

Eleanor looked from side to side. Then she stared at the flagpole in front of them.

"This is the only flagpole."

"That's right. This is Evering Square."

She studied the base of the flagpole.

"Well, it *is* square," she had to admit.

"Bob Evering was the only Silchester boy who didn't come back from the War Between the States. He was friends with my pa, Jack Darty, and Wally at the barbershop. As I recollect, he was supposed to marry Miss Baxter, over at the bookstore."

"Oh." Eleanor nodded.

No wonder the little lady kept her head—her very self—buried in books. In a book she could be every heroine. Her lost love could be every hero. For her, life was probably much better in a book than it had been in reality.

Shielding his eyes from the noonday sun, Josh looked to the flag waving at the top of the pole.

"We all erected this in his memory. I guess compared to some of your big city squares, it's not much, but that doesn't mean he's not missed just as much."

"I understand."

Her nerves had been much too overwrought lately, Eleanor decided. Why else did she feel like crying for two people she didn't really know? She held on to Josh's arm a little more tightly.

"We've met."

"Who? Bob Evering?"

"No, Miss Baxter. I think that bump on the head did more damage than Doc or Gussie had originally figured."

"Whoops! Here he comes. I guess Jack stalled him as long as he could," Josh said, turning quickly and pulling her into Moore's General Store.

"Hey, Josh," Unk called from his seat at the checkerboard. "Why, you burst in here so fast, I was reminded of the time York McCurdy's wife had triplets. Summer of fifty-one, I do believe. He liked to near fainted dead away right in the very spot where you and the lovely lady are standing now."

He pointed a gnarled finger at the floor at their feet.

"Don't know if it was the shock of having fathered three babies all at once, or the fact that them kids was the ugliest things I've ever seen on dry land. He wasn't sure whether to buy them cradles or cages."

"You must be Unk Moore," Eleanor said with a laugh.

"Well, since nobody else'll claim the dubious honor, then I guess I must," he replied. "And who might you be, pretty lady?"

"Eleanor Folsom. My father—"

"Ah, yes. Sure. If you don't know who Mr. Folsom is

on this island, you must've been hiding out in the oyster beds too long. He's the son of a gun who tore up the leeward side of the island.''

Eleanor opened her mouth to protest, but after having seen the untouched beauty along the Straiten Narrows, she was finally beginning to realize why these people were just a bit hostile to the summer folks.

"I hope you won't hold that against me," she said. She flashed him her best, city smile.

" 'Course not. Life's too short to hold grudges.''

"What would you know about a short life, you old codger?" came a woman's booming voice. "You're going to be around here forever.''

"Naw, I just want to outlive you, Augusta.'' He settled back against his chair with a deep chuckle. "Right about now, that's my one and only goal in life—to outlive you. Well, that and getting my store-bought teeth to fit right.''

"Miss Folsom, how nice to have you pay us a visit,'' Augusta said, smiling. She approached Eleanor with her hand extended and her head held high. They looked like two empresses encountering each other at a diplomatic function.

Eleanor blinked. The woman had no waist and no hips. She looked like the only person who could use a hollowed-out log as a corset.

"What can I supply you with today?''

"Nothing,'' Josh said.

Augusta's smile didn't beam quite so brightly, but she still held her head high with the greatest aplomb.

"We . . . we only came in for some shade,'' Josh said. "We really should be moving on.''

"Oh, do we have to go so soon?'' Eleanor protested. "This really is a wonderful place.''

"Why, thank you, Miss Folsom.'' Augusta was beaming again.

"How you managed to fit so many things in here!"

Eleanor wandered up and down the counters, and the rows of items on the shelves in the center of the store.

"It's just amazing. Fabric, shovels." She sniffed. "Cinnamon. Lilac water?"

She lifted a small bottle and sniffed at the stopper.

"My great-grandmother used to wear lilac water. She died when I was very young, so I don't remember too much about her. But every year for Christmas we'd get her a bottle. When grandfather's little mercantile expanded into a great big store, Father always complained that he could buy her more expensive perfume. But she always insisted on lilac water. She claimed she wore it when she got married, and wouldn't wear anything else."

She put the bottle down and moved along the counter.

"Peppermint drops. Licorice."

"Miz Augusta, why don't you give us a bag of the peppermint drops? Then we've got to be going," Josh told Eleanor firmly.

"Oh, very well."

Augusta handed the little brown paper bag across the counter to Josh.

"Thanks, Miz Augusta. Put it on my tab, won't you?"

Augusta gave a deep sigh. "Sure. Sure. That tab's getting awful long—and winter's coming," she warned.

"I'll take care of it. Can we use your back door?"

"It's the storeroom," she protested. "I don't think Miss Folsom wants to see that."

"Yes, she does," Josh insisted as he pulled Eleanor along after him. "It's an important feature on her tour of the island today."

"You are such a liar!" Eleanor teased as she followed him through the storeroom, with its shelves full of boxes and colored bottles.

The door chimes rang.

"Well, fancy seeing you again, son," Unk greeted the newcomer. "Say, you can take that scarf off now. Ain't none of them cottonheads ever did come in here, did they, Augusta?"

"Cottonheads?" Augusta demanded imperiously. "What in heaven's name are you talking about, you old fool?"

Josh quietly closed the door behind them. He didn't need to hear Bradley rant and rave when he found out he'd been fooled. But it had been a darn good joke while it lasted. Trust Augusta not to play along like everyone else.

"We're in the woods now," Eleanor said. "I really liked the store better."

"You're much safer in the woods, trust me," Josh assured her. He held the little bag out to her. "Here, have a peppermint."

"That was Bradley coming into the store right behind us, wasn't it?" she asked, dipping into the bag.

"Of course."

"Who else would wear a woolen scarf in the middle of July?" She eyed him suspiciously. "Now, why would Bradley be wearing a scarf here when he never did back in Baltimore? What are the cottonheads Unk Moore was talking about? Why is Bradley safe from them inside?"

"Because cottonheads don't come inside," Josh stated plainly.

They waded through the thin growth of bushes at the edge of the woods. Virginia creeper, black-eyed Susans, bayberry bushes, honeysuckle, saplings of maple, birch, and sassafras.

"Will they get us outside?" Eleanor asked as she followed in his footsteps. She made very sure she set her foot down in the exact same place Josh's foot had just vacated. That way she knew for certain there weren't any snakes there.

"Nope."

"I get the feeling they aren't outside, either."

Josh held his finger to his lips and urged her to shush, even though there was no one around to listen.

"I have to make a confession," he said. "I told Bradley—well, no, it wasn't just me. Aunt Audrey was in on it, too. We told him that the cottonmouth snakes and the copperhead snakes had gotten together to make this very poisonous critter called the cottonhead."

"You didn't!" She started to giggle.

"Of course, with a name like cottonhead, they're repelled by wool—"

"You didn't!" Her giggling grew worse.

"No, no. That part was Aunt Audrey's idea. If you don't want to get bitten by one of them, you have to wear wool. Of course," he added, polishing his knuckles against an imaginary lapel, "we island folks are immune to their bite."

"You're impossible! Both of you. Your whole family. Probably the whole island!" Her giggling turned into full-fledged, side-splitting laughter. She almost swallowed her candy whole.

"Probably. But, hey, Bradley's the one who actually believed us. Of course, at the time, we didn't want him dropping over dead in the middle of town from heat prostration, so we just told him to wear a little scarf. Believe me, if I'd known then what I know now, I'd have him wearing the entire flock of sheep!"

"I hate to say so, but Bradley deserves this."

"I had hoped he wouldn't find out just yet that we'd all been fooling him. Now there's no guarantee he won't be coming into the woods. But there's a lot of pretty things to be seen here. I guess it's just as relaxing as Gussie's walk along the shore."

"Josh," she asked cautiously, "there aren't *really* any copperheads or cottonmouths around here, are there?"

"Of course not. Do you really think I'd bring you back here if there were?"

"No."

"Good." He paused a moment. "Of course, there are probably a couple of harmless little green garter snakes."

With a squeal Eleanor rushed up closer to Josh.

He laughed and boldly put his arm around here.

"A clever trick, Claybourne," she scolded, settling comfortably into his embrace.

"A wonderful move," he corrected.

He drew her closer again to his body. The bright light of the sun didn't reach the floor of the woods directly. It filtered down through the translucent green leaves. Every once in a while a shaft of golden light pierced the misty green.

Crickets chirped in the undergrowth. Bugs hummed overhead. Occasionally the whirring of a bird's wings fluttered by. Squirrels chattered from the high branches.

The air was thick and sweet with honeysuckle and disintegrating leaves.

He wrapped his arms around her waist.

"You're safe here now with me. I'd fight off snakes, and grizzly bears, and even Bradley to keep you safe, my love."

He kissed her again. This time there would be no prying eyes from nosy neighbors in houses along the beach. He ran his hand through her loosened hair, fanning it out behind her.

He caressed the dark cascade down her back, into the indentation of her tiny waist, and out again to smooth over her slender hips.

She held his head with both hands, as if she was afraid to let him ago. Her fingers wove through his hair, and down his neck. Once or twice her fingertip dipped into the neck of his shirt.

He wanted her to unfasten each button. He wanted to

feel her soft cheek resting against his chest. He wanted her to hear how she made his heart beat.

He wanted to unfasten her buttons, too. His stomach tightened with desire as he imagined placing his own cheek against her soft white breasts, and listening to her heartbeat.

"I want to hold you," he said. "Caress you, make your heart beat faster for me alone."

"Oh, Josh, my love. I'm yours, and yours alone."

He couldn't do that to her—not now, not here. She deserved better than a roll on the forest floor.

"You deserve satin sheets, candlelight, and champagne—not dead leaves, sarsaparilla, and ants. You deserve a white lace gown and a golden wedding ring. Not a cottage with a kerosene cooker that doesn't always work, and fish every night for supper."

If her parents ever found out she was with him alone all day, they'd ship her back to Baltimore immediately. If he was lucky, they might allow her to come back to Silchester next year. Of course, by then she might have just given up and given in to Bradley's demands. Or she might be sent off to a convent.

Whatever the future brought, he wanted to cover as much of the island today with her as possible. Then, in the future, everywhere he went he'd have a memory of her there. He'd end up like old Miss Baxter—crabbing or oystering all day, then sitting with his head buried in a book, daydreaming of what might have been for the rest of his life.

"Come on. There's still so much more to see," he said as he urged her along a little path the playing children had worn through the woods.

"It's a little church," Eleanor said with surprise.

"Silchester Methodist. Did you think we were all completely heathen here?"

"No, no. But it's so tiny."

"But we fill it every Sunday—and Christmas," he said proudly.

A low hedge ran around the perimeter of the churchyard. She peered over the edge.

"There's a little graveyard, too."

"Well, what did you think? That we eat our dead?"

Eleanor let out a horrified little cry.

"We make great chicken sandwiches."

Eleanor's cry of horror increased. "You're insane! You're demented!" She reached out and slapped him on the arm.

He captured her wrist and pulled her roughly to him. His strong arms surrounded her within his embrace.

"You're beautiful," he told her as their faces came near.

"You're handsome."

"You're making me insane—wanting you," he whispered in her ear. He nuzzled the soft spot under her ear. "Not being able to have you."

He didn't wait for a reply. He kissed her again, with all the passion that waited within him. He moved to caress the corners of her mouth, then to her soft pink cheek.

"Who said you can't have me?" she whispered in his ear.

• 14 •

He RELEASED HER. What could he tell her? Your parents. My occupation. Your world versus mine. That doggone Rule Number One that started all the trouble in the first place. All of these things, and more. That's why I can't have you.

"Not in the churchyard," he said, pulling back slightly. That would be a good enough excuse. "Someone might see us."

"Now, who would be sneaking around a churchyard?" a short man wearing a clerical collar demanded as he strode boldly toward them.

"You, for starters, Mel," Josh told him with a laugh.

"Not me. See, I've reformed."

The man tugged at his tight white collar, as if he actually wasn't too comfortable wearing it. Whether it came from conscience or from his stocky form, Eleanor couldn't say.

"What? No more fish?"

"Only what Letty puts on my dinner plate."

Eleanor looked positively bewildered.

"Mel, may I introduce Miss Folsom?" Josh began. "Eleanor, this is Reverend Melvin Toomby, orneriest minister Silchester ever had."

" 'Orneriest kid ever to set foot on dirt,' I believe is the correct quote from Miss Zang," the reverend corrected.

"Can't say as I blame her, either." Josh leaned closer to Eleanor and whispered loudly, "Of course, that's the church version. I believe some of the other quotes involved the minions of Satan, the Spanish Inquisition, Benedict Arnold, and John Wilkes Booth."

Eleanor wasn't sure they were talking about an actual minister. It was even a little hard to believe this young man was a preacher. All the ministers she'd ever met never smiled, looked down on everyone else from lofty heights, had long white beards or whiskers of some sort, and had been almost as old as the Almighty Himself.

This fellow wasn't much taller than she was, had dark hair, was clean-shaven, and sported a twinkle in his eyes even more mischievous than Alice.

"Just because of a few fish," the Reverend Toomby complained.

"A few fish?" Eleanor repeated.

"Let me tell you what this character did when we were—what? Twelve years old?"

"Thereabouts."

Eleanor grinned with anticipation. If the Reverend Toomby was anything like any of the other people on Silchester, this was going to be a great story.

"The very last day of school, all the children had gone through their promotion ceremonies—"

"Except Walter Fletcher," the Reverend Toomby added, "who was always late for third grade because he had to shave."

"They filed out of the schoolhouse," Josh recounted.

He pointed across Mallard Street to the only red building she'd seen on all of Silchester Island—the schoolhouse.

"All the rest of the kids are cheering and running for home—like normal children. Mel tells Miss Zang he left a book he was reading in his desk. She's so delighted to think he was actually reading a book, she lets him back in and doesn't check up on him—which she should've known to do from many previous unsavory experiences with him.''

"It was her own fault," the Reverend Toomby pronounced, shaking his head gravely.

"Mel then proceeds to put several fish—"

"Nice, *fresh* fish, mind you," the reverend joined in. With pride he added, "I used only the best ingredients for all my pranks."

"Which he had been hiding all day in his socks."

"A cold, messy job—but it was worth it," the reverend interjected.

"Didn't anyone notice . . . well, a certain odor?" Eleanor asked.

"No. I always helped my dad with the fish before school. No one ever noticed."

"Then he slips them in Miss Zang's desk and closes the top," Josh finished. "Then, of course, the school is closed up for the summer, so no one notices the powerful smell that had been building up, until September first, when Miss Zang opened the front door."

"That's horrible!" Eleanor exclaimed.

"That's right."

"That was fun." Reverend Toomby chuckled.

"After Doc Whitaker got her to come to—"

"Not Gussie?"

"Oh, heck, no!" the Reverend Toomby exclaimed. "She wouldn't let Gussie touch her with a ten-foot pole."

"She claims she won't have any truck with anything that's not scientific," Josh said. "She claims that's not what the Creator gave us a brain for."

"So for that one little prank, I sat on the dunce stool in the corner until Christmas," Reverend Toomby complained. "And, of course, I had to clean up the whole mess before school could start that fall.''

"I can see where you needed reforming, Mel," Josh teased him. "You're just lucky she didn't use that hickory stick of hers on your bottom."

"It would've made the sitting a whole lot harder, but the worst thing was that dumb-looking hat." The Reverend Toomby nodded to Eleanor. "Well, nice meeting you, Miss Folsom. I'd best go back to writing my sermon for Sunday morning. If Elisha thought the cloak of Elijah was hard to wear, he should've tried following in Reverend Straiten's footsteps."

He chuckled as he walked away.

As they watched him returning to the small white manse with black shutters beside the church, Josh remarked, "If anyone can do it, Mel can."

"If not, he'll just put fish in the desk and leave. I'd hate to be his replacement."

"Oh, don't worry. Mel's calmed down a lot since we were kids. He's got a pretty little wife from the mainland. From around Richmond, I think. No kids yet, though."

He turned to her and grinned.

"See, I'm not related to *everybody* on the island after all."

And there is a history of wives from the mainland, he reminded himself. Of course, Letitia MacDonald Toomby herself was the daughter of a minister who'd been a missionary to India—and a far cry from the pampered daughter of a rich man. To her, Silchester must be like luxury itself. To Eleanor, it might only be Perdition.

"Why do you have big slabs of granite on top of every grave?" Eleanor asked.

"What?" Josh asked, roused from his initially encouraging, yet ultimately disappointing daydreams. "Oh, the tombstones."

"Yes. Except for Gussie, I didn't think you all were a very superstitious bunch."

"Gussie's not superstitious," Josh protested. "She's . . . well, she's . . . just different."

"Well, except for those of you who hide fish in odd places, you're all very honest people. So, are you afraid of someone getting out or getting in?"

"Getting out," Josh answered quickly and bluntly.

Eleanor looked at him with surprise. This was obviously not the answer she had been expecting.

"I know you Silchester folks are a bit bizarre, but—"

"See, even though the church and the lighthouse are on the two highest places on the island, the tides can get pretty bad in a big storm," Josh explained. "We honor and respect our departed loved ones, and would like to keep them around us. The big stones help us do that."

She nodded. "I can understand that."

"Besides, it wouldn't look too good to have our dearly departed floating around in the Bay, having caskets washing ashore in Baltimore or Annapolis, or all the way down to Crisfield."

"No, I guess not," she responded with a giggle. "But it looks to me as if we summer folks aren't the only ones concerned with social appearances."

"In Crisfield I think they really do eat their dead," he added with a chuckle.

"Oh, you *are* morbid!" she declared.

"I'd like to show you the lighthouse and have you meet our lighthouse keeper, Laurie Watts."

"Laurie?" she repeated. "The lighthouse keeper is a woman?"

"Sure."

"I'll bet my father doesn't know anything about *that*," Eleanor said with the hint of a triumphant smile playing about her lips.

"Sure. I'll bet a lot of folks don't know it, but there's a couple more women keeping lighthouses all along the Bay. It may not sound like much of a job, but a lot of sailors' lives depend on those women."

"I'd really like to meet her. Is she anything like Gussie?"

"Not a bit," Josh told her as they started to walk through the woods again.

"Or Miss Baxter?" she asked, thinking of the independent women she'd met on the island so far. "Miss Zang?"

"Good heavens, no!"

"Your sister Maddie?"

"Not at all. Just wait. You'll see."

The climb up the gentle slope was easy. Every once in a while, Eleanor could get a glimpse of large houses through the trees.

"That's the Ridgelys'," she said, pointing. "We've certainly made our way around the island."

"Actually, if we'd go that way," he said, turning around and pointing through the woods, "we'd end up at my house again, eventually."

The growth of trees began to thin. In a wide, circular clearing Eleanor could see the tall white lighthouse rising high above anything else on the island.

"Is that where Miss Watts lives?" Eleanor asked.

"Actually, she lives in that little square house attached to the side of the lighthouse there." As they drew closer he said, "Looks like she's home."

"How can you tell?" Eleanor asked. The whole place looked deserted to her.

"Laurie's got her little flag up."

He pointed to a small yellow pennant flapping wildly in the breeze.

"It's a long walk up here, and she doesn't like to think of folks coming all the way up here and her not being home,'' Josh explained. ''So she flies her little pennant to let us know when she's home. Of course, she's almost always home. And if she isn't, where else is she going to be?''

Eleanor had to admit, even though they'd been to many places on the island today, they were still on the island. It wasn't very far from any one place to the next here. Everybody seemed to know everyone else's whereabouts.

She just kept hoping they could continue to elude Bradley.

''Isn't she afraid to live up here by herself?'' she asked.

''I guess not.''

''Should we knock?''

''Of course not.''

''Why not? We're certainly not going to barge right in on her.''

''Of course not. But we're not going to knock, either. Suppose she's up in the top, and has to walk all the way down the stairs just to say 'howdy-do,' and then walk all the way back up again to finish her work.''

Eleanor nodded her understanding. ''I think she'd be a little perturbed. I would be, too.''

''So we'll just take our candy and sit out on the rocks.'' Josh indicated the edge of a small drop-off out past the lighthouse. ''If she comes by, she'll say hello. If not, well, there's always next time.''

He sure hoped there'd always be a next time with Eleanor. Josh led Eleanor to the rocky edge of the drop-off. It wasn't high enough to deserve the full-fledged name of cliff.

To her right, Eleanor could clearly see the Ridgely cottage now, and beyond that, the Hamiltons'. To her left, she watched the water ebb and flow at the mouth of the Straiten Narrows.

When she saw what was below, she held on to Josh more tightly.

"Don't worry. I won't let you fall," he assured her.

"It goes almost straight down," she said. The steep stone side dropped down to a pile of jagged, seaweed and barnacle-covered rocks. If anyone did survive that drop, they'd be crippled for life.

"That's why we call it a drop-off, but it's not really that far."

"I still wouldn't want to fall down it!"

"Me, neither, but with my luck lately, I just might."

"Oh, goodness. I hope Bradley doesn't know about this, or he's liable to try to lure you out here and give you a push."

Eleanor looked once again at the jagged rocks jutting up from below. The water splashed over them. A little farther out she could see the white froth on the tops of the churning water, and every once in a while a submerged rock exposed by the waves.

Just when she thought a wave was about to break on the rocks, an undercurrent would pull it out again, then splash up when she least expected it.

"See what I mean about it being dangerous?"

Eleanor just nodded.

"A sailor can never predict what the water will do in that area. Undertows come up and disappear and move all around. Eddies and whirlpools form, wash away. No way to predict it at all."

"Just promise me you'll never fish there."

"*Nobody* around here is that stupid," he assured her. "Anyway, the water's too turbulent to get good crabs and oysters."

"Well, do I call Chief Groves, or will you trespassers go quietly?" a woman asked.

Josh started to laugh even before he turned around.

Eleanor turned to see a stunningly beautiful woman in a plaid shirt and men's trousers bunched into a belt at the waist. Until now, Eleanor had been quite confident of her own healthy beauty. Never mind that the young woman had the boldness to wear men's clothing. She looked as if she should be wearing something diaphanous, have a glistening fishtail, and be singing alluring songs from the rocks below.

She was accompanied by one of the biggest dogs Eleanor had ever seen. He was a threatening-looking black and tan, with heavy jowls spread in what could only be called a doggy smile. His bright black eyes watched her curiously.

"Don't worry. The only person he's ever bitten is Red Taylor, and that was an accident. Red never should've tried to get me to dance at Suzanne and Oscar's wedding." Then she smiled shyly at Eleanor and said, "Miss Folsom, pleased to meet you."

"How do you know me?" Eleanor was too stupefied to make a coherent response.

Laurie laughed. "I'm not so isolated up here that I don't hear what's going on in town."

"Oh, my goodness. Who else knows?"

"Just the folks who won't tell. Well, I've got to go."

Without allowing for a word of persuasion to make her stay, Laurie headed toward her lighthouse.

"Does she always come and go so quickly?"

Josh nodded. "Usually. The longest I've ever seen her hang around any one place except here was at Suzanne and Oscar's wedding."

"She took the dog to the wedding?"

"She never goes anywhere without Bruce."

"His name is Bruce."

"Yeah, he'd get real cantankerous if we tried to call him Sally."

"What's she doing keeping a lighthouse anyway?" Eleanor managed to ask without sounding too jealous.

Certainly *she* was above being glad that Laurie Watts was keeping a lonely lighthouse on the edge of Silchester Island instead of capturing hearts in the salons of Baltimore, New York, London, or Paris.

"She's real shy," Josh observed. Then he sat down and patted the ground beside him. "Come on. Have a seat and we'll eat candy, and watch the tides and the boats coming in from crabbing."

Eleanor sat beside him and leaned against his strong chest as he leaned back against a tree stump. They shared the peppermint drops, watched the gulls and pelicans skimming the water. Occasionally a heron or swan would flap gracefully by, or a fish hawk would soar overhead. Eleanor moved to lean her head on Josh's knees and surround them with her arms. His legs were as muscular as his arms.

One by one, the small boats were gathering, heading toward the north end of the island to tie up at their own piers. No one dared approach Rocky Point.

"They really do stay away from Rocky Point, don't they?" she asked.

"I told you, nobody's that stupid."

"Hasn't anyone tried? Some drunk or silly daredevil? You know what my father would say about personal endeavor and the American way of success and making money."

"Sure, people have tried. They're all under those big stones in the churchyard, too."

"All of them?"

"Oh, I guess there's a few that they never recovered the body, but none to my immediate recollection. Unk could tell you about the older ones better than I could."

"No, thanks. I really don't think I want to know."

Josh shifted away from her and rose to his feet. "Oh, my golly. I've been enjoying myself so much, I lost track of the time."

"I haven't spent such a wonderful, peaceful day in many, many months," she said softly.

"I think you'd best be getting back home now," he told her. His expression was very serious. "I never thought to keep you out this late. Your father'll be waiting for me with a shotgun—shoot first, ask questions later."

She sighed with disappointment. Today had been the most wonderful day of her life—so far. She hoped for many more, but she still hated to see this one end.

But she knew very well that her mother would start to wonder where she was. She might get away with pleading having luncheon with Isabelle but, considering how everyone knew what almost everyone else was up to, she couldn't get away with hiding out through the dinner hour.

Besides, she couldn't put Isabelle in such a position to *really* have to lie for her. A fib might not do much harm, but right now she was bordering on profound mendacity.

"Will . . . will you at least walk me to my driveway?" she asked. "Just to make sure Bradley's not lying in wait for me."

"Of course," he said as he placed his arm over her shoulder and began to lead her through the woods.

Eventually they reached the backyards of the houses along Mallard Street. Children had left their swings and seesaws empty. Here and there a hobbyhorse rested in the sand. Someone had left a rag doll in a bright red wagon.

"I told you before, I'll *always* watch out for you, Eleanor," he promised. "The best I'm able, for as long as I'm able."

The setting sun was turning the leaves to a deep russet green. What magic could turn a leaf two colors at the same time as it fluttered in the breeze from the Bay? How could two people from two such different worlds find each other on a tiny island and fall in love? Eleanor wondered as she and Josh walked through last year's fallen leaves and twigs.

They stopped at the edge of the woods facing the Folsom driveway.

She didn't move away from him yet. She hoped it was too dark against the shadows of the tall trees for anyone to see them. She hoped it was too far from the house for anyone to notice them.

She wanted to stay as close to him as possible for as long as possible. But she knew the time had come to part.

"Will . . . will I see you tomorrow?" she asked.

"I certainly hope so," he answered.

"I don't know how I'll get out of the house . . . how I'll find you."

"Don't worry," he said. "I'll find you."

He took her in his arms again.

"I need to kiss you just one more time," he said softly as he looked down on her in the twilight.

"Don't make it sound so final," she pleaded. But deep inside she feared the same as he did, that this might be their last kiss.

"You know as well as I do that it all depends on what happens once you get home."

She nodded.

"A kiss for luck," she said, tilting her face up to his.

He didn't need a second invitation.

He hadn't shaved for two days. His beard was rough. She savored the maleness of him as his lips met hers. He was strong and good. He was bold and caring. He was everything a man could be. The firmness of his muscles felt good to hold. She wanted to hold him forever, and tell him she loved him with her dying breath.

At last she pulled away. Her fingers trailed along his as they tried to continue to touch each other for as long as possible. She watched him as she backed across Folsom Drive. When she reached her driveway, she turned and ran.

She tried to stay on the drive, so the tears that dimmed

her eyes wouldn't make her run into any trees. Her whereabouts would be difficult enough to explain. She could hardly come home with a black eye.

So there they were, Bradley noted. His eyes narrowed as he watched Josh and Eleanor making their way through the woods at the back of Bodine's. Standing at the window of his darkened room, partially hidden by the lacy curtain, he crossed his arms over his chest and reached up to stroke his chin in thought.

I chase after them all day. Aided by the rest of the people on this island, they continue to elude me. Now, when I'd all but given up, I find them.

That just shows me I must be persistent. I mustn't give up.

One day she will be mine. One day soon. As soon as I can rid myself of Claybourne.

How could I have missed last night? he berated himself. He pounded his fist against the wall. He was drunk, it was dark, the board was heavy. *I had a clear shot at his head. And no witnesses!*

Damnation! He'd actually hit him. How could he have missed not killing him? *He must have the hardest head in Christendom.* Or he was the luckiest son of a gun on earth.

He'd get him next time.

I really owe it to him now. Making me look like a fool in front of all those people. How could I have left my guard down long enough to be fooled by a stupid fisherman? I should have been more suspicious of those preposterous cottonheads right away. Well, he won't catch me napping again.

Just look at them, how he holds her so close. How can she allow him such liberties and cringe at my touch? I've tried so hard to show her what a good man I am, and she chooses a common, smelly, dirty workman.

Maybe he'd been mistaken. Maybe he'd treated her with too much love and longing. Maybe she didn't need gifts. Maybe she needed to be punished for refusing him. *Then* she would truly see how much he loved her.

He berated himself for not bringing a gun. He couldn't buy one at the General Store now, or he'd attract too much attention or suspicion.

But he was a supremely resourceful man. There were lots of other ways of ridding himself of Claybourne. Claybourne was not invincible.

Next time, Bradley wouldn't miss. And Eleanor would be his.

Eleanor slipped around to the side of the house. The servants' entrance was usually kept open until a bit later. She hoped she could quietly go up to her room, undress, and be fast asleep. Or at least she could claim a headache or the vapors when dinner was announced.

Oh, my goodness! she silently exclaimed when she bent to take off her shoes. She still had on Maddie's Sunday shoes. They didn't look anywhere near as well kept as when she'd first borrowed them. How was she going to explain where her own walking shoes had gone?

She should try to clean these up the best she could, she decided. It was the least she owed Maddie.

She tried to pump a little water to wash off the sand and forest litter. Oh, why did that darn pump have to squeak so loudly? Even if they did only use it two months out of the year, couldn't someone have fixed it before they arrived for the summer?

They'd hear her, and she'd be found out for sure. If worst came to worst, she wondered, did she have enough spit to clean a pair of shoes?

As soon as the cloth was wet enough with the little bit of water she'd managed to pump, she began polishing.

She had plenty of shoes she could wear instead. As soon as she returned to Baltimore, she'd buy Maddie a new pair and send them to her. Maybe she could lend Maddie a pair or two for Sundays until her own new ones arrived.

She held the one shoe out to examine it. Yes, already it looked a lot better. Maybe Maddie wouldn't be so upset after all.

She set it down beside her, picked up the other one, and started to scrub.

"And just where have you been all day, miss?" Father demanded.

Eleanor dropped the shoe. She tried not to look at all guilty when she turned to answer him. "I was with Isabelle . . ."

Father didn't look convinced.

"With Alice—"

"Don't lie to me, Eleanor," he warned.

"With Josh," she told him with an apologetic grin.

"Captain Claybourne?"

Eleanor nodded and bent to pick up the shoe. Right about now, she felt like something she'd just scraped off the bottom.

"So, it's Josh now, is it?" he demanded.

She nodded again. She thought she detected a note of softening in his voice. But Father's face remained as impassive as stone. She still had a lot of explaining to do.

"Well, I suppose I should have foreseen this."

Eleanor began to breathe a little more easily.

"And taken the proper precautions against it."

"Oh, no. You're not going to lock me in my room like Hilda Wallace's father did to her, are you?"

"Don't be silly. That's positively medieval and barbaric."

Eleanor took another little gasp of relief.

"I knew I shouldn't have allowed you girls to learn to

read—much less allowed you free choice of your books.'' He shook his head with an exasperated sigh. ''Just look at what kind of silly ideas you come up with.''

Eleanor wisely refrained from reminding her father that *Mr.* Wallace was the one who thought up locking Hilda in her room.

Then she shuddered again.

''You're not going to send me back to Baltimore tomorrow, are you?''

''No. I won't send you alone, and I see no reason for the entire family's holiday to be ruined just because you have the brains of an addled rabbit.''

''Then what . . . oh, no!'' Until now, she'd only been concerned with mere physical punishment—imprisonment, exile, starvation—those she could handle.

Her eyes grew wide with horror as she pleaded. ''Oh, please, Father, don't do that! Please!''

''You brought this on yourself, Eleanor,'' he told her. His voice was cold and emotionless. ''Don't blame me if you can't accept the consequences of your actions.''

There was only one punishment more dreaded than anything else. Thumbscrews, the rack, the Iron Maiden—none could compare with—

''Oh, please, Father. Don't set Mother on me.''

❖ *15* ❖

"A SENSE OF duty. Yes, indeed. That's what everyone ought to have. Why, the world would be a far better place if everyone had a sense of their proper duty—to themselves, to their family, to their position in society, to their town, their country, their God. Women as well as men ought to have a sense of duty. Women *especially* ought to have a sense of duty, as they are the mothers who bear the children and raise the children in the way they should go. A child needs to be raised with a sense of duty. And then, come flood or Perdition, they *do* their duty."

Mother paraded up and down Eleanor's bedroom. Eleanor watched the carpet, prepared to grab a pitcher of water should her mother's constant tread back and forth ignite the carpet by simple friction.

Of course, should her mother wear the carpet and the floorboards down completely, and fall through into the dining room, well, there was very little she could do then but laugh herself silly.

But the carpet was expensive and thick. The floorboards were sturdy hardwood. There was very little chance of either event happening in the near future. Eleanor could only sit and listen, with no hope of pardon or reprieve.

At least her father had sent her immediately to bed last night without rousing her mother, and Eleanor had been able to get some sleep before her mother had come to her room immediately after breakfast.

Her father had said he wouldn't lock her in her room, but she'd been served breakfast in her room—which was very unusual. She imagined lunch would be pretty much the same—if they didn't forget she was up here.

If she heard this lecture from her mother one more time, she believed she would scream and throw herself into the Bay. With her dying breath, she'd ask Alice to return Maddie's shoes and to tell Josh she'd always love him.

"A sense of honor. Yes, indeed. That's what everyone ought to have. Why, the world would be a far better place if everyone had a sense of honor. Everyone ought to honor their own body, as the temple of the Holy Spirit. Everyone ought to have a certain amount of honor for our duly elected city, state, and federal officials—even if they are a bunch of pompous, filibustering idiots only interested in lining their own pockets and finding sinecures for their relatives—and the beautiful country for which they stand. Certainly, honor is due your parents—doesn't it say so right in the Bible?"

After all these years Mrs. Folsom had timed her lecture perfectly to coincide this portion with a stop directly in front of Eleanor to ask that pointed question.

"Yes, Mother," Eleanor answered automatically.

Oh, she hated when Mother brought religion into her scoldings.

"I see very little sense of honor or duty in my elder daughter."

"I'm sorry, Mother," Eleanor repeated by rote.

Although this truly was an unusual scolding and ought to be noted in her journal. Usually Eleanor received a scolding for mischief that she had not been able to stop Alice from perpetrating. This time she had actually done what she was being scolded for.

And she'd *enjoyed* it! She'd do it again if she ever escaped this prison. She'd do it all over again even if she had to listen to this lecture throughout eternity.

Eleanor had all she could do to look properly penitent, and not break out laughing.

"A sense of responsibility. Everyone ought to have a sense of responsibility. Why, the world would be a better place if everyone knew their responsibilities—to their family, to society, to their country. Women especially ought to have . . ."

What? She left God out of this part? Eleanor noted with amazement as her mother continued to drone on and on. Either Mother was entering her dotage, or the world would shortly come to an end. Should she be prepared to duck in case lightning came shattering through the window?

"A sense of loyalty. Everyone ought to have a sense of loyalty. Why, the world would be a better place if everyone remained true and loyal to their friends, their family, the values that family holds dear. Women especially ought to have a sense of loyalty to their family while they are in their care, and to her husband once she comes under his control. You need to think long and hard about your own misguided loyalties, Eleanor."

Mother left out one very important loyalty, she noticed. She failed to make any mention of the fact that she must be loyal to her own heart.

"But, Captain Claybourne—"

"Captain Claybourne—ha! 'Captain,' my aunt Tilly's hairpins!" Mother declared. "If that man truly is a captain, then I'm the commanding officer of the Army of the Potomac! That man is not a fit person with which to associate. Not fit for *my* daughter, at any rate. If you think by taking up with this unsuitable man, you'll force me into no longer encouraging you to marry Bradley Randolph . . . well, you're right."

Mrs. Folsom's tone of voice softened considerably.

"I promise I won't badger you about him anymore. I promise not to even *hint* anymore. But surely, Eleanor . . ." She laid her hand on Eleanor's and patted gently. "Surely, somewhere in between those two wretched extremes, you could find a suitable husband."

Mrs. Folsom stepped back from this unusual display of motherly affection and drew herself up again to her usual regal bearing.

"I shall leave you now to contemplate your inadequacies."

The only thing I'm inadequate in, Eleanor silently planned, *is I need a ladder to get out of here.*

"I can only hope and pray that you will come to your senses."

"Coming to her senses" ultimately meant "agreeing with Mother."

"I hope you'll also contemplate your duty to your family to uphold the strict moral standards we have always tried to abide by."

"Like Cousin Doris Fenster, who had that house out in Frederick, with lots of lady boarders who had lots of gentlemen callers?"

"Eleanor! I believe we had all agreed not to discuss Cousin Doris."

Good heavens, I'm turning into Alice, with no gate between my brain and my mouth!

"I hope you will contemplate the honor of the family, and your own personal responsibilities to see that this family remains the pillar of society that it has always been."

"Like the time Uncle Stanford tried to sell that pickled beef that had gone bad to the Army?"

"Oh, Eleanor! I thought younger sisters were supposed

to imitate their elder sisters, not the other way around. You're becoming as bad as Alice.''

Eleanor was beginning to wonder if Alice was really as terrible as everyone made her out to be.

Mrs. Folsom slammed the door behind her when she stormed out.

"So, here I am," Eleanor spoke to herself. She slapped her arms loosely at her sides. "Left alone to contemplate my inadequacies."

She rose from the bed and began to pace her room. She tried to pace in a ninety-degree angle from her mother. She didn't want to wear out the carpet in only one direction.

She also didn't want to take the chance that her mother had indeed weakened the floorboards, and her tread, although much lighter, would be the straw that broke the camel's back. Of course, if she survived the fall into the dining room and was still able to run, that would be one way to get out of the house.

She paced over to the window.

"I need a ladder to get out of here."

She looked down two stories to the brick walk surrounding the house, to the bushes growing next to the house, to the bricks set on edge and painted white that bordered the bushes.

She shook her head as she pulled her head back in. She'd never survive that fall. She might as well jump off Rocky Point.

"Is she gone?" Alice asked.

Eleanor looked around. No Alice. Listening to Mother rant for several hours had indeed caused her complete and total dementia. She was now having auditory hallucinations.

"Is she finally gone?" Alice demanded, poking her head out from under Eleanor's bed.

"What are you doing under there?" Eleanor demanded.

She'd been wrong, Eleanor decided. She'd been too lenient. Alice truly was as bad as everyone made her out to be.

Alice pulled herself out, stood up, and brushed the dust off her dress.

"You missed one in your hair," Eleanor said, pointing.

Alice reached up and pulled that one out, too, crossing her eyes to make sure she got it.

"I repeat, what were you doing under my bed? How did you get there? Why would you want to be there anyway?"

Alice sat on the bed. She held up three fingers and, as she answered Eleanor's questions, she ticked one down each time.

"I've been under your bed eating licorice whips. I crawled under there. I wanted to be there so I could hear Mother scold you."

Eleanor held up one finger. "When did you crawl under my bed?" She held up another. "Why would you want to hear Mother scold me?"

"Early this morning before anyone else was up. It was the only time I could sneak in unnoticed. You snore, you know."

"I do not!"

Alice held up two fingers. "Because I wanted to hear all about what you'd been up to yesterday. I guess you're not such a Goody Two-shoes after all."

"Does that raise me greatly in your estimation?" Eleanor asked with a wry grin.

"Not really."

Alice chomped on the end of a licorice and tore it off with her teeth. Eleanor expected to hear her growl.

"However, it does show that you have promise, and I've decided to take you under my wing."

"Why?"

"So you can have Josh—if you really want him."

"Of course I do."

"If he really wants you."

"Of course he does." *He does, doesn't he?* she had to ask herself.

He'd kissed her, he'd told her how much he wanted her. But he'd also been a bit unclear on whether or not he'd actually marry her and bring her to this island—or come live with her and her family in Baltimore. Or whether he'd actually marry her at all.

Now that she was out of the first golden flush of infatuation, and back in the semi-loving arms of her family, the cold light of reality was making that lovely golden glow fade rapidly.

"Of course he does," she tried to repeat, as if the more times she said it, the truer it would be.

"Well, the first thing you have to do is figure how to get Mother and Father to let you out of here and leave you alone again."

"Oh, of course. That's so simple, why didn't I think of that?" Eleanor demanded sarcastically.

"Because your brains are clouded and your thoughts are impaired because you're in love," Alice answered, completely straight-faced. "Perdition! I hope I never fall in love!"

"Me, too. I can't imagine you bearing children just like yourself to inflict upon this world."

Alice ignored her completely.

"What I want you to do is sit here and think up a really good, believable apology," Alice ordered.

"Along with contemplating my inadequacies?"

Alice eyed her mischievously. "Can't do two things at the same time?"

"Oh, stop. How can I stay here?" Eleanor demanded in disbelief. "I thought you were going to get me out of here."

"I am. *My* way." Then she paused for a moment. "Well, no, not really my way. But a sort of namby-pamby way that suits you better."

"Gee, thanks."

Alice headed for the window.

"Where are you going?"

"Out and down."

"Why?"

"Door's locked. Remember?"

"But you can't!"

"Sure I can. Bradley did it. I'm lots better than him."

"You'll fall and die. Then how will I explain that to Mother?"

"That's *your* problem. *I'll* be dead."

Alice's dark braids disappeared over the window ledge.

Eleanor settled back on her bed. If she heard a crash, of course she'd come running. But right now she didn't want to see the untimely demise of her younger sister as she plummeted to her death from the rickety trellis.

Somehow she had to see Josh. She had to know he loved her—that this wasn't just some summer romance that ended when the geese flew south.

What if that was all it was? she asked herself.

How could she leave his sea-blue eyes, shining in the morning sun? His sun-touched hair blown in wisps by the breeze across his bronzed face. His strong hand resting gently atop hers. His lips blending with hers until she lost herself in him.

She had until September. And then what would she have? Only memories? Regrets? Recriminations from her parents? Baltimore with all its bustling activities—and she lonely in the midst of it?

"Say, son, you look like somebody shot your dog," Unk Moore said as he rocked back and forth on the front porch of the General Store.

"I feel like somebody shot me," Josh replied. He sat on the edge of the porch, his elbows resting on his knees.

"That knock on the head do that much damage? Or was it that knock to your heart?"

Josh turned around and eyed Unk.

"Oh, come on. I know I'm old. I know my last wife died back in sixty-nine, and I ain't seen fit to marry again 'cause the only other ladies around here my age are Miss Zang and Gussie, and I can't see myself saddled with either one of them harridans—although Miss Zang would teach me good manners, and Gussie would keep me healthy. But that don't mean I don't remember real good." He gave Josh an audacious wink.

"I haven't seen her in three days, Unk." He picked a blade of grass that was growing up between the porch floorboards and proceeded to tear it into little pieces.

"Is that why you been waiting on this porch like it was feeding time at the hog trough and you was starving?"

"She said she'd try to meet me. Every time I go to her house, I'm told she's not home or she's not receiving today. I've left lots of messages—which I highly doubt she gets. I haven't heard anything from her."

Unk grunted and nodded.

"What if she's changed her mind? What if she had a bit of fun on the poor side of the island and went back to all her rich friends and forgot all about me?"

"Do you really think that of her?"

"No. Of course not."

Josh picked up a rock and hurled it out into the street.

"I took a couple of bottles of beer up to the coachman, thinking we could kind of talk, get friendly, and he'd be able to sneak me in somehow."

"What happened?"

"Turns out he's a real Bible-thumper. Doesn't hold with

any drinking. No gambling. Doesn't smoke. Doesn't drink. Probably doesn't—''

"Uh-uh-uh, son," Unk warned.

"Either," Josh finished anyway. "I was out of luck."

"What'd you do?"

"Went home, drank both beers, and fell asleep on the couch. Ticked Maddie off in the process."

"Darn, son! You could've at least shared them with an old man who never knows when one drink'll be his last."

"Sorry, Unk."

"That's all right. I know you ain't thinking right in your head, son."

"I've done everything short of breaking into the place," Josh complained. He picked up a pebble and heaved it at a clump of grass.

"Well, then, why don't you?"

"Because I don't like the thought of sitting in Bo's jail, even if he does keep it cleaner than Maddie keeps house. It's probably cleaner that Doc's surgery."

Unk chuckled.

"Come to think of it, if Mr. Folsom catches me breaking into his house, he might not let Bo take care of it. You know how those rich folks are."

"Can't say as I do."

"I'm liable to find myself on a chain gang in the Dismal Swamp!"

Josh threw another pebble at another clump of grass, this time with even more force.

"So, what're you going to do, son?"

"Wait," Josh answered plainly. He heaved his shoulders up and down in a gesture of futility. "That's all I can do. But I'm here, and they're here on this island until September, and I'll know when they're getting ready to set sail. *Somewhere* in between, I'll find her."

Josh set his jaw with determination and stared at the for-get-me-nots at the base of the flagpole in Evering Square.

"I can't say I'm displeased with you any longer," Mrs. Folsom said to Eleanor as they were climbing the stairs to retire to bed.

"I'm glad to hear that, Mother," Eleanor answered list-lessly.

"I know we've kept you awfully busy these last few days—such a round of gay summer activities! I hope you've been enjoying yourself."

She hadn't missed Bradley's company, though. Part of her was very relieved not to have seen him for the past three days. But there was a suspicious little voice in the back of her mind, warning her. Bradley wasn't a man to give up so easily. He was up to something—she just knew it! The longer he took, the worse she knew it would be. And she was powerless to do anything about it. She could only hope and pray Josh would be there to help her again.

"They've been very entertaining," she replied with ap-proximately the same amount of joy she'd have had if she'd been watching executions the whole time.

"I suppose if I were a martyr, I might put the blame on myself for your unfortunate little . . . um, escapade," Mrs. Folsom said. "I suppose you were extremely bored when you first arrived. Perhaps if I had arranged more good, clean fun for you with the other young people, you wouldn't have felt the need to look elsewhere for enter-tainment."

"Perhaps not, Mother."

Mrs. Folsom reached out and patted Eleanor's cheek.

"That's a good girl. Now, that lovely brunch at the Stew-arts and the exciting croquet tournament afterward must have worn you out. Why don't you get some sleep? Then tomorrow afternoon, the McGruders are having a party alfresco at the Yachting Club.''

''I can't wait.''

Eleanor closed her bedroom door. She waited and listened. Yes, no matter how dutiful, loyal, honorable, and responsible Eleanor had tried to be these past three days, her mother still turned the key in the lock.

Eleanor bent down at the side of her bed and peeked under. No Alice. She was disappointed. For once she could have used her sister's bouncy, indomitable company.

Without undressing, without even removing her shoes, Eleanor threw herself back on the bed. She couldn't sleep. She'd done enough sleeping at those horrible gatherings—she could hardly call them parties.

Weren't parties supposed to be fun and lively? She felt as if she'd been set down in the midst of a gathering of corpses. If Josh were there, they could have set big rectangular stones on top of everyone so they wouldn't wash out into the Bay.

Josh! Oh, Josh! How I wish you were here! I know you'd come to me if you could. I'd go to you if . . .

Well, what's keeping you? she asked herself.

Duty, honor, loyalty, responsibility.

Eleanor sighed. She turned out the lamp at her bedside and closed her eyes in the darkness.

Crickets, katydids, and cicadas trilled in the night air. Mosquitoes buzzed overhead. An owl perched in the branches of a tree outside called ''Who?'' In the distance she could hear the waves lapping against the shore.

She heard the church bell ringing. She sat bolt upright in bed. Another bell joined it. That must be the school bell. There wasn't another on the island. They continued to clang wildly.

''What is it?''

Church and school bells did not ring in the middle of the night for no reason. Were they under some sort of attack?

Had all those seagulls come back? Did they have enough bread to fend them off?

The bells continued to ring.

She ran to her door. Damn! No matter how she twisted or turned the knob, the door remained locked.

She rapped on the door. "Let me out! Let me out!" she cried.

No answer.

"What's wrong? Somebody, please, let me out!"

She hammered on the door with her fist. Still, no one came to release her.

The bells continued to ring.

"Ellie!" Alice's voice came muffled through the thick wood. "Ellie, it's all right. There's some kind of fire on the other side of the island."

"The islanders' side?"

"Yeah."

"Do you know where?"

"Wait a minute."

Eleanor waited in the deafening silence of the clanging bells while Alice went in search of information. It seemed to take an eternity for her sister to return.

"Ellie? Are you still there?"

"Yes. Where else would I go?"

"Reed said it looks like the fire is around maybe the end of School or Doc Street."

"Doc Street?" Eleanor hammered more fiercely. She had a horrible feeling deep inside. "Alice, you've *got* to get me out of here."

❖ 16 ❖

"MOTHER HAS THE only key," Alice replied.

"Can't you steal it from her?"

"Don't you think I've tried?" she countered.

"Can you find Father's gun and shoot the lock off?"

"You've been reading too many penny dreadfuls," Alice scolded.

"You've got to get me out of here."

"You've got to figure a way to get yourself out," Alice told her.

Eleanor stopped hammering on the door. She stopped listening to the bells. She tried to just think.

Mother paces and talks, she thought. *Father paces and makes money. Alice doesn't think. I've been taught* not *to think.*

"I've been taught to be dutiful, honorable, responsible without thinking why and to whom," she said aloud. "Did I forget one? Oh, yes. Loyal."

Right now, she realized, she was being very disloyal to herself—and to the man she loved. If he was only a summer romance, he was a darn good one! But the truth was, to her he was a love that would last her a lifetime. She had to be sure he was safe. She couldn't wait until she heard the news secondhand from someone else tomorrow. She must know now.

How?

She turned to the window.

Alice was an idiot, and Bradley was a fool. That was how they had managed to climb down the trellis without killing themselves.

She leaned out the window. *She*, on the other hand, was very sensible, and not adventurous at all. *She* would fall to her death.

If she was going to do this, she'd better get to it, then. Josh could be dying of injuries even now, gasping her name with his last breath, and she wasn't there to hear him and comfort him.

She reached under her dress and tore off all her petticoats. She'd resew all the tapes tomorrow. Right now, to save Josh, just to be with him, she'd throw the whole darn apparatus on the fire.

She unfastened her bustle and dropped everything to the floor. She took off her shoes and dropped them out the window. Those, she would need.

She took a deep breath and stuck her leg out the window. Feeling around in the darkness with her toes, she managed to find a rung of the trellis. Clinging to the windowsill, she eased the rest of her body out and slowly lowered herself.

She tested her weight on the wood. It held. It had held Alice and Bradley. Why shouldn't it hold her? Just her luck, she would set foot on the one rotted strip.

In spite of Bradley, she was glad now she hadn't taken an ax to the trellis. He might have used it to get in, but she really needed it now to get out.

As soon as she set foot on the ground, she leaned against the side of the house and breathed a deep sigh of relief. She'd made it in one piece. Now if she could only manage to stop shaking.

The bells continued to toll. She couldn't waste time indulging in silly dramatics. She drew in a deep breath and felt around for her shoes. They'd landed practically directly beneath where she'd dropped them. She slipped them on quickly, lifted her skirts and ran.

Black smoke against an eerie orange glow churned into the sky as she sped down Doc Street. The farther down Doc Street she ran, the possibility that it was someone else's house steadily diminished. She knew she was too close to Josh's house for it to be any other.

A crowd had gathered around. Practically the entire town. How would she ever see what had happened?

She stood on tiptoe behind someone, trying to see over his shoulder. The man turned around. It was Jack Darty.

"Go on in front," he told her.

With his hand on her back, Jack urged her forward. At the same time he placed his other hand on the shoulder of the man in front of him. She didn't know who he was, but when he saw who she was, he moved aside, and another man made room for her to move through. She found herself passed from hand to hand through the crowd almost as if she were one of them, until Gussie took hold of her and drew her to the front.

Josh stood in the road in front of his house, his arms wrapped around Maddie and a smaller girl, obviously Winnie. He kept his hand on Bill's shoulder. Winnie was holding a big gray cat.

The volunteer fire company had hauled out an ancient pump and was just squirting out the last of the smoldering embers of what used to be their kitchen. The rest of the house appeared undamaged.

"Josh?"

"Oh, Eleanor!"

He gave his brother and sisters a quick hug as he released them and ran into Eleanor's arms. He swept her up into his embrace. He pressed his cheek against hers.

He'd missed her so, he never wanted to let her go, and yet he was afraid he'd hurt her fragile beauty if he held her too tightly.

"How'd you know?" he asked.

"I heard the bells. I just knew. . . ."

He wanted to hold her and kiss her forever, but not in front of all these people.

"I'm so glad you're alive—all of you."

"We were getting ready for bed when Bill smelled smoke. Winnie grabbed the cat, and we all ran outside."

"Well, Josh," a grimy firefighter said as he approached, "best we can figure, it was that darn kerosene cooker of yours." His wiped his perspiring forehead on his sleeve.

"Darn thing never did work right," Maddie grumbled.

"Take a good airing to get rid of the smoky smell."

"No problem," Maddie grumbled, throwing her hands into the air. "We'll just open the kitchen window."

"You know we'll all help you rebuild."

"Thanks, Norm."

Norm started calling out orders to the volunteers to put the old pump away.

Maddie walked up to Josh. "Gee, do you think we can all stay with Archie in his new house while our kitchen gets rebuilt?"

"I'll sleep on the beach, thanks."

The crowd moved in to surround Maddie, Winnie, and Bill with offers of help—a place to spend the night, clean clothes, fresh food.

Josh quietly took Eleanor off away from the crowd.

"Kerosene cooker, my foot!" he grumbled, kicking at the dirt with his bare feet.

"What . . . what do you mean?"

"I mean there was nothing wrong with that cooker." Josh stabbed his thumb angrily back toward the house. "I mean, there used to be, but . . . but when I didn't see you for a few days, I kind of went on a fix-it spree. I repaired the cooker, I nailed down loose shingles on the roof, weeded the tomato patch. Maddie thought I'd gone crazy from that bump on the head. I did anything I could think of that might help me not think about how much I'd rather be kissing you.''

"Oh, Josh, you *do* love me?"

"Of course I do." He looked at her as if she'd just said the silliest thing in the world. "I love you. I want to marry you."

He gave her a broad, apologetic smile.

"I'd hoped to bring this up at a little more romantic occasion—moonlight, roses, pickled eggs—but . . . How could you ever think otherwise after—?"

"Just . . . no, nothing. Just blame it on me being a very insecure woman."

She knew now all her doubts and fears were foolish. She smiled and watched him, her eyes glowing more than any embers.

"So, what could have started that fire?" he asked.

"What?"

Only a man could make undying protestations of love and think about a faulty kerosene cooker in the same breath!

He was scratching his head, as if that would help him think better. Eleanor noticed he specifically avoided touching the back of his head.

"What—or better yet, who—started the fire in a cooker that worked perfectly well?"

"Oh, you don't think—"

"I certainly do."

"Bradley," Eleanor said with a gasp. "But why? Why would you think that when he hasn't bothered us for . . . for several days?"

He shook his head. "Who would suspect him now of wanting to hurt either one of us?"

"You're right. Oh, Josh, what will we do?"

He was silent for what Eleanor thought was a very long time.

"You will go back home," he told her.

She opened her mouth to protest, but before she could say a word, Josh continued, "Bradley couldn't suspect you were here tonight, so he won't be lying in wait for you. Even if he were, the whole town is awake. He wouldn't dare try anything."

"But what about later?" She was still worried. "I've got a million things Mother has planned for me to do."

"Then do them," he told her.

"But—"

"I know I won't be able to be by your side every minute. But I'll be there," he promised. "I'll be watching out for you. Right now I'm going to try to clean up some of this mess and help Maddie get the little ones settled in someone else's house for the night."

"Aren't you going to the police chief?"

"No."

"Why not?" She was fairly screaming with frustration and desperation. "Bradley tried to kill not just you this time, but also your whole family—and your cat!"

"Because right now, I don't believe Bradley thinks we suspect him, and I want to keep it that way," Josh said in a whisper. "He still thinks we'll blame this on a bad cooker and let it go at that. But we know better—and I'll be watching for him."

"Oh, Josh, just be careful. You can see now why I've been so worried. Bradley's not just annoying. He's downright dangerous."

"I'll keep you safe."

Eleanor looked over to the damaged house and squeezed Josh's hand.

"Who'll keep *you* safe?"

Alice snickered all through breakfast.

"What's so funny?" Mrs. Folsom demanded.

"Nothing." Alice stirred her scrambled eggs round and round, stared at Eleanor and giggled again.

"Alice, you're becoming annoying," Mr. Folsom pronounced from behind his newspaper.

"Alice has always been annoying," Mrs. Folsom said.

"I'm just looking forward to what a wonderful time Eleanor and I are going to have today with the McGruders. That's all."

Eleanor watched her sister arrange her sausage and blobs of jelly on the scrambled eggs so that the whole mess looked like a face.

"I'm glad you're so happy. Eleanor, on the other hand, looks very morose to me."

"I'm still a little tired from yesterday, I suppose," Eleanor admitted.

Alice began giggling again.

"Shut up, Alice," Eleanor snapped.

Mrs. Folsom's eyebrows rose. "Oh, my. We are cranky today, aren't we? Well, I'm sorry, but you'll just have to put all that behind you. The McGruders have gone to a great deal of trouble today to provide us with food and entertainment. We have an obligation to them to try to make their party enjoyable for them as our gracious hosts, their other guests, and ourselves."

If Eleanor heard one more word that had anything remotely to do with duty or obligations or responsibilities of any sort, she'd scream. She'd just about used up all the patience she'd packed to bring here for the summer. They'd have to lock her away for good.

"I just hope the weather remains fair," Mrs. Folsom said. She leaned over to watch the sky out the window.

Eleanor thought the sky looked fairly clear, from what she could see. But there was also a certain misty blueness that hinted of rain.

"Yeah, rain sure can spoil an outside party," Alice said.

"Mr. Folsom, what have you heard regarding the weather?" Mrs. Folsom asked.

Eleanor didn't care what her parents or anyone else did. When she finally married Josh, she refused to refer to him as Mr. Claybourne, or anything else—except maybe Daddy.

"The fishermen around here are looking for rain," Mr. Folsom mumbled from behind his newspaper.

"But are they going to find it?" Mrs. Folsom persisted.

The newspaper moved up and down as if Mr. Folsom had shrugged. "Who can say?"

Eleanor wondered what Gussie would have to say about that. Someday she'd have to get up enough nerve to ask her.

Once Eleanor and Alice had escaped from the breakfast room, Eleanor gave her sister a punch on the shoulder.

"What in the world were you laughing at?" she demanded in a hoarse whisper.

"You."

"What's so funny about me?"

"You." Alice started to giggle again.

She dashed up the stairs with Eleanor close behind.

"I can't believe you really did it," Alice declared as she bounced onto her bed. "You actually climbed down that trellis, went to Doc Street all by yourself in the middle of the night, and met Josh."

"Yes. Well, the whole town was there, so I wasn't exactly by myself," she modestly admitted. "It wasn't exactly the middle of the night, either."

"That's good enough for me. And then you climbed back in again. I've got to admit now, I'd taken you all wrong, Ellie. You're nowhere near as goody-goody as I'd thought. I think I really like this Josh fellow, too. He brings out the best in you."

Eleanor stopped frowning at her silly sister and actually smiled. "I think so, too."

"Oh, save me! She's in love!" Alice rolled over across her bed, hung her head out over the edge, and pretended to vomit.

"That's what I like about you, Alice. You're so refined."

"It's like old times again, like before that wretched Bradley started bothering you."

"Almost," Eleanor responded softly.

She headed toward her room. She could never be exactly the same again. She'd suffered too much too long from him. But she had an entirely new life with Josh that she could look forward to.

She guessed she could manage to suffer through this party at the Yachting Club. Now that she knew Josh truly loved her and wanted her, she could manage to suffer through almost anything.

Bradley lay on his bed at Bodine's, hands behind his head, staring up at the blank ceiling. Anything was better than those maudlin pictures Mrs. Bodine had hung on the walls.

Who would have imagined the people of Silchester could rally so quickly? Who would have imagined that old pump could actually work well enough to put out a fire? Who would have believed that he could be thwarted once again in his efforts rid himself of his nemesis?

Well, if he couldn't keep Josh away from Eleanor, he'd just do the next logical thing. He'd take Eleanor away from Josh. The beauty of his plan was its simplicity.

It was so simple, he thought, laughing to himself, and yet no one would be able to stop him. Once he and Eleanor were man and wife, he'd come back here every year, just to thumb his nose at Claybourne.

This time he wouldn't fail.

"You'd think for once the man could put away his fishing lures," Mrs. McGruder complained.

She shot some dagger glares at the small group of men who were congregated at one end of the long pier at the club. They were avidly examining and discussing Mr. McGruder's extensive collection of fishing lures. He'd even set up several poles in the obvious hope of showing his guests how well his lures worked.

"I just hope he doesn't catch something and flop it on the table, expecting us to eat it," Alice whispered to Eleanor.

"Oh, come now, Clementine," Mrs. Folsom said. "He so dearly loves this pastime of his—and it does keep him out from underfoot, doesn't it?"

Mrs. McGruder nodded. "I suppose I should be grateful for the small things."

"It keeps some of the men occupied today as well," Mrs. Stewart added. "They're not expounding about capital investments, and stocks and bonds, and all those other boring financial matters."

"Well, I still wouldn't be all that broken up if it did rain, and he had to pull in all his lures," Mrs. McGruder grudgingly conceded.

"Oh, don't say that!" Jemima declared. "I have a new hat, and I'd just *die* if it got wet."

Jemima held on to her hat and lifted her head to search the sky for dark, threatening clouds.

"I think I'd just die if this food got wet," Michael Stewart said. "If it starts to rain, I volunteer to eat it all up before it gets soggy."

"Thank you, Michael."

"What a sacrifice!" Alice commented.

"This is truly wonderful, Clementine," Mrs. Ridgely said. "Someday I'll have to hire that chef away from you."

Isabelle, Eleanor, and Alice strolled along the pier.

"Are you interested in fishing lures, my dear?" Alice asked with mock sophistication.

"No."

Isabelle leaned closer to Eleanor and whispered, "Me, neither."

"I don't think we'd be very welcome in that bastion of male exclusivity, anyway," Eleanor observed.

"You're very right." Isabelle turned toward the other end of the pier. "Do you think it'll rain soon?"

"Yes."

"Did some of the old fishermen—"

Eleanor opened her mouth to correct her friend.

"Oh, all right. Watermen—heavens, Eleanor, you really *are* becoming one of *them*, aren't you? Did one of them tell you?"

"No. I can see the clouds gathering over to the south all by myself." Eleanor pointed discreetly in that direction. "As a matter of fact, they're coming this way pretty fast, aren't they?"

Isabelle shrugged. "If you say so. Shall we go find something else to eat?"

"I think I've tried one of everything."

"Let's go back and try one more. He's really a terrific French chef."

"They only call him a chef because his last name is LeJeune," Alice said.

"Well, that's French."

"He comes from Ohio," Alice told them. "His accent is about as genuine as some of P. T. Barnum's exhibits."

"How do you know?" Isabelle asked.

Alice just smiled.

Eleanor shrugged. "That's anyone's guess."

"Well, he's still a good cook," Isabelle said as she helped herself to several more of his confections. "And if he gets by with telling people he's French—well, why not?"

"Yes," Eleanor agreed. "Why not?"

"Come on, Ellie," Isabelle urged. "You're not eating."

"I'm fine."

"Are you too nervous to eat, Eleanor?" Isabelle demanded in a whisper. "Are you expecting Josh to show up again? Oh, how exciting."

"No, not really."

Eleanor didn't know what to expect right now.

While Isabelle and Alice were uttering "oohs" and "aahs" over Chef LeJeune's masterpieces, Eleanor was busy watching the watermen's boats.

Some of them sailed close to marshes and sandbars, pulling up crabs in clumps of grasses from the bottom with huge metal tongs. Then they'd sail farther out to meet the market boats that took their catch to Baltimore or all the way to the Fulton Street Fish Market in New York City.

She noticed one of the boats was going a little faster than the others. Her hull was sleeker, trimmer. She looked brand new. She sat higher in the water than the others. Obviously she wasn't loaded down with anything. Someone was going home with empty pockets and an empty stomach tonight.

The boat was still coming rapidly to shore. Eleanor watched it, but she didn't think anyone else was paying it any attention at all.

It was heading straight for the Yachting Club pier. It even looked as if it was heading straight for Mr. and Mrs. McGruder's party. It wasn't slowing down.

She didn't recognize the pilot until it was too late.

❖ 17 ❖

Bradley was wearing plain old clothes, something a waterman might wear, with a hat pulled low over his face. That was why she hadn't recognized him.

"Randolph!" Mr. McGruder exclaimed as Bradley pulled himself onto the dock. "Haven't seen you in—"

Bradley pushed roughly past him.

"What's the meaning of this—?" someone else demanded.

Bradley pushed him aside as well.

He strode boldly past all the ladies until he stood face-to-face with Eleanor.

"Go away, Bradley," she told him in a voice that still quivered.

Josh had told her he would always be there to protect her. Where was he now? She wanted to look around for him, but was afraid of what Bradley might do if she took her eyes off him for even one second.

How could she expect Josh to be here, today, at this exclusive party? She wished her parents were as good at keeping Bradley away from her as they were at keeping Josh away. If they had been, she wouldn't be in this mess right now. Of course, Josh had integrity, respect, and a sense of honor—things that Bradley had no concept of.

"I'll go away," Bradley told her, keeping his gaze as steady as hers. She almost relaxed with relief, until he added, "But you're coming with me."

"No!"

She backed away quickly. Alice and Isabelle tried to step between them, but he was still too fast. He captured her wrist in his grasp and pulled her toward the edge of the pier, knocking Alice and Isabelle out of the way.

She hit at his wrist with her fist, but he didn't loosen his grasp. He held her at arm's length, so she couldn't strike out at his face.

"Let my sister go, you dirty rotten—" Alice's words were lost as she picked up a tray of sandwiches and threw the entire thing at Bradley.

The sandwiches scattered over the pier. The silver tray went crashing off his arm and into the water.

With a wicked laugh, Bradley gave Eleanor a rough push. She fell off the side of the pier and landed in the boat. She landed on her arm. The pain shot all the way up into her shoulder.

She'd hit her head. Stars danced and fell before her eyes. The sides of her world started to turn black, but she shook it away. She couldn't afford to pass out now, like the heroine of some bad melodrama, just when the villain had her in his clutches so that the hero could come to her rescue.

She knew Josh would protect her if he were here. But she didn't know where Josh was. If she was going to outwit Bradley, she might just have to do it herself. She'd need all her wits about her. She had to stay awake.

She rubbed her arm and tried to wiggle her fingers. They all still moved. She was glad to think she hadn't broken anything. Trying to escape with a broken arm would probably be a lot more difficult.

She tried to make her way to the side of the boat. The

water couldn't be that deep here. She'd jump out and wade ashore.

Before she could move, Bradley jumped into the boat and landed beside her. She was in enough pain already. She was glad he hadn't landed on her.

"Bradley! Oh, Mr. Randolph!" Mrs. Folsom cried, clasping her hands to her bosom. "Stop, stop! I beseech you as a mother, do not harm my child. For the sake of she who bore you, return my daughter to me unharmed."

Mrs. Folsom, surrounded by the other matrons, sank in a swoon to the planks of the pier. They surrounded her with beating fans and vinaigrettes.

Eleanor hoped her mother was unharmed, but also hoped she stayed unconscious just to keep her quiet. She didn't need any more bad melodrama from her very own mother to make this moment even worse.

The men still paced the docks anxiously, shouting threats that she knew very well Bradley wasn't paying a bit of attention to.

Isabelle had now joined Alice in pitching anything and everything they could lay their hands on at Bradley—cakes, cucumbers, celery sticks, and the trays and dishes they were served on. Their intentions were very good. Their aim wasn't. Most of the dishes sank to the bottom. Most of the food was swallowed up by fish.

The red-and-white-striped canopy overhead began to flap more vigorously in the approaching storm. The small waves that lapped the shore came in faster and higher.

"Randolph!" her father cried angrily, shaking his fist at Bradley. "Stop! This is kidnapping! I'll see you executed for this. I swear! I'll have your own uncle pass sentence on you."

"I'm sure he'd like that very much," Bradley replied.

"I'll put the noose around your neck myself and pull the lever that drops you to Perdition!" Mr. Folsom threatened.

"But first you must catch me." Bradley gave another one of his evil laughs.

Eleanor wanted to pick up some of the food that had landed in the bottom of the boat and throw it at Bradley. But it would hardly do him any harm.

Steering away, he opened the throttle of the little steam engine, caught the wind offshore in his sails, and headed out into the Bay.

"He got her, Josh! He got her!" Edgar came running and shouting up to Josh. "Just like you said he would."

"Damn!" He hated being right at a time like this. "Thanks, Ed. I owe you." Josh started the small engine of his bugeye.

"Hey, what's family for?"

Josh had kept the *Lady Claire* waiting on the other side of the public dock. He couldn't risk being seen too close to the Yachting Club. He wasn't sure what Mr. and Mrs. Folsom would do, but that was the least of his worries. He didn't want Bradley to see him. He didn't want Bradley to suspect a thing.

On the other hand, since Ed was harbormaster, no one would think it was unusual if he was there. He'd been keeping a sharp eye out for anything that looked suspicious.

Darn if Bradley hadn't come in too soon. If Josh had only been able to stay closer to Eleanor, he might have been able to step in while they were still onshore. He might have stopped Bradley in time.

Well, now was no time to play "if only." He had to keep his mind on the chase. Especially now, with the storm approaching and the waters turning choppy, and the wind taking the sails at odd angles.

Josh watched closely as he hoped to gain on the other boat. But Bradley's boat was new, and a lot sleeker and faster than his could ever be. How was he going to catch them? How was he going to save Eleanor?

Where was the darn fool going, anyway? Josh wondered as he followed him past the Yachting Club. He should be heading in the other direction if he hoped to take her back to Baltimore.

Maybe he thought he was taking her to Washington. He might be able to make it up the Potomac in that boat, but he'd have to be awful careful with the crosscurrents and riptides. Josh just prayed he could, too.

Bradley couldn't be thinking of taking her all the way down to Virginia, could he?

Josh shook his head. Who could figure out where that madman was taking her? He had to be crazy just to try to take Eleanor away with him. The best Josh could do right now was not try to outthink him, but just follow him.

Josh heard the sound of other boats gaining behind him. By now, the men at the Yachting Club had collected their wits and their crews, got their big boats out of mooring, and taken off after Bradley, too.

He just hoped that with their big, lumbering yachts they wouldn't get in his way.

They were rounding the side with all the big houses now. He'd give what each one of them was worth to catch Bradley and make sure Eleanor was safe.

Suddenly Josh's heart bounded into his throat. Where was that maniac taking her now?

Bradley's boat was rounding the south end of Silchester. If he didn't try to veer off southward soon, he'd be heading straight for Rocky Point.

"Bradley, why are you doing this?" Eleanor asked.

"To prove I love you."

"I'm not understanding what you're doing here."

She tried to keep her voice calm and sensible when all she really wanted to do was cry and cringe in a corner. She couldn't let Bradley see he scared her that much. She had to try to talk him out of this. And if she couldn't talk him out of it? Well, she'd have to find some way.

"Come now, my sweet. I know you're not completely stupid."

"Kidnapping me proves you love me?"

Bradley nodded.

"Wrenching me away from my parents who love me proves *you* love me?"

Bradley nodded.

"Scaring my poor parents half to death, and worrying them about my welfare, proves you love me?"

"Yes, yes, yes!" he shouted. "Can't you see I would do anything for you? Doesn't that prove I love you?"

"You'd do anything for me?" she repeated.

"Yes," he declared.

"Then take me home."

"No."

"I thought you loved me."

"If I take you home, you'll never see me again. I must be with you to show you every day, every hour, every minute exactly how much I love you."

"Bradley, you're giving me a headache."

Eleanor lay back against the seat of the boat. It was hard and uncomfortable, but it was all she had. What else could she do?

Jumping out of the boat now was out of the question. The water was far too deep here. She had on shoes and skirts and petticoats that would only weigh her down. If she tried to take them off, she only ran the risk of falling overboard. She couldn't swim, and she didn't stand a chance of trying to wade to shore.

Overpowering Bradley was out of the question, too. He was far too strong. Obviously talking did no good with this madman, either. He was completely insane.

She might hope that in an unguarded moment, Bradley would turn his back, and she could smack him over the head with something. She kept looking around the boat for something to hit him with, but anything she could take, such as an oar, would only be too readily noticed, and the element of surprise—the only thing she had in her favor—would be gone. She had to think of something else.

Anyway, if Bradley were unconscious, that meant she would have to sail the boat. She knew absolutely nothing about boats except they bounced on the waves, and she hated the bathroom—or head—or whatever nautical folks called it.

"Where are you taking me?" she asked.

"Away, to our little love nest."

Oh, brother! More of that silly, melodramatic talk.

"Where's that, Bradley?"

"It's a surprise."

"I hate surprises, Bradley."

"Don't worry. You'll learn to love them, just as you'll finally learn to love me."

"Bradley, unless you tell me where we're going, I'm already learning to hate you," she warned.

Bradley said nothing.

Lightning flashed, and thunder rolled overhead.

"We're insane to be out in a storm like this," she told him. "We'll be struck by lightning and die."

"Then we'll die together, my love."

Was there *nothing* she could say to discourage this man? She just hoped, if the authorities recovered their bodies, they wouldn't bury them in adjoining lots. Maybe Josh would put in a good word for her with the Reverend Toomby.

Eleanor noticed the Ridgelys' cottage to her left.

"Bradley, you must turn immediately," she ordered as sternly as she could. The man hadn't listened to her about anything else. She could only pray he was listening this one time.

"I won't go back, my love."

"Bradley! We're heading for Rocky Point. You've *got* to turn back!"

Bradley shook his head and sailed on.

"Bradley, no one has ever successfully navigated Rocky Point."

"Ha! I'll bet none of those ignorant fishermen can. But I'm a seasoned, professional yachtsman. I'll show these bumpkins a thing or two about how real men sail."

"Bradley, if you're going to die, go ahead, but don't take me with you."

"I can't stop now, my love. You see, they're all behind me."

He tilted his head slightly backward. Even in the beginning of the drizzle Eleanor could see a smaller boat followed by several yachts chasing after them.

"I'll navigate the point, they'll all crash upon the rocks, I'll safely pass through the narrows, and we're heading back to Baltimore with no one to follow us."

"So we are going to Baltimore."

"For a while."

"Then what?"

"I told you, my dear. Surprises, surprises."

"Bradley, you must turn. Now!"

The rain was getting worse. The wind was blowing harder. Eleanor could no longer hear what Bradley was saying over the flapping of the sails and the roaring of the thunder. She might as well save her breath. If they capsized, she was going to need it.

The waters grew rougher. Just when she thought the boat was going to rise on a wave and slip down the trough to the other side, it hit the bottom like a rock, only to be tossed up again.

The bottom of the boat was filling with water. Was it because of the heavy rain, or had they hit an underwater rock and put a hole in the bottom of the boat? After all the efforts of the others chasing them, would they meet their doom because of a hole in a boat?

If she had a bucket, she'd start to bail. Heck, if she had a bucket, she'd hit Bradley in the head with it and try to turn this boat around. If Bradley could sail, she ought to be able to figure it out, too. In a matter of time. Time was the one thing she no longer had.

Josh was rapidly gaining on them now. He didn't know where all the underwater rocks were, but he was familiar enough with a few from the days when he was crazy, and had done a few crazy things. But he'd never been stupid enough to try to navigate Rocky Point. If Bradley kept going, he'd find out.

The yachts behind him were gaining, too. He could only hope they knew the dangers of Rocky Point, too, and were smart enough to stay away.

He was drawing closer. Through the salt spray he could see her face clearly now. He could see the fear and worry drawing her lovely mouth into a frown. He could see the desperation in her eyes as she warily watched Bradley, apparently seeking any opportunity to escape.

His heart lurched within his breast. She appeared so delicate, so vulnerable, and yet so brave in the face of this peril. He had to save the woman he loved.

Suddenly she turned and saw him.

Eleanor had only supposed that, out of desperation, she'd imagined the sound of another boat approaching. When she turned and saw Josh in his boat, making his way toward her through the dangerous, whitecapped waves, she let out a shout of surprise and relief. Then she quickly gasped as she realized that, to save her, he was putting his own life at the mercy of the wind and waves.

The prow of Josh's boat was almost to the stern of Bradley's. A few more inches, a few more, a few more. If only he could manage to pull alongside and pull her into his boat!

Suddenly a wave lifted both boats into the air. The *Lady Claire* slid down one side. Bradley's boat disappeared into the trough on the other. When the wave receded, Bradley's boat was completely out of sight.

"Eleanor!" he cried to the wind and rain. His heart stopped until he saw the bottom of the boat. They'd flipped over! Where was Eleanor? Could she swim? He doubted it. Of all the things they'd talked about, why hadn't he asked her that?

There was so much else he'd never get to say to her now.

"Eleanor."

A dark patch bobbed in the water near him. It wasn't a rock. It was her head! He reached out. Her face broke the surface, and she drew in a great breath of air. She was clinging with a desperate grasp to the oar still in the oarlock.

Before the wave could sweep her under again, Josh had seized the back of her collar. One hand reached up, clasping firmly around his wrist. He gave a tug harder than any he'd ever made. She released the oar. The upper half of her body flopped into the boat.

"Get in, get in!" he cried as the *Lady Claire* continued to ride the heaving waves precariously.

Afraid to release the tiller completely and relinquish his boat to the wind and tides, he used one hand to bunch up her skirts and pull her legs into the boat.

"Why do they have to wear all this?" he muttered angrily. If she hadn't been clinging to the oar, all the sodden fabric would have pulled her under. She'd have sunk like a rock.

She coughed up a bit of water, then gagged over the side of the boat. She fell back against the seat and brushed her stringy wet hair out of her face.

"Bradley?"

"I don't see him. I'm so glad you're safe."

"Oh, Josh!" She was too exhausted to say any more, but too afraid—or too smart—to relax completely. She grasped the sides of the boat and held on.

"There he is," Josh said, pointing out into the water.

He tried to get his boat to sail closer to Bradley. The water kept washing him farther away.

"Bradley," Josh called. "Can you hear me?"

Bradley made no sign that he had heard.

"Bradley, we're trying to come for you," Josh called out louder. "Hang on, Bradley. We're coming."

"No."

"What do you mean, no? Hang on! We're coming."

"Go away."

Eleanor roused herself. "Bradley, don't be a proud, dead fool."

She held out her hand to him. He refused to take it.

"I thought you hated me."

"I only hate what you've been doing to me. I . . . I can't just let you die."

"But you still love him, don't you?"

"Yes."

Bradley's head went under a wave. When he resurfaced, he looked to her again. "I've told you before, my sweet," he said. "If I can't have you, life isn't worth living."

His head sank beneath the raging currents of Rocky Point. Eleanor waited, holding her breath, her hand still extended, watching to see him surface again. Josh stood poised, waiting to pull the man into his boat.

Bradley never reappeared.

"Oh, merciful heavens!" Eleanor gasped.

Josh heard her voice crack and knew she was about to cry.

"No time! No time!" Josh yelled. "We're caught in the current."

"What can I do to help?"

"Hold on," he warned her. "And pray! We'll just have to ride it through."

◆ *18* ◆

ELEANOR CLUNG TO the seat of the boat. Josh held on to the tiller, praying all the while that the current wouldn't dash them up on the rocks, that a wave wouldn't catch the underside of his boat and flip them over as it had Bradley's.

Just so long as they didn't get caught in a crosscurrent, washing in and out of the mouth of the narrows, batting his boat back and forth until it was just a few sticks floating on the water—and he and Eleanor would be two more of the bodies that had never been recovered.

If he could just make it past Rocky Point, he knew he could navigate the Straiten Narrows. In a few seconds he would know.

The waves washed over the top of his boat, soaking him to the skin. Eleanor was already drenched. He could see she was beginning to shake, but couldn't tell if it was from cold or fear.

The spray and the rain slapped his face. The salt waves stung his eyes. He had to squint to see anymore. The rain was coming down so heavily, he could hardly see past the prow of the boat. Maybe this was good. Maybe then his doom would come upon him suddenly, and he wouldn't have time to be afraid.

If only he had time to kiss Eleanor one more time. Of all the things he held dear, Eleanor and the life they might have shared would be his only regret.

Everything in front of him was white and blue and green. Everything stayed white and blue and green. He knew he had the strength to keep the rudder on course, but he couldn't even see where he was going to tell which way the course was. He was sailing blind through a sea of air and water combined.

The boat gave a shuddering jolt. Everything in front of him was still white and blue and green. There seemed to be more blue. He could tell he was still seated upright. Eleanor was still clinging to the seat. She was still breathing and shuddering.

Somehow they had made it through. Was it his own piloting skills? Sheer luck? Eleanor's prayers?

The way through the narrows was still difficult to see through the pouring rain, but they'd made it past Rocky Point. They were in the narrows. The next pier up was his own.

"Eleanor," he said softly. He reached out to touch her shivering body. She was cold and soaking wet. After surviving Rocky Point, he didn't want her catching her death of cold.

"Eleanor, we're safe."

Slowly Eleanor lifted her head from the seat.

"We're alive?"

"Yes."

"Oh, Josh."

She sat up and threw her arms around his neck. She kissed his soaking cheeks and lips. She ran her fingers through his hair. Rain fell on them. She didn't care.

"As much as I love this, can we wait just a moment until I dock my boat?"

"Oh, yes, yes. I'm sorry," she said, pulling slowly away.

"I always get so silly when I narrowly escape death."

She smiled and brushed away a tear—at least, she thought it was a tear. She was so darn wet now she could hardly tell the difference, and everything tasted salty. But her breath was catching in her throat each time she looked at Josh and knew they were both safe and alive. She figured she must be crying.

Josh pulled the *Lady Claire* into the small shed at the end of the pier. It was dark inside, but everything was dry. The thunder rumbled overhead, shaking some of the tools hanging on the sides of the building. The lightning flashed through the gaps in the wooden planks and through the broad opening onto the narrows. The rain was falling so hard, Eleanor couldn't even make out the distant shore.

"I think we'll just sit here a moment," Josh said.

He moved up to sit beside her in the prow of the boat. They looked out over the narrows, watching as the rain slowly abated, keeping each other warm until they could go up to his house.

He held her close to her. She snuggled into the warmth under his arm. The nearness of his body, his strength and power, made her stop shivering with fear. In a little while she stopped shivering from cold, too.

"I don't know what to say, Eleanor," he finally said.

"I guess this is one of those moments when it's hard to figure out what to say."

"I know I want to say I love you."

"I love you, too. I want to thank you for saving my life."

"I told you, I'll always be there for you."

She snuggled closer to him.

"The *Lady Claire* is a good boat."

"The best," he agreed. "I wish you could have met my mother. You two would have liked each other."

"I'm sure."

"You know, Audrey Bodine is my mother's sister."

"I didn't know that."

"They looked a lot alike. My mother was very pretty. I guess we'll have very beautiful children."

"I'd like that more than anything else."

The rain had stopped completely. Eleanor still didn't want to leave the shelter of the shed, or of Josh's arms. But she had been raised to fulfill duties and responsibilities. She still had lots of things yet to do.

"I need to go back," she said, pulling away from the nest of his arms. "Everyone's probably wondering what happened to us."

"You mean your parents want to know what happened to you."

"Yes. I think after this, they'll be glad to see you alive, too."

"Maybe."

Josh stretched his long legs out of the boat. He helped Eleanor out, then walked with her to his house. The kitchen door was tightly closed, keeping out the rain. The smell of smoke had pretty much disappeared. After their soaking, the little house was warn and dry—and very comforting.

"Nobody's home," she said.

"They're all at Aunt Audrey's, I guess. She's got plenty of room. I'll get some dry clothes. I keep mine in Bill's room." He continued talking as he fished around in the chest of drawers. "Then we'll see what Maddie's got in her chifforobe that'll fit you."

"Oh, I've already got the poor girl's shoes," Eleanor protested. "I can't take her dresses, too."

"Just one. And it's only a loan," he assured her.

He threw his own selection of shirt and pants down on Maddie and Winnie's bed. He opened both sides of the chifforobe. Then he pulled out a plain green dress.

"There." He held it up to her shoulders. He was watching her carefully, judging the fit. "This ought to do it."

He held the dress in front of her. She knew his gaze rested on her throat, then wandered down to her breasts. She could feel her breasts warming under his gaze, as if he were caressing them. She could feel her stomach tightening as she imagined him seeing her in fact, caressing her with his hands, moving across her body.

"The green matches your eyes."

"You probably need a little more pink to match my nose after what we've been through," she said with a little laugh. It was hard to laugh, it was even hard to speak when she felt so incredibly naked and alive in front of him.

He reached up and gently tapped the end of her nose. "I love you just the way you are. All pink and green," he said with a laugh of his own. His hand smoothed over her cheek and reached up into her dripping hair. His voice grew deeper, more serious, more intense. "All white and gold."

She could feel his fingers as they ran through her damp hair to the back of her head. He drew her to him, and placed a kiss on her lips.

He tasted salty. He smelled of salt and seaweed. He felt warm with life and passion.

She reached up and entwined her arms about his neck.

She heard Maddie's dress fall to the floor. Both of his arms enveloped her in his strong embrace.

Her fingers traced an undulating pattern across his neck as she moved forward. How brazen, how bold, how daring! She traced a path to the top button of his shirt and unfastened it.

She had set her course with this simple act. Just like navigating Rocky Point, she knew there was no turning back.

Well, yes, there was. All she had to do was say no. Josh wouldn't force her.

But she didn't want to say no—she never wanted to say

no to Josh ever. She knew exactly what she wanted, and wouldn't turn back.

She unfastened the next button.

"Are you sure?" he whispered.

"I'm sure."

Reaching behind him, he gave the door a shove so that it closed with a resounding click.

He began to unfasten the line of small buttons down the back of her dress.

"You know these things are a nuisance," he muttered. "And it's not fair. You get to watch what you're doing. I have to go by touch."

"Isn't that what you were planning on anyway?"

"Not completely. Not like this."

She finished the last button and pushed back the damp fabric. His chest was muscular and deeply tanned. She reached up and placed her hand in the center. She could feel his heart pounding. She ran her palm over his muscles, enjoying the delicate tickle of the hairs on his chest against her skin.

She bent her head slightly and kissed his chest. For just a moment, he pulled her to him. She rested her cheek against his warmth, listening to his breathing become faster, more ragged.

"Don't tell me I'm not fair," she said as she turned around. She lifted her hair out of the way. Josh rapidly undid the remaining buttons.

He slid the dress from her shoulders, exposing her narrow back and white skin.

His hand slid down to cradle the gentle curve of her buttocks.

She turned to face him.

"Are you sure?" he asked again.

"No. I've gone this far just to slap you, call you an unprincipled cad, and get my father to shoot you."

Josh grinned. "All right. Just so you're sure."

Reaching up, he held the delicate fabric of her dress between his fingers and slowly lowered the bodice.

His eyes softened and grew misty with desire as he watched her. Carefully he unfastened the front clasps of her corset until she stood completely exposed to his loving gaze.

He was shaking his head.

"You're beautiful. Absolutely beautiful. I look at you and I can't believe anyone so exquisite could possibly think of loving me."

"You're perfect. How could I not love you?"

She pushed his shirt from his shoulders. Quickly he pulled his arms from the sleeves and threw it to the floor.

With several swift motions he pulled the tapes of her petticoats and drawers. They fell in a sodden lump to the floor. He offered her his hand to help her step out of them. He kicked them aside.

Still holding one hand, as if he were afraid she'd suddenly disappear, he reached down and pulled back the quilt on the large bed.

She sat on the edge of the bed, then pulled her feet in. She reached for the sheet and began to pull it up to cover herself.

"It's a little late now, don't you think?"

She laughed and pulled it up anyway.

He turned his back to her and unfastened the buttons of his trousers. They fell to the floor.

She reached out and, with her fingertip, traced the line between the deep tan and the bare whiteness of him. He twitched.

"Don't tell me you're ticklish."

"No, no, of course not. *Men* aren't ticklish," he answered gruffly.

Pulling at the sheet to cover himself, he slid in beside

her. Then he reached over and pulled her closer to him.

He was warm and soft, and hard—all at the same time, and in all the right places.

"So I can feel it but not see it?" she asked.

"Later," he whispered as he kissed her cheek. He moved to kiss her lips, her neck, the little hollow at the base of her throat. He held her at the waist, but slowly moved his hand up and down just enough to caress her hip.

His hand slid up to cradle her breast.

"I can't believe how soft you are. All white and pink."

He placed a very tiny kiss on the tip of her breast.

"I can't believe how beautiful you are. I keep thinking maybe I didn't survive Rocky Point, and I died and this is heaven—just being here with you."

"Then we both died. I never expected this wonderful a reward."

"I never thought this was considered good behavior."

"I think it's *great* behavior."

She ran her hands over the firm muscles of his arms and back. She tentatively meandered down to feel the smooth skin of his buttocks. He was firm and tensed. He was ready for her.

She knew she was ready for him.

His warm body covered her. She smiled as she welcomed him to love her.

Later, cradled in Josh's arms, Eleanor watched the sky out the window. The gray clouds moved on, like beasts migrating across the sky. Piles of white clouds drove them away. Patches of bright blue began to appear between the white.

"I love you," Josh said. "I need you in my life, Eleanor. I want to marry you as soon as we can."

"I can't think of anything better."

"I just need to talk to your parents."

"Why? We love each other, and that's all that matters."

"No, it isn't, and you know I'm right," he said, sitting up in the bed.

He looked around at the tumble of damp clothes and rumpled sheets. He reached up and scratched his head.

"Boy, Maddie's going to be even more angry about this mess than about the fire."

He reached down, rummaged through the piles of fabric, and pulled out his dry trousers. He stood and slipped them on.

"I know you're willing to give up your family, your friends, the life you've been living for me. You know I'd give up my family and friends, too—my very life for you."

"I know."

"But family is important, Eleanor. You know how important it is to me. In spite of your differences I think it's important to you, too."

Silently Eleanor nodded.

"You don't have to give up anything for me. I'm going to try my best to convince your parents of that. You can understand why I *need* to talk to your parents."

"What if they won't listen?" she asked. Her eyes were dark with worry.

❖ 19 ❖

ALL ALONG, ELEANOR had always imagined that she might be walking back up Mallard Street again someday, heading for the Yachting Club and the public dock. She never imagined she'd be welcomed with all the pomp and ceremony of a big brass band—on such short notice, too.

"It's them! It's them!" everyone started to shout and came running toward them.

Mrs. Folsom threw her arms about Eleanor and began weeping. Alice and Isabelle ran up to surround her with hugs.

"We've been worried out of our minds!"

"Where've you been?" someone demanded.

"In the water," Josh replied.

"You're dry."

"We made it through Rocky Point," he began.

"Get on!"

"No, we did. We docked my boat—you can check if you want. We stopped in my house to get dry clothes. . . ."

"What happened to the other fellow?"

There was a moment of awkward silence. Then Josh answered, "His boat capsized. I hope he washes up soon."

"I'll write to his family. We'll conduct a memorial," the Reverend Toomby offered.

Mr. Folsom stepped forward. "I must thank you again for saving my daughter. We're so grateful—"

"I didn't do it for you, Mr. Folsom. I did it because I love Eleanor. So don't try to offer me any money this time," Josh warned with a little smile.

"I know better than that now," Mr. Folsom admitted. He gave Josh a hearty pat on the shoulder.

"But there is something else very important I need to talk to you both about." Josh nodded toward Mrs. Folsom as well. "Mr. and Mrs. Folsom, I've come to request your daughter's hand in marriage."

"No, no," Alice declared. "You have to take all of her!"

"Shut up, Alice," Isabelle said.

Mrs. Folsom just stared at Josh with cold, disbelieving eyes. Mr. Folsom looked as if he were going to chew his tongue off, thinking so hard.

"You want to marry my daughter?"

"Yes, sir. I love her very much, and she loves me."

"Is this true?" Mr. Folsom demanded of Eleanor.

"Yes, Father." Before, Eleanor would have only studied the ground as she confronted her parents. Now she looked each one confidently in the eye.

"While I know I can't provide her with all the material comforts you've given her, I'll give her the best I can, and love her and cherish her until my dying day."

"Well, that *sounds* good, Captain, in theory. But in reality, I must admit, I'm a bit concerned."

"She'll never be cold or hungry. She'll always have shelter and clothes. She'll always have my love."

"She'll be working in your house, caring for the children, while you work yourself day and night trying to buy a fleet of fishing boats," Mr. Folsom stated bluntly. "Isn't that true?"

"Yes, sir. I have certain ambitions, and I'm willing to

work very hard to achieve them. But it's only to try to make life better for my family."

"Admirable, Captain. Admirable, but not entirely practical."

"I'll still marry him, Father," Eleanor said. "No matter what you say."

"I know you will," Mr. Folsom answered without batting an eye. "That was never a question in my mind. You see, I realize you've got more of my spirit in you than you even realize, my dear."

Mr. Folsom turned to Josh.

"So, I have a little proposition for you, Captain."

"I won't take your money for marrying your daughter, sir," Josh proudly insisted.

Mr. Folsom drew back and stared at him. "I wouldn't offer you money to marry her. This isn't the Dark Ages, you know. Women aren't chattel to be bartered, bought, and sold." He turned and gave Eleanor a wink. "As my son-in-law, however—"

"I don't think I should take your money under those pretenses, either."

"Now, now, don't be so proud and cocky, son," Mr. Folsom said. "Listen to what I've got to say first, before you go jumping to conclusions."

He placed his arm over Josh's shoulder and drew him aside.

"What I have for you is a business proposition."

"I think I told you before, also, that I want to be my own boss. I won't work for any man—even a father-in-law."

Mr. Folsom shook his head.

"There you go, jumping the gun again. I'm not talking about you working for me. I'm talking about you working *with* me."

"With?"

"A partnership."

"Partnership?"

"Are you hard of hearing, son, or just dense?"

"Neither."

"Then listen. I intend to start a company—seafood from the Bay and the like—crabs, clams, oysters, fish. I can buy boats. That's not a problem. But I need a good partner— full and equal—who can carry on the daily workings of the company. A man who knows all about the way these watermen think, and feel, and work, and about how the Bay works. I can't think of a better man for the job than my future son-in-law. What do you say, Josh?"

Mr. Folsom extended his right hand. It only took Josh a moment to decide. He clasped Mr. Folsom's hand in a hearty shake.

"I warn you, I am very good at making money with *all* my companies," Mr. Folsom said. "I think you should prepare yourself to be very, very wealthy."

Mrs. Folsom sat at the edge of the pier, shaking her head.

"I just can't do it. There's no time, no time. Why, it'll take me months to make up the guest list, choose the appropriate attendants—you know you'll *have* to have your cousin Cecily as a bridesmaid—even if she is as big as a house," Mrs. Folsom fretted. "It'll take *weeks* to have the gowns made—after we've chosen an appropriate style. We'll have to rent the big ballroom at the hotel, find a decent caterer, and a florist. Oh, dear, I suppose we ought to have a minister, too."

"I don't want to wait," Eleanor insisted.

"Oh, oh, dear. Don't tell me . . . No, no. You haven't been here long enough."

"Oh, Mother, don't be silly," Eleanor said, feeling her cheeks flush. "I just don't want to wait months and months."

"Oh, people will gossip about a hurried wedding," Mrs. Folsom lamented.

"People will gossip about anything anyway, Mother. And at least mine turns out a good bit better than Cousin Doris or Uncle Stanford."

Mrs. Folsom sighed. "I suppose you're right."

Josh came to stand beside Eleanor. He placed his arm over her shoulder. She wrapped her arm about his waist.

"Our life is going to turn out better than anything you could possibly imagine," Josh whispered in Eleanor's ear.

"It already has," she whispered in reply.

Author's Note

In 1885, the oyster catch from the Chesapeake Bay was fifteen million bushels; in 1984, less than one million were caught. Part of this is caused by overfishing, part by failure to reseed oyster beds, and part by pollution.

Between 1965 and 1985, over half of the submerged aquatic vegetation in the Bay disappeared because of sewage, agricultural runoff, and sediment caused by sawmills, fires, and diseases that have ruined the Bay's forests.

Soil erosion is a problem. In 1742, a royal grant indicated 1,286 acres comprising Bodkin Island. Today, Bodkin Island consists of less than one acre with one loblolly pine and one residence surrounded by a continuous bulkhead.

Wildlife, waterfowl, and fish are rapidly declining. In 1986, the Chesapeake Bay's black bears of Virginia's Dismal Swamp were placed on the endangered species list.

Josh was only joking. The good people of Crisfield do *not* eat their dead.

Our Town

...where love is always right around the corner!

__Take Heart__ *by Lisa Higdon*

0-515-11898-2/$5.99

In Wilder, Wyoming...a penniless socialite learns a lesson in frontier life—and love.

__Harbor Lights__ *by Linda Kreisel*

0-515-11899-0/$5.99

On Maryland's Silchester Island...the perfect summer holiday sparks a perfect summer fling.

__Humble Pie__ *by Deborah Lawrence*

0-515-11900-8/$5.99

In Moose Gulch, Montana...a waitress with a secret meets a stranger with a heart.

If you enjoyed this book, take advantage of this special offer. Subscribe now and...

Get a Historical

No Obligation

If you enjoy reading the very best in historical romantic fiction...romances that set back the hands of time to those bygone days with strong virile heros and passionate heroines ...then you'll want to subscribe to the True Value Historical Romance Home Subscription Service. Now that you have read one of the best historical romances around today, we're sure you'll want more of the same fiery passion, intimate romance and historical settings that set these books apart from all others.

Each month the editors of True Value select the four *very best* novels from America's leading publishers of romantic fiction. We have made arrangements for you to preview them in your home *Free* for 10 days. And with the first four books you receive, we'll send you a FREE book as our introductory gift. No Obligation!

FREE HOME DELIVERY

We will send you the four best and newest historical romances as soon as they are published to preview FREE for 10 days (in many cases you may even get them before they arrive in the book stores). If for any reason you decide not to keep them, just return them and owe nothing. But if you like them as much as we think you will, you'll pay just $4.00 each and save at *least* $.50 each off the cover price. (Your savings are *guaranteed* to be at least $2.00 each month.) There is NO postage and handling—or other hidden charges. There are no minimum number of books to buy and you may cancel at any time.

FREE

Romance
(a $4.50 value)

Send in the Coupon Below

To get your FREE historical romance and start saving, fill out the coupon below and mail it today. As soon as we receive it we'll send you your FREE Book along with your first month's selections.

Mail To: **True Value Home Subscription Services, Inc. P.O. Box 5235**
120 Brighton Road, Clifton, New Jersey 07015-5235

YES! I want to start previewing the very best historical romances being published today. Send me my FREE book along with the first month's selections. I understand that I may look them over FREE for 10 days. If I'm not absolutely delighted I may return them and owe nothing. Otherwise I will pay the low price of just $4.00 each: a total $16.00 (at *least* an $18.00 value) and save at least $2.00. Then each month I will receive four brand new novels to preview as soon as they are published for the same low price. I can always return a shipment and I may cancel this subscription at any time with no obligation to buy even a single book. In any event the FREE book is mine to keep regardless.

Name _____

Street Address _____ Apt. No. _____

City _____ State _____ Zip Code _____

Telephone _____

Signature _____
(if under 18 parent or guardian must sign)

Terms and prices subject to change. Orders subject
to acceptance by True Value Home Subscription
Services, Inc.

11899-0